dot.dead

dot.dead

a.silicon.valley.mystery

keith.raffel

MIDNIGHT INK
WOODBURY, MINNESOTA

First Edition
First Printing, 2006

Book design by Donna Burch
Cover design by Gavin Dayton Duffy
Cover photo © age fotostock / SuperStock
Author photo by Douglas L. Peck

Midnight Ink, an imprint of Llewellyn Publications

Library of Congress Cataloging-in-Publication Data
Raffel, Keith, 1951–
    Dot dead : a Silicon Valley mystery / Keith Raffel. — 1st ed.
        p. cm.
    ISBN-13: 978-0-7387-0833-1
    ISBN-10: 0-7387-0833-X
    1. Computer industry—Employees—Fiction. 2. Housekeepers—Crimes against—Fiction. 3. Murder—Investigative—Fiction. 4. Santa Clara Valley (Santa Clara County, Calif.)—Fiction. I. Title.

PS3618.A375D67 2006
813'.6—dc22   2006042015

This is a work of fiction. Names, characters, places, and incidents are either the product of the author's imagination or are used fictitiously, and any resemblance to actual persons, living or dead, business establishments, events, or locales is entirely coincidental.

Midnight Ink
Llewellyn Publications
2143 Wooddale Drive, Dept. 0-7387-0833-X
Woodbury, MN 55125-2989, U.S.A.
www.midnightinkbooks.com

Printed in the United States of America

To my mother and father

ONE

I didn't see who knocked me out. Two steps into the foyer and a blow to the head brought me to my knees. A kick in the face finished me off. He must have been waiting behind the front door. Now, groggy and queasy, I grabbed the closet doorknob to hoist myself up. After the throbbing subsided, I teetered over to the bathroom and looked into the medicine cabinet mirror. My lips and chin were covered in the thickening blood that still seeped from my right nostril. I held a wad of Kleenex up against my nose and winced as the fingers of my other hand explored the bump on top of my head.

After a few minutes, I had stanched the blood and washed it off my face. Then I rechecked my reflection in the mirror to determine if the two blows had done lasting damage. My nose was now veering to the left a little. I shrugged. Women hadn't been lining up to date the owner of the old face anyway.

Moving over to my bed, I sat down and dialed 911. Though born and raised in Palo Alto, I had never called the local police before.

"911 operator."

"Hello, someone just hit me over the head and knocked me out." Not bad, I thought—my voice sounded pretty steady.

"Oh, my. Are you at 807 Lincoln?" Her tone of concern reminded me of Miss Winston, my old elementary-school nurse.

The 911 system had pinpointed my location. "Yes. I'm Ian Michaels, and it's my house."

"Do you need an ambulance?"

"Not necessary. I'm okay."

"Is the person who hit you still there?"

"No. He's gone," I said, and then wondered how I knew. Maybe I hadn't been completely unconscious when he'd left.

"You hold on, dear. I'll get someone right over."

The dispatcher's sympathetic voice rose in alarm at such goings-on in our fair city. It was just bad luck that had me home early on a Wednesday afternoon. During lunch, I had looked down at my feet and noticed my left foot clad in a navy sock while my right wore brown. Each looked fine with my glen plaid suit, but together the effect was not pleasing. Since I had a meeting at four to close a big sale—that's why I had on the dressy clothes instead of my usual khakis—I raced home during lunch to rectify my fashion faux pas.

I checked my watch—1:20—and figured I'd been out of it for just two or three minutes. A shudder of fear coursed through me. Despite my confident answer to the dispatcher, could I have been wrong? Could the guy who conked me still be here?

I began a quick but cautious tour, peeking around corners. The DVD player, TV, and stereo stared at me from the wall unit in the second bedroom, which I used as a den. The Macintosh still sat on my desk, and the screen saver's aboriginal figures still pranced across the screen, shaking their spears. My brief inspection showed the house the same as I had left it. The uninvited guest hadn't left much evidence of his stay, except on my head.

Fear abated; anger and indignation began to build. Attacked in my own house. In Palo Alto?

What the hell?

What had my unknown assailant wanted, anyway?

The sounds of sirens, faint at first and soon earsplitting, interrupted my thoughts. I hustled out to the front porch. No sense having Palo Alto's finest burst in with guns drawn. Two squad cars careened up. One of them aimed for my driveway but squealed to a halt with two tires resting on the front lawn. The other parked more politely across the street. After a lifetime in the city, I saw a Palo Alto police officer with a gun drawn for the first time.

His weapon pointing only at earthworms and moles, the policeman came toward me, asked to see my driver's license, and introduced himself. Officer John Mikulski, who looked like an overage surfer boy, took charge of what little investigation there was to be. The second officer, a sturdily built woman in her twenties, remained mum after introducing herself as Fletcher.

Notebook in hand, Mikulski apologized for the inconvenience. I liked that. He was taking personal responsibility for what had happened to me. We stood in the front yard under the shade of the pepper tree. No, I hadn't seen who had hit me. No, I hadn't noticed anything missing. Yes, I was happy to have them look around. I showed them where and how I had been bushwhacked.

"Did you leave the door unlocked?" asked Mikulski.

"No, I unlocked it and opened it just before I was hit."

"Now, we could dust the place for fingerprints, but . . . ," started Mikulski.

"Yes, please."

"I was going to say that we would leave a mess. There probably aren't any of his, and even if there are, it's probably just a teenage kid."

"I don't mind the mess. I have a maid. If there are fingerprints, we should get them. Otherwise, we'll never know, if you catch the guy breaking in somewhere else, that he was the one who did this to me." I pointed to my head.

"Okay, sir." Mikulski nodded his longish blond hair. In Palo Alto's stratospheric real estate market, even my little bungalow would bring well over a million bucks. That meant I fit the profile of solid citizen and taxpayer, so Mikulski humored me. Pounding head or not, I studied Fletcher brushing dust over a window frame. No sign of prints. None on the window handle either.

"No indication the door was forced. Who has a key, besides you?" Mikulski asked.

I explained how I had hired a maid named Gwendolyn Goldberg through a house-cleaning service about six months before. She came on Wednesdays and used the key I'd sent the service. I had never met her.

"We communicate by notes."

"Today's Wednesday."

"Said she'd be here Thursday this week. I still have her note if you want to see it."

I walked to the kitchen without swaying too much, peeled the Post-It off the refrigerator door, and held it out for inspection. The note was written in a delicate, spidery hand:

Ian, next week I'll be in on Thursday if that's okay with you. I've left some oatmeal raisin cookies on the table. Good luck with your presentation.   —Gwendolyn

Again Mikulski's eyebrows lifted.

"She's like my mother. She cleans, she looks after me."

"How'd you find her?" Mikulski asked.

"She's from Mindy's Maids. I got a service so I wouldn't have to worry about social security taxes and stuff like that."

I'd always kept my place neat, but keeping it clean was another matter. Since Gwendolyn had been coming, an immaculate house greeted me every Wednesday evening. Soon after she started, she began leaving little notes asking where I wanted this or that put. Now we had a full-fledged correspondence. As we became better acquainted that way, the cookies began to show up. The name, the handwriting, the maternal tone of her notes, and her meticulousness had me imagining a woman in her fifties or sixties, a Jewish Shirley Booth.

"We'll need your prints and hers, too," Mikulski said.

The taciturn Fletcher opened an inkpad and turned to me. Time to be fingerprinted. She grasped each finger, rolled it in ink, and rolled the ink off onto a card. The prints belonging to me could be eliminated from further consideration.

Mikulski promised that he or Fletcher would call the next day after interviewing neighbors, and I gave him my work and home numbers. Fletcher nodded her adieu, and the two of them were out the front door and speeding off in their white cruisers.

Knowing Gwendolyn would be coming the next morning, I did not spend much time cleaning up the black fingerprint powder Fletcher had left behind. I showered, gritting my teeth during the hair washing. While rinsing off, I rejected the idea of seeing a doctor. Yes, my nose was probably broken. But I'd broken it as a kid, playing basketball. The doctor had just wiggled it from side to side, pronounced, "You broke it," and informed me he could do nothing about it. Why go through a long wait at the doctor's office for that? Anyway, I needed to get back to work. I had that customer meeting this afternoon, plus a presentation to get done for the board meeting next week. On top of that, I was scheduled for jury duty tomorrow.

———————

A clerk called out my name first as fifty or so of us milled around the waiting room. A sheriff's deputy escorted me into the courtroom. Palo Alto Police Department yesterday, Santa Clara County Sheriff's Office today. I wondered if the presiding judge would be Stanley Cohen, a family friend, but once seated in the jury box, I spotted a placard reading "Judge Franklin Carollo."

I had left my pile of industry magazines at home. How many more articles did I need to read bemoaning tapped-out tech firms, see-through buildings, and dissolved law partnerships? So, as the jury box filled up, I was scanning *The Economist*, not *E-Week* or *InfoWorld*. *The Economist* weighed little, but its small print and flimsy pages packed enough news and analysis to keep me occupied for a couple of hours. Anyway, I preferred reading about Christian-Muslim acrimony in Nigeria to contemplating my swollen skull or the upcoming board meeting.

Twenty minutes later, a collection of prosperous-looking men and women had filled the box. At thirty-five, I was the youngest sitting in the jury box by about three decades—my peers apparently had a leg up on me in avoiding their civic duty. A black-robed judge swirled into the court and stepped up to his perch. Looming over us, he asked, "Would you each tell the court your name, occupation, and the occupation of your spouse?"

"Ian Michaels," I said when my turn came. "I'm a manager at a networking company. I'm not married."

A round robin of recitations from the other prospective jurors ensued. Then the prosecutor, a Ms. Ishiyama, began questioning us. Around my age, she was slender and petite with an intelligent face and long, straight black hair. Her double strand of pearls clicked as she leaned forward. Her voice quivering with earnestness, she asked, "Do you believe it's your job as the jury to determine whether the defendant is guilty or not guilty?" She pointed her index finger at the hulking man sitting next to the opposing lawyer.

As she repeated the question for each of the other eleven in the jury box, all intoned a reverential affirmative. When my turn came, the prosecutor hesitated. I could tell she didn't want to ask me and take a chance on me breaking the spell she had cast. But she did, and I did. "Don't I have an individual duty to determine whether the defendant is guilty or not guilty? I'll listen to what everyone says, but in the end I figure it's a personal decision." I'd never been on a jury, but I had seen *Twelve Angry Men*.

"Just what this court needs—a jurisprudence lesson from a high-tech manager," said the judge in a voice laden with sarcasm.

After a few more minutes of questioning other prospective jurors, the prosecutor turned to the judge. "Your honor, I'd like to exclude Mr. Michaels from the jury." She could excuse up to six jurors without explanation. Ah well. First in, first out.

"Mr. Michaels, you're dismissed." The judge winked at me. No hard feelings.

Outside the courtroom, I blinked in the spring sunshine and checked my watch. Just after noon. I'd pick up some lunch on the way to the office. Wait. Rather than eating takeout, I could stop at home and eat leftovers from Tuesday night. I hadn't felt much like eating last night, and half a delicious Tony and Alba's mushroom pizza called to me.

Ten minutes later, I pulled up in front of the house. A Toyota Corolla I had never seen before sat in my driveway. With a start, I realized I'd be meeting Gwendolyn face to face for the first time.

After a light knock on the front door, I put my key in the door and swung it open. The aroma of freshly baked cookies wafted out to me. My upright vacuum stood before me. "Gwendolyn? It's Ian," I called out several times. No response.

My first thought was that I had indelicately walked in when she was in the bathroom, but three steps later I saw the open bathroom door. I turned right and walked into my bedroom. The blinds were closed. It took a moment for my eyes to adjust to the gloom and then for my brain to adjust to what it saw. On my bed, face-down, sprawled a woman with her hands reaching up toward the pillows over her head. Her long, lean body was clad in a short jean skirt and a green polo shirt. I shook her shoulder.

No response. More shaking. I turned her over. On her chest, through a gash in her shirt, spread a reddish brown stain. I put my hand on her neck, searching for a pulse. Nothing. I pushed the hair off her face. Her high cheekbones, dark brows, and wide mouth made an impression, but my gaze locked onto her vacant blue eyes. I staggered back and stumbled over my best German carving knife. Then I reached for the bedside phone—it rang before my hand touched the receiver.

"Hello." My voice sounded hollow to me.

"Mr. Michaels, this is Officer Fletcher. I'm glad I reached you. I couldn't tell from John's note which was your daytime number."

"Maid . . . dead," I rasped into the phone.

TWO

I LURCHED TO THE toilet, fell to my knees, and vomited up my breakfast. Again I heard the wail of an approaching siren, but this time I did not hurry to meet the police. My diaphragm convulsed a second time, and out came a stream of bile. I flushed the toilet and made it to the door. There stood Mikulski, disbelief plastered across his open face.

"She's in here," I said.

We skirted the vacuum and turned into the bedroom.

"Who is she?" he asked.

Just then came more loud knocking on the front door. My head felt like an echo chamber. I opened the door, and Fletcher walked in. It had taken her only five minutes to drive here from the station downtown, and she hadn't turned her siren on.

I swung my head toward the bedroom, and the three of us took the short walk in single file.

"Must be my maid, Gwendolyn Goldberg." I pointed to the figure recumbent on the bed.

"You don't know it's her?" asked Mikulski.

"I explained yesterday . . ."

"Oh, right. You communicated by notes."

"But I figure it's her." I pointed again. "The ring on her right hand has two Gs on it."

Fletcher went to the window and raised the blinds with a clatter. Mikulski felt Gwendolyn's neck, shook his head, and took two backward steps.

"Dead, but still warm," he muttered.

I scanned the room. The blade on the floor gleamed in the sunlight coming in through the window. Gwendolyn must have cleaned the room. The passes of the vacuum had left the rug looking like a newly mowed lawn. The oak floor around its edges shone. There was no sign of the coins, pens, and other detritus that I emptied from my pockets onto my dresser each evening. I would find them where Gwendolyn always put them—in the mahogany box on the dresser with the pennies, nickels, dimes, and quarters stacked in precise columns.

"Anything missing?" Mikulski asked.

"Didn't look. Gimme a minute, and I'll look around."

The three of us wended our way through the narrow hallway into the den. We heard the eerie boing of a didgeridoo as two-dimensional aborigines ran across my Mac's screen. The murderer had not taken the computer, then. The wall of shelves was still crammed full of books. Next we looked in the kitchen. Microwave, telephone, KitchenAid mixer, all there on the white countertop. A heap of two dozen oatmeal cookies sat next to the mixer, their sweet scent an incongruous jolt in a house of death. Mikulski laid his beefy hand on the oven door. "Still warm," he muttered again.

Mikulski scribbled a note on a pad and then turned to me, "She bake for you every time she comes?"

"Just sometimes."

"Anything unusual in here besides a plate full of cookies?"

I pointed at the empty slot in the knife block. "Only that." My voice was a croak, and my mouth tasted sour. I opened the cupboard where I kept the glasses.

"Would you like some water?" Ever the good host was I.

The two officers shook their heads and then scrutinized me as I ran the tap, filled the glass, and drank.

"How do you feel?" Mikulski asked.

My skin stretched taut across my skull. My head pounded. My stomach muscles ached from the vomiting. Gwendolyn Goldberg, my maid, had been murdered in my house. I had just lost a good friend, a friend I had never met. My dowdy, caring, maternal pen pal was slender, young, and beautiful. And dead.

"I feel okay," I replied.

"Should I call a doctor?" Mikulski asked. "You look pale."

"No, I'm fine," I said.

"My cell's not getting a signal. Can I use a phone?" Fletcher asked.

"You can use the one in the den."

"Sue is calling in to get help," Mikulski said. "We'll need a special ID unit."

"She brushed for fingerprints by herself yesterday," I said.

"That was routine. This isn't. She'll do it again but this time with help from our best print guy, and she'll get a videotape. And we'll need an ambulance from the county coroner."

Fletcher returned. "The lieutenant wants to give the place a once-over himself, so we're gonna have to wait a bit. He asked you not to leave, Mr. Michaels. Said he wants to be here when we interview you."

Conversation died away. At another time, there might have been some awkwardness, but I was pursuing my own train of thought. I didn't get far. A minute later came a quick rap on the door.

"Do you mind?" Fletcher asked.

I shook my head, and she headed over to the door and opened it. In walked a man at least five inches taller than my six foot one. He extended his hand. "Lieutenant Tanner. Robert Tanner."

"Ian Michaels. We've met. You were a senior when I was a sophomore at Paly High. I wrote about you in the school paper." Tanner had been a wide receiver, an outfielder, and an all-state forward who led the Paly basketball team to winning the Central Coast Championship. The school hero, he had accommodated me when I needed a story for the school paper. He'd shown well-founded cynicism about his prominence as an African-American sports hero in an almost all-white school. For the months between our interview and his graduation, he acknowledged my presence in the hallways with a wave or a "Hey, Ian." That made him different from most of his classmates, who figured themselves too cool to say hello to a sophomore.

"Sure, I remember, Ian." He smiled, yet whether he did remember, I couldn't tell. He had gone on to greater glory as an All-Pac-10 guard at Berkeley before blowing out his knee. "I'd like to catch up, but later, okay? Do you mind waiting here with Officer Fletcher while Officer Mikulski and I look around your bedroom?"

After they left, Fletcher's eyes darted toward the bedroom every few seconds. She leaned forward to try to hear what Mikulski and Tanner were saying on the other side of the door. Fletcher was aching to be with them, I knew.

"What's going to happen?" I asked.

She didn't answer. No wonder. In her mind, I could be a suspect. I took a shot at breaking through her reserve. Tilting my head toward the bedroom, I asked, "Male bonding going on in there?"

She snorted. "No way they're going to let me stick to this one."

"Wouldn't they assign it to detectives?"

"Our department doesn't have a permanent detective bureau. Once anyone gets a little seniority, he or she can rotate in and out of

ISD—the Investigative Services Division. That's what we call plain-clothes."

"So does the lieutenant take charge now?"

"No. Officers can supervise, but they can't take over a case."

"Like in business. Workers do the work and managers watch."

"Right," she said, a faint smile crossing her lips. "We'll either turn it over to the guys in ISD or the lieutenant can pull us off the beat and move us to ISD to handle the case. John has done a stint in ISD, so that's bound to happen for him."

"But you haven't?"

Lips pressed together, she shook her head. "Only been on the force three years. I'll probably be back on my beat tomorrow." I sensed rather than heard a quiet curse.

Tanner and Mikulski emerged from the room.

Even amidst the macabre circumstances, Mikulski's voice sounded almost cheerful. "Sue, the lieutenant wants to move us to ISD to take care of this case."

She must have felt like running outside and whooping down the street. Instead, without saying a word, she went out to her squad car to get the equipment. I heard another car screech to a stop. When Fletcher returned, she carried a camcorder case, and a second officer held a gray plastic tackle box; they headed back to the bedroom.

As Tanner settled in at the other end of the couch, I felt the cushions under me rise as if I were sitting on the high seat of a seesaw. He slouched a little. Seeing Gwendolyn's body had dimmed his aura of energy.

Tanner looked at me. "Tough break."

"Worse for Gwendolyn," I said.

Tanner grunted.

Mikulski, who had slipped out earlier, came through my wide-open front door with a small tape recorder. "You mind?"

"That's fine," I said.

Mikulski laid the recorder on the coffee table between us.

"You sure that's Gwendolyn Goldberg in there?"

"No. I figure it's her because she was supposed to come today. And then there's the ring with the two Gs."

"Who can ID her?"

"I guess Mindy's Maids, where I hired her."

"Why were you home today?"

The questions went on and on. I explained and re-explained everything I knew about Gwendolyn. Finally, forty-five minutes later, Mikulski snapped off the recorder and said, "I guess that's about it for now."

"Okay. May I ask *you* a question? What do *you* make of this?" I asked.

"Don't know," Mikulski said. "Normally, I'd figure the maid surprised a prowler, but I don't think so. Two days in a row someone breaks in here. That's more than coincidence."

"What, then?" I asked.

Mikulski shrugged.

"And what happens next?"

"I'll have to check with Officer Fletcher, but I'd guess we have a few more hours of looking around your place. We'll dust for prints again. We'll take samples of any blood we find. The medical examiners will want to go over your bedroom and the unattended body themselves."

"Unattended body?" I asked.

"That's someone who died without an attending physician. We'll get some more officers here and have them start knocking on doors in the neighborhood to see if anyone noticed anything."

"I guess I should figure on staying somewhere else tonight?" I had no great desire to sleep in my place anyway.

"Makes sense," Mikulski replied.

14

"Can I grab my razor, toothbrush, and some clothes?"

"Be better if you didn't. We don't want to take a chance that anything is disturbed."

"Okay, then. I'll be back tomorrow. You'll lock up?"

"Sure. And if we want to get hold of you tonight, where will you be staying?"

"I'm going to go by work now. After that, I'll either be at a hotel or a friend's. You can reach me by cell phone." I hadn't given them my cell number the day before, but I did now.

When I stood, a wave of dizziness washed over me. My head was moving in circles before Tanner grabbed my arm and steadied me.

"You've had a tough day. You need to go to the doctor?" he asked.

"No, just got a little dizzy when I first stood up. I'm okay now. Thanks."

I climbed into my Acura and moved the rearview mirror so I could see my face. Its pallor intensified the purple splotch under my right eye. Behind my reflection, I saw the lonesome Toyota parked on my driveway.

I put the car in gear and pulled away from the curb. My car seemed to navigate on autopilot; my mind focused anywhere but on the road. I had only a vague awareness of the throbbing of my skull or the soreness in my midsection. Doubtful whether I would get much done at the office this afternoon, but trying made more sense than driving around in a daze. I needed to work on next week's presentation to the board.

As I entered the building, Juliana, our receptionist, was talking on the phone. Her cheery greeting served as a shot of caffeine most mornings. Not this time. I gave her a little wave, and she frowned, looking concerned. I walked up the stairs and into the only private office in the company. Paul Berk, Accelenet's founder, president, CEO, chairman, and largest shareholder, hunched over his keyboard like Beethoven at his piano. Accelenet had no secretaries, and even Paul did his own typing.

I spoke to his back. "Hey, Paul. Have a minute?"

"Yup." Paul's fingers continued dancing across the keys. I waited.

While not quite at the level of Bill Hewlett or Dave Packard, Paul still rated as a Silicon Valley legend. Born in Hungary, Pál Békés had been a baby when his parents carried him across the border into Austria during the 1956 revolution. Paul Berk, as his parents rechristened him, graduated from the Bronx School of Science at sixteen and from Stanford with a Phi Beta Kappa key four years later. A poster boy for the American dream, he started Berk Technology at age twenty-seven. When he sold it fifteen years later, his eight percent of the company amounted to some $200 million. The capital gains meant less than the loss of his métier, high-tech CEO. Restless after four years of retirement, he started Accelenet because he knew PC users would never be satisfied with current networking speeds. As Paul liked to say, "In our business, too fast isn't fast enough." He saw the first-mover advantage in implementing the ASF 2.0 standard and moved fast in integrating peripheral components on-chip. As a result, Accelenet was making practical and affordable the multi-gigabit speeds needed to bring full-motion video conferencing to millions of desktops.

I first met Paul at a cocktail party when he was still running Berk Technology. Despite his celebrity, Paul stood alone near the drinks, sipping a martini. When my date wandered off, he and I began talking. Less than forty-five minutes later, I agreed to abandon my consulting job at McKinsey and come to work for him as director of business development. We shared interests in politics, world affairs, art, the latest novels, and, hopelessly, the Golden State Warriors. We even seemed to have a familial resemblance: in airports and at trade shows, strangers grabbed my hand and called me Paul even when the man himself stood ten feet away. Fifteen years my senior, Paul relished the occasions when this happened. "Do you look that old, or do I look that young?" he would ask me.

I remained at Berk as a general manager after Paul sold the company. Then the call came from Paul saying he was starting Accelenet and wanted me to join him. Now, nine years after that cocktail party, here I stood in his office. There wasn't anyone whose advice I would value more.

"Paul," I said again.

Paul whirled around on his seat, and his face contorted in surprise. He leapt up and brought his face so close to mine that I smelled the woodsy fragrance of his aftershave.

"Jesus, Ian, what's up? You looked like hell yesterday at the RBC meeting, and you look even worse now. Sit down."

He gestured to one of two facing armchairs. I sank into it.

"What the hell's the matter?" he asked. He sat down in the other chair.

"Today my maid was killed in my bed."

"Yeah, right."

I didn't answer.

He leaned forward. "No shit?"

"No shit."

His eyes widened, and I launched into the full story. He listened, his elbows on the armrests of the chair, saying only the occasional "uh-huh" to show he was paying attention.

When I finished, he asked again, "Are you okay?"

"I keep seeing her body on the bed. But yeah, physically, I'm okay."

"Shouldn't you have gone to Dr. Dubitzky after you were knocked unconscious?" Paul asked. He and I shared a doctor.

"Why? Am I babbling?" Paul just stared back at me, so I continued. "My eyes aren't dilated. I have a headache, my stomach muscles are sore, and the top of my head has a goose egg. No reason to spend a few hours in the doctor's waiting room, though."

"Let me drive you to Urgent Care."

"I promise I'll go after work."

He squinted at me, then said, "Fair enough. Now let me ask this. Don't you think you should have called a lawyer immediately?"

"What for?"

"There's been a murder in your house."

"I couldn't be a serious suspect. The guy who killed her today must be the same guy who knocked me out yesterday. I want to help catch him."

"You're not a serious suspect? Who knows if the cops will see it that way? What if your maid's husband sues you? Call Bryce. He can give you advice on how to handle any more questioning." Bryce Smithwick was Accelenet's lawyer now and Berk Technology's lawyer before. His firm had grown with Berk Technology and other hot start-ups in the Valley. He now headed a three-hundred-lawyer firm.

"She wasn't wearing a wedding ring." I looked at Paul. "Calling Bryce sounds like good advice, though."

"Now, where are you going to stay tonight?"

It was decided that I would spend the night in the guest room at Paul and Kathy's. I thanked him and stood up. No dizzy spell this time.

I maneuvered my way back to my cube and sat, just thinking. Why had I been bopped on the head yesterday only to find Gwendolyn's dead body on my bed today? As Mikulski had said, more than a coincidence. Was someone after me and found Gwendolyn instead? I had my share of people who weren't fond of me. Steve, for example, whom I'd fired when he came to work stoned for the umpteenth time. He'd sworn he'd get even. Yeah, right—so he came after me at lunchtime and killed Gwendolyn.

After ten minutes sifting through the events of the past two days, I shook my head and started listening to accumulated voicemail messages, routinely responding, forwarding, and deleting them. Then I heard the canned voice of the messaging system announce, "Call thirteen was received today at 11:45 a.m." Next came an unfamiliar woman's voice. "Hello, Ian. I need to talk to you. If you hear this in the next hour, just call me at your house. Otherwise, call me tonight at home." The speaker called out the seven digits and then paused. Prickles marched up my spine to my scalp like an army of angry ants. The message resumed. "Oh, this is Gwendolyn." I heard the click.

I stared at the phone receiver in my hand as if it were a gateway to the afterlife. After a few seconds, I hung up.

THREE

Paul Berk tossed the paper across the breakfast table. It just missed my glass of orange juice and plate of buckwheat pancakes. I looked down and saw my own face peering back at me from the front page of the *Palo Alto Times*. Or rather not my own face, but the face of a person I had been half a lifetime ago. One of the perquisites of the editorship of my high school paper had been a job as a stringer for the *Times*. Someone must have rooted around the paper's morgue to find the eighteen-year-old likeness that had topped my "High Times" column.

Evidently, the enterprising *Times* had managed to get a high school picture of Gwendolyn as well. The face was the same as I had seen on my bed the day before, but here she looked out at readers wide-eyed. The way our pictures were juxtaposed made it appear as though we'd been named king and queen of the junior prom. But the grotesque headline that rested over those photos drove away any such fanciful thoughts: "Maid Killed in PA Exec's Bed." Now, the *Times* was no *National Enquirer*, but the size of the headline type looked about as large as I had seen since the 49ers' last Super Bowl victory. My eyes strayed back to the picture of Gwendolyn.

"She was beautiful," Paul commented.

I jerked my head up and met Paul's gray eyes. Was there an implication in that remark? "I never saw her till yesterday. I told you that."

He gave me an exaggerated nod as if to humor me and then pointed down at the newspaper.

I lowered my eyes again and began to read. The article had been written by a Marion Sidwell with "contributions from the *Times* staff."

> Stanford student Gwendolyn Goldberg, 23, was brutally stabbed to death yesterday as she worked as a house cleaner in the Palo Alto home of high-tech executive Ian Michaels.
>
> According to the Palo Alto police, Michaels said he surprised the murderer and was knocked unconscious when he returned home at lunchtime. Apparently, Michaels could offer no description of the murderer.

I snorted. Conflating the events of Wednesday and Thursday, Ms. Sidwell had resolved that a rendezvous with the murderer had more sensationalistic appeal than a simple discovery of the body.

> Fanning through the neighborhood around the murder site at 807 Lincoln Avenue, a team of more than a dozen police found no evidence of the killer. "The only two people that neighbors saw going into the house were the maid and homeowner," Lieutenant Robert Tanner reported at an impromptu news conference at police headquarters, around seven last night. Tanner promised that the police would be "unrelenting" in their efforts to find the murderer but admitted having no firm leads as to the murderer's identity.
>
> "There is something wrong when citizens cannot be safe in their houses in the middle of the day," Palo Alto Mayor Frances

Lister declared. She vowed to expand the new community policing program, in which officers patrol neighborhoods on bicycle. "I think Palo Altans want to see more of their police officers. It will make them feel safer and deter this kind of violent act."

I could just see Fran's indignation at the nerve of anyone roiling her tenure as the young mayor of our fair city. I had known her since high school, when she rescued the drama club from years of somnolence with a rousing production of *Carousel*. Her Mickey Rooney–ish enthusiasm and organizational talent had won her election as senior class president. A sense of humor could not be numbered among her many commendable qualities, however.

The article continued on the back page, where a picture of my house covered most of the paper above the fold. In the foreground, two white-coated men from the coroner's office rolled a gurney topped by a dark body bag. My eyes ran over the words of the next paragraph, but seeing that bag blocked any chance of comprehension. I took a gulp of juice, exhaled, and tried again.

> A neighbor who prefers her name not be disclosed reported seeing the victim enter Michaels's house around 10 a.m. and Michaels returning to the house two hours later. "I was knitting by the living room window and saw that nice Mr. Michaels come home a few minutes after noon," she told the *Times*.

I sighed and muttered, "Thanks a lot, Mrs. O." Mrs. O'Flaherty had lived in the house across the street for close to half a century. A retired schoolteacher, she spent much of each day on a red paisley chair overlooking the street while she knitted baby sweaters and listened to Beethoven on her surprisingly up-to-date stereo system. She was a busybody, no doubt about it, but a nice, caring one. She had caught me out front washing my car and inveigled me in for homemade scones just the previous Saturday. Bad luck that she hadn't spotted the killer entering or leaving.

Gwendolyn Goldberg was a student at Stanford University majoring in English. According to the university registrar, she had returned to complete her studies in September after two years overseas. Ms. Goldberg was class valedictorian of Torrey Pines High School north of San Diego. While there, she also served as student body president and was voted most likely to succeed.

The deceased was working part time as a house cleaner. "Some other college girls work for me," said Mindy Mitchell, owner of Mindy's Maids in Mountain View. "The hours are flexible and the pay is good, but Gwendolyn was the only one from Stanford. You'd never know it, though. She was a hard worker, not stuck-up at all."

Last night Ms. Goldberg's parents, who were unavailable for comment, went to the county morgue in San Jose to identify the body. Reached in Del Mar, Harold Marshall, a longtime friend of the Goldberg family, said, "The entire neighborhood is in shock. Gwen was just about the smartest and prettiest girl we ever had around here, and I cannot believe she's gone. It's not fair."

Michaels, 35, a former editor of the Palo Alto High student newspaper, is a graduate of Harvard College and Stanford Business School. He currently works at Accelenet, the high-speed-networking company in Mountain View headed by Paul Berk. Mr. Michaels could not be found for comment.

The police urge any citizens having information on the murder to call the police hotline number and ask for Officer Fletcher or Officer Mikulski.

I left my head between my hands for a moment and then heard Paul ask, "Did you call Bryce?"

"I'll call right after breakfast." It was only seven thirty—a little early to be trolling for a lawyer. But still, judging from the article, Paul's fears of yesterday afternoon were on the money. The writer hadn't said I was a suspect, but that implication ran throughout the article. I "apparently" could not identify the murderer. And then there was Mrs. O'Flaherty's less-than-helpful testimony. Last of all, the report that I had been unavailable for comment made it sound as though I were halfway to Rio.

I finished the orange juice. The writer had done a good job working the phone last night, but the article still left a raft of unanswered questions. What did Gwendolyn do overseas for those two years? What was she doing working as a maid?

Roger, the Berks' cook, came waddling out with another stack of pancakes. After any meal or party at the Berks', I made sure to compliment him on his culinary talents, and he knew I thought of myself as his biggest fan. So when he saw my barely touched plate, he lowered his head and shuffled back to the kitchen.

The phone rang, and I heard Roger's muffled voice. He came back holding the portable phone by its antenna as if dangling a dead mouse by the tail.

"It's a Marion Sidwell, who wants to ask a few questions about Ian."

"I'll take it," Paul said. Surprised, Roger handed him the phone. He and I both knew Paul rarely took calls from the press at home.

"Hello, this is Paul Berk." Paul covered the mouthpiece. "Pick up the phone in the kitchen," he whispered.

I pushed open the swinging door, ignored Roger's startled stare, and carefully lifted the receiver. Paul was saying, ". . . known Ian for ten years. I would testify to his integrity under oath."

"Are the police going to arrest him?" asked a deep voice. This Marion was not a woman.

"For being bopped on the head in his own house?" Paul asked.

"Police sources indicate that he could be a suspect."

"Why?"

Sidwell sidestepped the question. "Do you know where he is now?"

"Yes, I do. He stayed with friends last night after stopping at a doctor's to have his skull repaired." Paul told the truth, just not everything he knew.

"Can you give me a phone number?"

"I can get a message to him."

"Please have him give me a call, then. I want to be sure we report his side of the story, too."

"Will do."

I walked back into the dining room. Paul started to say something, and I held up my hand. "I know. Call Bryce."

"You got it."

"Right after breakfast," I said, chomping on a pancake.

The phone rang again. I looked at Paul and guessed, "Reporters from the San Francisco or San Jose papers?"

Roger's expanse again filled the doorway. "Bryce Smithwick," he announced.

"Hello, Bryce. Glad you called." Paul tugged at his ear as he listened to Bryce's response. "No, no. Don't worry about the company. I've talked to the press already and made clear where I stand. Ian's with me, and he's going to need some help."

No matter how long we'd worked together, Bryce's first loyalty was going to be to Accelenet, his client.

"Here he is," Paul said, gesturing at the portable handset on the table.

"Hi, Bryce. Ian Michaels," I said into the receiver.

"Hello, Ian," said Bryce's crisp tone. "Figured I'd find you there, or that Paul would know where you'd holed up." I winced at his phrasing.

In the course of the next several minutes, I agreed not to talk to a policeman or assistant DA without a lawyer present. Bryce himself specialized in securities law, not criminal defense; he promised to make some inquiries and get back to me with a recommendation for a lawyer.

But I did not want to wait for Bryce to find representation for me. "Okay if I use the phone?" I asked Paul, and when he nodded, I took my old Handspring Visor out of my shirt pocket. A few taps on the screen and the number of Stanley Cohen, the family friend and local judge, appeared. He answered the phone himself.

"Whoa, Ian. Just reading the paper. You okay?"

"Yeah, but I can sure use a favor."

"What can I do?"

"Tell me the name of the best criminal lawyer you've seen in your courtroom." Stan had been a judge for twenty years, so that question encompassed a boatload of attorneys. Unlike Bryce's recommendation, his answer would be based on personal observation.

"It's like that, is it? Y'know, the best damn lawyer I've seen in years is a prosecutor, Ellen Ishiyama. She spent five years as a defense attorney before the DA recruited her."

"I've sort of met her. She questioned me for jury duty, uh, yesterday. She questioned me yesterday. But the last thing I need is a prosecutor."

"Today's Friday, her last day in the DA's office. I'm going to her goodbye party this afternoon. She's returning to the defense bar on Monday at Goodsell and Higgins. You've got a chance to be her first client and get her undivided attention."

"I'll call her Monday then."

"Can't see why anytime after five today isn't okay. And Ian, I'd rather my name didn't come up with Ellen."

I reassured him about my discretion, thanked him, and hung up. Stan hadn't done anything wrong, but he wouldn't want a lawyer appearing before him to know he thought she was that good.

At eight, Paul's wife, Kathy, appeared. Blond and slim, no more than an inch short of six feet, she glided over to me. As I stood, she clasped my hands in hers and inspected my face with an intent blue-eyed gaze.

"So how is your head?" she asked. She had been ready to call an ambulance after one look at me the previous night.

"Not as bad as it looks. The doctor at Urgent Care told me my skull must be petrified."

"Did he give you anything?" Kathy asked.

"Just ibuprofen."

"Had enough to eat?" she asked, moving to more mundane matters.

"Roger is always good to me."

I counted Kathy a close friend as well as Paul. They lived about a mile away, and I found myself over there for dinner several times a month. Paul and Kathy had no children, and so I reckoned, cliché or not, that I was the son they'd never had—even if Kathy was only twelve years older than me and Paul fifteen. Kathy took my status as an unattached thirty-five-year-old as a personal affront; she had, therefore, set me up with a string of attractive, well-educated women with good jobs. Not one had yet made my heart flutter—or vice versa as best I knew—although all seemed pleasant enough. Did my unattached status stem from an unwillingness to commit to a relationship? Or from the knowledge that none of the candidates came close to matching Kathy herself?

"No need to come into the office today, Ian. We can manage without you this once," Paul said.

"He wouldn't think of going to work," Kathy said, turning to me.

Paul looked at me and then his wife. "He has a screw loose. Even after what happened yesterday, he came in."

"I have that presentation to the board coming up," I replied. Six months before, Ray Qi, one of our engineers, had mentioned the possibility of a new encoding scheme to speed I/O on one of our new networking boards. With Paul's okay, I rented space in a building about a mile away from our main building. That way, Ron, along with seven other engineers, a product manager, and a couple of support people, could focus on getting a working prototype done as fast as possible. In Silicon Valley speak, we had set up a "skunkworks," named after the moonshine still in the Li'l Abner comic strip where something interesting was always cooking. Preliminary tests had been promising, and I would be presenting the results to the board on Tuesday. If I had my way, what we now called the Bonds project would move Accelenet into the major leagues. "Gonna see what's happening at my house and make a few calls, but I should be in this afternoon."

I wanted Paul to know that I was as focused on Accelenet as ever.

FOUR

Driving up, I expected to see yellow tape pulled across my house, saying, "Crime Scene—Do Not Enter," like in those detective shows. But the house stared out at the street impassively, showing no signs of what had happened inside it just the day before.

I walked up the front steps and put my key in the door. My last two daytime entries had been less than propitious. This time I would be cautious. I pushed the door all the way open. Nobody behind it. In a superstitious way, I persuaded myself that as long as I kept looking for a stranger in the house—alive or dead—I would find no one. So I walked a few steps forward and turned right into the hallway.

Out of the corner of my eye, I saw someone in my bedroom. I opened my mouth to cry out but clamped it shut when I recognized Officer Fletcher in her blue uniform.

"You scared me." I knew I sounded defensive and probably a tad embarrassed as well.

"Understandable." She raised her eyebrows. "How else could you react after what's happened?"

I shrugged. People told me that I came across as self-assured. Fletcher would have a different view, knowing that I had vomited yesterday and almost screamed today. I said, "I didn't see your squad car out front."

"One of the guys brought it back to the station last night. Mikulski will be here soon if I need a lift. Anyway, it's only a twenty-minute hike back downtown."

"You got stuck guarding the house all night?"

Now she shrugged.

"Is the house back to being mine?"

"You ready to be here alone?"

"I thought so until a second ago."

"If it's okay with you, I'd like to look around some more. See if there's anything we missed, take some more photos, kind of pick up the vibes."

"So you didn't get stuck here, you volunteered."

She shrugged again.

"When can I come back?" I asked.

"Tomorrow?"

"That's fine. Can I pack a bag?"

She raised an eyebrow.

I explained. "With clothes, toiletries. That kind of thing."

"Sure, but I'll have to watch."

"Why?"

"Just procedures." She held out her hands, palms up. "Where did you stay last night?"

"At Paul and Kathy Berk's. I kept my cell phone on."

"You going to spend tonight there, too?"

"Yup." Staying with the Berks did not constitute hardship duty, and they'd told me I could stay over as long as necessary. Fletcher asked for the Berks' number, and it joined my home, work, and cell numbers in her little notebook.

"You might want to check your answering machine. Your phone's been ringing off the hook."

I figured she'd probably listened to all the messages as they came in.

"Thanks," I said. "I have a few calls to make, too. Coffee?"

"That wouldn't be so bad. With just a little cream, please."

"I have some Kona from Peet's. Don't drink the stuff myself. I'll have some tea."

Fletcher leaned against the wall and watched as I busied myself with boiling water, a coffee pot, a tea infuser, and such. "How come you have fancy coffee around if you don't drink it yourself?"

"A couple of months ago, I picked some up when I had friends over for dinner. Gwendolyn found the leftovers in a thermal carafe the next day. She left me a note telling me that she'd finished up the coffee, that it was delicious, and that she hoped I didn't mind. I wrote back telling her to make some whenever she wanted. I've been stocking it for her ever since."

"Still have those notes?" she asked. Her offhanded tone was almost endearing. While I was rooting for her to be the one to catch the murderer, I had to be careful. I'd agreed not to talk to the police without a lawyer present. So far, though, this conversation could not have done me too much harm, and at the end of it I was going to get what I wanted: clean clothes.

"No, sorry. Threw them away. Didn't expect anyone to ask for them."

Pungent coffee fumes wafted through the kitchen, and the kettle whistled. I filled the infuser with my favorite tea, Fortnum and Mason's Queen Anne Blend. I walked to the refrigerator and pulled out some nonfat milk.

"Hope this is okay," I said, holding the carton up for Fletcher's inspection.

"Better for me than cream."

I poured the milk into the steaming mug and handed it to her.

"If you want more later when I'm not around, just help yourself."

She thanked me, I grabbed my tea, and we walked toward the den.

My answering machine's red light glared at me without blinking. That meant twenty-five messages had filled the machine to capacity.

Fletcher hung back at the doorway and said, "I don't need to hear you, you know, if you want to deal with those messages. I'll just camp out in the hallway. But leave the door open, okay? I just need to make sure you don't tamper with the evidence. Uh, not that I think you would. Er, tamper, I mean." With her stammering, a pink flush appeared on her neck and began to migrate north to her face.

"Thanks." Maybe her fluster offset my fright of a few minutes before. Even-steven now? I grabbed a message pad and sat down to listen.

I heard friends and coworkers express sympathy and support. A woman Kathy had set me up with offered to help "however I can." But newspaper, radio, and TV reporters had left most of the messages. The last two recordings were from the San Francisco bureau chief of the *New York Times* and a producer on CNN. While not the OJ case, Gwendolyn's murder was a big story even beyond the Bay Area. The potent mixture of murder, a beautiful woman, Silicon Valley, and Stanford was bound to get the media beating on their tom-toms.

With Fletcher sitting less than ten yards away, I didn't want to stay in the den and respond to all twenty-five messages. But there were two calls I did need to make. My mother was just three days into a four-week tour of art galleries in Europe. If word reached her, it would be via my sister, Allison, who lived with her husband and two children up the peninsula in well-to-do Hillsborough.

I dialed Allison's number.

As I expected, she had no inkling of what had happened. She went to bed too early to have seen the news and didn't read a daily paper. Allison cried at weddings, in movies, when upset, and when happy—practically anytime. I outlined what had happened in a low-key manner, omitting a few details such as exactly who had found Gwendolyn. Between her sobs, I assured her I was fine and made her promise to tell Mom nothing. Altruism and self-interest motivated me in equal measure; I just wasn't up to dealing with Mom's reaction. I spent a few more minutes reassuring Allison as to my rock-solid emotional state. I think she actually believed me.

Next I dialed directory assistance for Del Mar, the beach town twenty miles north of San Diego, and asked for the number of Harold Marshall, the Goldbergs' neighbor quoted in the newspaper story. Unlike my sister, Mr. Marshall recognized my name immediately. "Oh, Ian Michaels? The person who found Gwendolyn. And you want to come to the funeral? How well did you know our Gwennie?"

"Well enough." She was sure as hell haunting me now. "Do you know where the funeral will be held?"

"No. Jack and Caroline went up north to identify her last night. I'm sure there will be a funeral once they get back."

"You know where?"

"No. We belong to the Methodist Church on the Pacific Highway, but they're Jewish."

I hung up after giving the curious Mr. Marshall my number and thanking him. Down the hallway, I saw Fletcher sitting on the bedroom floor making notes in a small notebook and then looking up at me. I checked out the room as I entered it. The fingerprint powder had vanished; maybe Fletcher had cleaned it up during her overnight sojourn. Sheets and comforter gone, the bare mattress was exposed. The imprint of Gwendolyn's body could be sensed if not seen. I shuddered.

Fletcher continued jotting notes, glancing up at me every few seconds. I dangled a razor from my hand for her inspection. She nodded, and I dropped it in an athletic bag. A toothbrush, a robe, and some clean clothes followed.

As I turned to leave, I asked, "Got anything?"

She looked straight at me. "We have a couple of theories we're working on. If anything pans out, we'll call you at"—she looked down at her pad—"the Berks'."

"Thanks. Appreciate it. Let me know what I can do to help. I'll be back tomorrow." I walked out. It gave me a funny feeling to leave someone else in possession of my own house. It added to the sense of insecurity and violation I'd felt ever since the unknown intruder had knocked me unconscious.

I drove over to the main branch of the public library, sat in front of an available computer, and logged on to the Yahoo! Yellow Pages. I found a listing for a synagogue in Del Mar. From the car, I called on my cell phone.

"Congregation Sukkat Shalom," a woman answered in a flat tone.

"Hello. This is Ian Michaels. I've heard about the death of Gwendolyn Goldberg. Are the Goldbergs members of Sukkat Shalom?"

"Yes. We've just heard down here. Isn't it terrible?"

"Did you know her?" I asked.

"Of course. Everyone did. It's such a shock." The woman sniffled.

"Do you know what arrangements are being made for the funeral?"

"No. Just a minute. Let me see if Rabbi Kahn is available."

I waited for only a few seconds.

"Hello. This is Sam Kahn."

"Hello, Rabbi. This is Ian Michaels from Palo Alto. I was wondering if plans have been made for Gwendolyn Goldberg's funeral."

Unlike Mr. Marshall, the rabbi gave no indication that he knew who I was. "I just spoke to Jack and Caroline," he said. "We plan on having services here Sunday afternoon."

Just two days away. "Won't the authorities want to keep the body longer than that?"

"Caroline is confident she'll get her back here by Sunday."

"What's the hurry?" I asked.

"Are you Jewish, Mr. Michaels?"

"Yes, I am."

"Have you heard of *kavod hemet*?"

From the sound of the rabbi's voice, I should have. "No," I replied.

"That means respecting the dead," he explained. "We believe that Gwendolyn was made in God's image and that to desecrate her body or to let it remain unburied more than two days violates *kavod hemet*."

"Oh, right, the burial within two days. But wouldn't an autopsy desecrate her body?"

"I think that upsets the Goldbergs tremendously, but they didn't have a choice. And Jack and Caroline want the authorities to catch the person who murdered their girl."

"So do I," I said.

FIVE

THE RAINING DIRT THUDDED against the cherrywood casket.

After Gwendolyn's father, mother, sister, and three surviving grandparents had each thrown a shovelful of dirt into the grave's maw, Rabbi Kahn told us that anyone else who wished to do the same should step forward. I recognized that I had not known Gwendolyn well enough for such an intimate gesture, but when the other few dozen mourners had fallen in line, I felt too conspicuous to stand apart. I cursed myself for coming from the service at the synagogue to the actual burial.

My shovelful was the last.

I had taken a morning flight down to San Diego and driven a rental up I-5 to Congregation Sukkat Shalom. As the service had begun, I'd sifted through my motivations for being among the four hundred mourners. A sense of obligation. A desire to absolve guilt for putting Gwendolyn in harm's way. More than anything, an intense curiosity about the person she had been. I concentrated on what the eulogists told me about her. Their words of memory and sadness helped lift the mask of death for me and made me believe I was getting a glimpse of the real woman.

Art Levine, a longstanding family friend, painted the picture of Gwendolyn's early years. She had been precocious, reading *Goodnight Moon* at three, enjoying the Sunday comics by four, and graduating to the *Little House on the Prairie* series at five. In school, she had a reputation as a bookworm until she ran the fifty-yard dash in sixth-grade PE. She beat all her classmates, boys and girls alike. "That was her first step down the road to track stardom," Levine said. "But even though she was an All-American long jumper, track was not Gwendolyn's passion. Words—reading and writing—were her first and deepest love."

As Levine went on, I shifted in my seat and looked around. The sanctuary was built of bleached wood and had a wall of windows looking out onto a hilly landscape. The ceiling, dotted with skylights, arched thirty feet above us. The room was shaped like a piece of pie with a bite taken from the sharp end. While the room itself gave a sense of light and space, I felt claustrophobic. Seated at the end of a row that would seat ten comfortably, I counted a dozen others jammed in with me. Turning my head enough to see latecomers bunched in the back, I jostled my neighbor, a stout woman dressed in black, and whispered an apology.

"You Gwen's boyfriend?" she whispered back.

"Just a friend," I replied. The woman looked skeptical. I turned back to listen to the next eulogist.

"It was time for her third and final jump at the state track meet," her high school coach, a woman in her early forties with a short Afro, was telling those crammed into that small sanctuary. "She'd done her lifetime best on her first jump and was in the lead. But another girl jumped exactly twenty-one feet in her third try. When it was Gwen's turn, I found her reclining in the cushions of the high-jump pit reading. She couldn't have been there more than five minutes, but she was so absorbed that I had to shake her shoulder to get her attention. Then she hopped up, strolled over to the runway, and took off. I'll never forget that jump. She went twenty-one feet, four inches."

Islands of younger people, who must have been Gwendolyn's friends, were scattered throughout the middle-aged sea of men wearing dark suits and women in somber dresses. All cried right along with the coach.

Next came Gwendolyn's freshman roommate, Monica Hyde, blond, short, and squeaky-voiced. Monica had met Gwendolyn her first day at Stanford. Having grown up in conservative Del Mar, Gwendolyn at first found Stanford a smorgasbord of delights: trips to San Francisco, campus politics, and, best of all, people as interested in literature and writing as she was.

Monica said her roommate feared she was at Stanford under false pretenses. Gwendolyn came to Stanford to study, to discuss, and to learn, and she worked hard at all that. But what most people wanted from her were track medals—what they talked to her about was long jumping. "I never understood Gwendolyn's insecurity," Monica said, pushing her bangs back. "Her accomplishments on the track gave her a certain notoriety even at Stanford, where we are used to Olympic-medal-winning swimmers and future NBA starters. She accepted it gracefully but thought it superficial. Gwen worried she wouldn't have been admitted on the basis of intellectual talent alone. Her straight As didn't reassure her all that much."

After Monica stepped down, a woman of twenty-six or twenty-seven stepped up to the *bimah*. Even though I had seen Gwendolyn only in pictures and on my bed, I did not need to hear the rabbi introduce the next speaker as Gwendolyn's sister to know who she was. Gwendolyn and Rowena Goldberg had the same dark hair and brows, the same prominent cheekbones. But where Gwendolyn had left me with the impression of the tall frame that you would expect in a championship long jumper, Rowena appeared no taller than five foot five.

"For twenty-three years, I had the best little sister in the world," Rowena began. I blinked. Her voice sounded eerily like the one her sister had left on my voicemail. I listened to how the two girls had shared a bedroom growing up. When their parents asked about separate rooms, Gwendolyn complained that she'd be lonely.

After her first two years at Stanford, Gwendolyn decided to take her junior year abroad at the Stanford campus in Paris. Maybe she was trying to get away from what was bothering her at Stanford—she left the track team. Anyway, after she completed that program, she managed to get a summer internship at the *International Herald Tribune*, which turned into a second year in France. She had just returned to Stanford the previous September to finish her degree.

Rowena retained her composure throughout her eulogy. Still, I suspected she would feel this loss for the rest of her life in ways the other speakers would not.

After Rowena, the rabbi himself made a few remarks. Rabbi Kahn, a gaunt, bespectacled man in his fifties, had been at the synagogue long enough to have presided over Gwendolyn's bat mitzvah. He had stayed in touch with Gwendolyn when she was at Stanford and during her two years in France. He revealed a spiritual side of Gwendolyn that no one else had remarked on. She regularly attended Friday services at Stanford's Hillel Society and even found a synagogue to attend in Paris.

"She took to heart God's command that we do *tzedakah*." The rabbi's voice echoed through the sanctuary. "That word is usually translated as 'charity.' That's not what it means. It means 'justice.' Giving to those who have less than you do is God's commandment. In high school, she volunteered at the Special Olympics. At Stanford, she visited patients at Packard Children's Hospital."

I realized that eulogists did not dwell on the flaws of the deceased. Nevertheless, the woman being described was someone who I wanted to meet—who I wished I could have met. A woman with her résumé should have been insufferable. Instead, she had been beautiful and talented, compassionate and spiritual, intellectual and warm, and maybe a little insecure, too. A sense of gloom and loss came over me. When the rabbi announced that all mourners were invited to the cemetery for the burial, I followed.

After the dirt flew off my shovel into the grave, I found myself in a small reception line on the grass. I shook hands with Jack Goldberg, whose long face was discolored by dark patches under his eyes, and Caroline Goldberg, who resembled Rowena in her ability to control herself even while hinting at the true depth of her feelings. Then I shook Rowena's hand and said my name. Her hand tightened around mine.

"You? You're Ian? Gwendolyn's Ian?"

SIX

ROWENA WAS WAITING FOR me by the front door. As we walked into the Goldbergs', I saw women in their fifties and sixties setting out brisket, chopped liver, stuffed cabbage, and the Jewish ravioli called *kreplach*. The smells reminded me of summers at my grandparents', Hanukkah feasts, and baby namings. But here, mourners murmured greetings, clasped hands, and shed tears. I felt like an intruder in this house overflowing with sadness. With a tug on my sleeve, Rowena led me to the kitchen.

"Coffee?" she asked.

"Do you have tea?"

I watched her step over to the cupboard. She held out a box of Fortnum and Mason's Queen Anne Blend. "When she came home last month for Passover, Gwennie told us this was her favorite tea, and Mother laid in a stock."

I knew she must have learned about the tea back in my kitchen on Lincoln, but all I said was, "Perfect."

Rowena filled a kettle and turned on the stove. I looked out the window. Perched on a hillside, the house offered a sweeping vista of the Del Mar beaches. The sun, suspended just a few degrees above the horizon, gave each cresting wave a sparkling cap.

"Milk or lemon?"

"Milk, please."

"I've been so anxious to hear about Gwennie's life in Palo Alto from one of her friends. Tell me."

I looked away from her penetrating glare. "This may sound peculiar, but I never really met Gwendolyn."

Rowena cocked her head. "What are you talking about?"

"She just cleaned my house. To help pay for school, I suppose. But we never met."

"No." Rowena's voice was raised and brooked no contradiction. "I remember when she told me she met you. Didn't you speak at the Stanford Business School last October?"

"Yes." I searched my memory banks. "My boss had been invited to speak at the Entrepreneur's Club. He had the flu. I went instead. It was no big deal, since I had written the speech for him anyway."

Rowena's head bobbed up and down. "Right. She told me she went up to you after the speech and introduced herself. She asked if the hard work required to start a business was worth it."

I scrunched my eyes shut. "A bunch of students came up to me afterward. They all told me they liked the speech, but I figured most were looking for jobs. Gwendolyn was one of them?" I opened my eyes.

"Must have been," she said.

"Did she tell you what I told her?"

"Yes. You told her it was kind of a Catch-22. To found a successful company, you had to think it was more important than anything. But if you were intelligent enough to run such a company, you had to know it wasn't. Realizing that, you couldn't have the drive needed to start the next Sun, HP, or Berk Technology. She told you she liked your answer."

"I've said that before and must have said it that night, too. Let me think." I had met Gwendolyn? Talked to her? Just about when she started cleaning for me?

"Did she mention any other time we'd met?" I asked.

"I had the impression you talked all the time." She must have seen a puzzled expression on my face. "Uh, weren't you dating?"

"Did she say we were?"

"No. She was a little mysterious about you. But I figured that meant she liked you a lot. We're sisters and didn't have to spell everything out," she explained, scrunching the left side of her face. "Anyway, she told me about your house, what you were doing at work—that sort of thing."

"I didn't know I'd met her. I hired her through a cleaning agency. We started exchanging notes, and before long we were pen pals. Her handwriting and name made me think she was much older."

We sat without talking, staring at each other. Rowena broke the silence. "My mother said she wanted to meet you. Do you mind?"

"No, of course not." I wondered what Gwendolyn had told her mother about me.

I stood up, and Rowena laid her fingers on my upper arm and guided me through the door. A moment later, I found myself amidst five women clustered around Caroline Goldberg. Her dark brows, wide mouth, and curly hair reminded me of Bess Myerson, the first and only Jewish Miss America and, for that reason, the idol of my grandmother and her sorority sisters half a century ago.

"Mr. Michaels, isn't it?" she said.

She held out her hand to me palm down, fingers extended. Giving a gentle squeeze to a hand that felt unnaturally warm, I said, "Yes, that's right, although I usually think of my father as Mr. Michaels. I'm Ian." I let go of her hand.

The corners of her mouth started to form a smile but did not get very far.

"I didn't know your daughter that well, but I feel her loss deeply." If only I could have come up with something less hackneyed and more comforting. I wondered if Mrs. Goldberg knew that her daughter had been killed in my house.

"Will you be okay, Caroline?" asked one of the women who had encircled her. She nodded, and her five attendants melted away.

"What was Gwen's life like in Palo Alto?" Mrs. Goldberg skipped a beat before adding, "Ian."

"I don't know. She cleaned my house, and we kind of met that way."

"She was your maid," Mrs. Goldberg stated in a matter-of-fact tone. Gwendolyn's choice of part-time employment did not embarrass her.

"We exchanged notes. She baked me cookies. I felt like she looked after me."

Her eyes dropped, and she shook her head. "When Gwen went back to school, she wasn't on the track team, so she lost her scholarship. But she didn't want help from us. She felt it had been *her* decision to leave school, and it wasn't fair for a twenty-three-year-old to depend on her parents. She told us she had savings from Europe and that she would work during the term and in the summer. When we asked about her finances, she told us she was doing just fine. I didn't press her. She was an adult. And she was working cleaning houses." Mrs. Goldberg shook her head again.

It was obvious to me from their house, their clothes, and their car that the Goldbergs could have afforded even the extortionate fees Stanford charges for a decent education.

"Maybe she had something to prove to herself."

Mrs. Goldberg went on, looking not at me but past me. "She did have something to prove. To an outsider, she seemed to have had the perfect life. She had intelligence, looks, athletic ability, and even" —she took a breath—"a family who loved her. But she needed to finish up without an athletic scholarship or any help from us. She wanted to earn her degree, not be awarded it. We stepped aside to let her do it her way."

Gwendolyn certainly differed from the pampered progeny of my friends, who paid tuition at fancy schools and bought their children BMWs to tootle around campus, only to find them moving back into their old bedrooms after graduation.

"I wish I'd been given the chance to know her better," I said, at least partly to myself. "She always seemed to be very upbeat and giving. I looked forward to her notes. They were cheery. And, like I said, she made me cookies."

"What do you do, Mr. Michaels?" she asked.

"I work in high-tech, for Accelenet. I'm responsible for marketing there."

"Is that Paul Berk's company?" she asked.

"Yes. Do you know him?"

"No, no. We were lucky enough to have bought some shares in his last company a number of years ago." Berk Industries had gone public at $12 per share. After three two-for-one stock splits, Paul had sold the company for $43 per share. An investment like that might explain the Goldbergs' comfortable circumstances. Part of Paul's legend was that he had made so much for so many.

Rabbi Kahn came up to us, and Mrs. Goldberg introduced me.

"Oh, so you're the gentleman from Palo Alto who called last week. I'm glad to see you made it." His deep, gravelly voice marked him as a heavy smoker. I looked at his hand as I shook it. No tobacco stains.

45

No odor of tobacco either. I moved him from the category of heavy smoker to former heavy smoker.

"Thank you for your help. I needed to say goodbye to her." I wished I could come up with a better response.

"You found Gwendolyn's body?" the rabbi asked.

I looked at Mrs. Goldberg. She had known. "Yes," I answered. "When I came home at lunchtime."

"Officer Fletcher told Caroline they would catch the person who did it."

"God, I hope so," I said, and then brought myself up short. "Sorry, Rabbi."

"That's okay. I myself am praying to God that justice is done." He paused. "Do you know Rabbi Frankel from Congregation Beth Or?"

"Of course. He bar mitzvahed me. A wonderful man."

"Oh, you're Jewish, Mr.—I mean, Ian?" Mrs. Goldberg asked.

Before I could answer, Rowena's voice broke into the conversation from over my shoulder. "Mother, if it's okay with you, I wanted to have a few more words with Mr. Michaels."

"Certainly, dear."

I spoke up. "I wish I could have told you more, Mrs. Goldberg. Is there anything I can do for you?"

"It might surprise you, but I'm going to say yes. Someone has to go pack up Gwen's belongings. Rowena has said she'll go up after we've sat *shivah*." I nodded to let her know I understood. My mother and I had discussed whether to observe this formal seven-day mourning period following the death of my father. She had decided no. "I'd like to come with Rowena, but I should stay with my husband. Rowena has said she'll fly up and make arrangements to ship some stuff here, give some to charity. Perhaps you can give her a hand."

"Mother." Rowena's cheeks flushed pale pink.

"I'd be glad to," I said to them both. I had the impression that Mrs. Goldberg was protecting her husband from going through Gwendolyn's things. She must have also been worried about Rowena's ability to handle that macabre task without support. I was impressed with the obvious strength of will in this woman whose life had been shattered, whose drawn face bore witness to her suffering, but who could still continue with the business of life. As for me, ghoulish though it might be, I wanted to look through Gwendolyn's things. I wanted to know her better.

After I said goodbye to the rabbi and Mrs. Goldberg, Rowena guided me back toward the kitchen. Behind us, the women were flocking back to Mrs. Goldberg; I suspected as much comfort and support flowed from her as to her.

"Feel like you were getting the third degree?" Rowena asked.

"A little. She even enlisted Rabbi Kahn in checking me out. But it's understandable."

"In the car, we discussed how we ought to gather up Gwendolyn's things. I told Mom I might ask you for help packing them up," Rowena said, "but she wanted to look you over first."

"And she did."

"I'll call to let you know when I'm coming up there."

SEVEN

Sitting in the lobby of Goodsell and Higgins on Monday morning, I riffled through the pages of the *San Jose Mercury*. The hullabaloo must have died down: I saw nothing about Gwendolyn's murder. A door swung open, and I stood up when I saw Ellen Ishiyama, ex–assistant DA, striding toward me, hand outstretched. She was dressed in a blue suit, again with a double strand of pearls.

"Mr. Michaels?" I couldn't tell whether she remembered me from last week in the jury box. I nodded, and she shook my hand with a firm grasp.

"You know, Mr. Michaels, I've scarcely had time to find my way around here, but follow me. I do know the way to my office."

We walked through a long hallway lined with worn volumes of California judicial decisions. She led me into a spacious office with dark wood paneling decorated mainly with unopened cardboard boxes. There were only three pieces of furniture in the room: two open folding card chairs, one in front of and the other behind the third piece of furniture, an imposing Oriental-style desk.

"You must excuse me, Mr. Michaels, but I just moved my boxes here Saturday. I didn't expect to be meeting with prospective clients on my first day here."

"I don't mind. That's an impressive desk."

"It came over on the boat from Japan with my grandfather. He did the accounts for his farm on it before the war."

"Where was the farm?" I asked.

"My father tells me the Great America amusement park is sitting on it now."

I whistled. That was acreage right in the midst of Silicon Valley, surrounded by Intel, Siemens, Advanced Micro Devices, and other high-tech powerhouses. "Too bad he didn't hold on to it."

"Yes, too bad."

From the tone in her voice, I knew what had happened.

"He lost it during the war?" I asked.

"Yes."

Hardworking first-generation Japanese immigrants and their American-citizen children had been put in camps after Pearl Harbor. There were no trials. Earl Warren, the future chief justice and California's attorney general at the time, had thought it was a swell idea. Nobody ever uncovered a scintilla of evidence indicating disloyalty among those rounded up.

"My dad's whole family was sent to Arizona. Hearing those stories about the camps was why I became a lawyer. I wanted to do justice." Her right hand flicked out as if to chase away her words. "Excuse me, but my return to the defense bar is making me maudlin."

"Hardly. Anyway, in a manner of speaking, I'm here to talk about justice."

"Of course. I've read about Ms. Goldberg's death in the papers," she said.

"My experience is that everything I read in the papers is true except for that occasional story I have personal knowledge of."

She appeared so elegant and her words had been so carefully modulated that I didn't expect what came next. The skin at the corners of her eyes crinkled, white teeth flashed, and then she emitted a throaty chuckle. "The press wasn't always that accurate covering the cases I handled in the DA's office either," she said, still laughing.

What do you know? Her carapace of competence hid a sense of humor.

We had been standing. She gestured to the folding chair in front of the desk, walked behind the immense heirloom, and sat down on her own folding chair.

She leaned forward. "Let's hear what really happened."

She let me tell my story in my own way. She prompted me with an occasional question, steering me back on course several times when I wandered off the subject, but I pretty much told her the whole story. When my voice quavered as I described what I saw in my room last Thursday, she told me to take my time.

At the end of my forty-minute monologue, she said, "Thank you, Mr. Michaels. Your description of the events was coherent and thorough. Do you need a break now? Something to drink, perhaps?"

"I could use something."

She rose from her chair and walked to the near corner of her office. She moved some boxes out of the way to reveal a half-size refrigerator. "Coke? Mineral water?"

"Mineral water would be great. Thank you."

We sat without speaking for a minute or two, each sipping a bottle of Calistoga.

"If you don't mind," she said, "I'd like to ask a few more questions."

"Okay."

"Did you save the voicemail from Gwendolyn?"

"Yes. I could play it for you from here if you'd like."

"Yes. Why not?" she said, and passed me the phone.

I pushed the speaker button, dialed into Accelenet's voicemail system, and skipped through the prompts to the one saved message. Hearing Gwendolyn's voice again, I inhaled so fast the air whistled through my teeth.

"Does anyone else know that you received this message?"

"No. I had talked to the police already. I promised Paul Berk I wouldn't talk to the police again without an attorney. Here I am."

"It helps set the time of the murder pretty precisely," she said. "The police would like to know about that. On the other hand, if they did hear it, it would sound as though Gwendolyn did know you." After staring into space for half a minute, she refocused her eyes on me. "If you don't mind, please give me your password to voicemail, and I'll get another recording of this message. For backup."

"The password is I-A-M-I."

Ms. Ishiyama raised an eyebrow. "You are you?"

"No, no. It's the first two letters of my first and last names. It's easy to remember because it's the mark the laundry has stamped on the collars of my shirts."

"Okay, but why would Gwendolyn call you for the first time ever on the day she was murdered?"

"I just don't know."

Ms. Ishiyama bombarded me with questions for another hour, testing my memory even while gathering facts.

When we finished, she asked where I thought I stood.

"I'm uneasy," I said. "When Paul Berk first told me to get a lawyer, I thought he was being overly cautious. Now I'm not so sure."

"Mr. Berk gave you good advice."

"I think Officer Fletcher is hoping it's not me, but that won't mean anything if she finds evidence to the contrary. She's dedicated and ambitious. And her partner's surfer-boy facade hides a pretty shrewd mind. What the two of them have is Mrs. O'Flaherty seeing me enter the house, just me and nobody else. I don't know if the police have found other suspects, but if they haven't, then I'm in trouble big-time. That's why I'm talking to you. The other reason I'm here is that you got me into this mess, and now I'm counting on you to get me out of it."

"Yes, of course. If I hadn't excused you so quickly from the jury Thursday, you would have had an alibi."

She got it.

"Do you know what worries me most?" she continued.

"How about this? I told the police I'd never met Gwendolyn. If I had never met her, there would be no motive. But now I've learned her sister can point to an occasion when we did meet. Her sister even thought we had some kind of relationship. The police have a note Gwendolyn wrote, and I have a message from her—both could be construed to indicate we knew each other well. All that gets the police close to thinking I had a motive."

She pointed her index finger at me as though it were a gun. "That's it. The police will try to prove you *did* know her."

"I'm just getting to know her now," I said.

"But if they think you are lying about that . . ." She left the obvious unspoken.

"Is it time to talk business? Could you give me an idea what this is going to cost?"

"My time is three hundred seventy-five dollars an hour. If we go to court, the rate goes to five thousand per day."

"I can see why you left the DA's office." I had a nest egg from selling my Berk Technology stock, but at those rates it would melt away faster than the NASDAQ Index in 2001–2002.

She read my thoughts. "This may not cost you much. Who knows? You may not be a suspect at all."

"Really?"

"You're right to think you will be," she conceded.

"If I need to say something official, I do want you to represent me."

"Good. My first step is going to be to call my old colleagues in the DA's office and see what they're thinking. And I'll try to talk to Officers Fletcher and"—her eyes went down to her notepad—"Mikulski. I've met them before. I'll call you and let you know what I find out."

"Do you need a retainer now?"

"My instinct tells me the risk of flight is low."

"I didn't kill Gwendolyn, Ms. Ishiyama."

"That should make my job easier, Mr. Michaels."

I climbed into my car, grateful to Judge Cohen for recommending a lawyer as smart and competent as Ellen Ishiyama. Pulling out of the lot, I knew where I needed to go next: work. Tomorrow was my big board presentation. I believed we had a chance for the kind of technical breakthrough that comes once or twice a decade. And we needed to move fast. Silicon Valley companies had a long history of letting others exploit their most important developments. Microsoft bought an operating system from Seattle Computer Products for $50,000 and turned it into the underpinnings of almost every personal computer in the world. Xerox developed Ethernet, the heart of today's networking technology, and watched while Cisco and others thrived as it flirted with bankruptcy. I had no desire to stand by while Accelenet was consigned to the dustbin of technology history.

Normally, I would have spent all weekend on the presentation. Now, seated at my desk at one o'clock, I had just twenty-one hours until the board meeting. I began downloading information from the corporate database, then putting it into bar graphs and pie charts. Thoughts of

Gwendolyn, Rowena, and Ms. Ishiyama faded. This presentation was important to the company and to me. I had something to prove.

Nine years I had been working for Paul. I had put together a deal with Sun that furnished more than ten percent of Berk Technology's revenues and earned me a promotion to vice president of business development. So advancement came fast at first, but for the past four years I had served as Paul's VP of marketing at Accelenet. I wanted to be Accelenet's chief operating officer. And I wanted it badly.

Eighteen months earlier, Accelenet's revenue had failed to meet plan when the newest release of our product, code-named Edison, fell behind schedule. Paul had turned to me to head up the crash effort to get the key chipset working. I could not let the project fail after Paul had shown such faith in me. In the end, thanks to luck and round-the-clock work by a team of twenty, we made up three months of the slip and showed a beta version at Supercomm in Atlanta that won a best in show award. Corporate revenues got back on track. My picture even appeared in *Fortune*'s technology issue with a caption calling me "the hard-driving head of marketing of Paul Berk's latest venture." My mother and sister had loved it.

Every so often, though, Paul would let drop that he had been talking to so-and-so who had suggested a candidate for the COO slot, the same position I wanted more than anything. In hindsight, I could see that hiring a more experienced executive might have made sense once, but not anymore. Just ten months ago, Paul offered the job to a senior VP from Cisco. To me, the entire interview process represented weeks of torment. Relief came only when the candidate turned Paul down in favor of a CEO slot at a well-financed optical-switching company.

So far I had told the headhunters who called from time to time that I remained committed to Accelenet. I knew I owed Paul. He had transformed me, the eager young consultant, into a high-tech executive. But I couldn't wait forever. I deserved the promotion. I just needed Paul to acknowledge it. And if not, I was ready to leave the nest. Just two weeks before, I had met with Paul. I had told him how much I owed him for the past nine years but that I wanted to be COO here at Accelenet and, if that wasn't possible, that it might be best if I looked around for another opportunity. "Let's talk after your board presentation," he had said.

EIGHT

Somewhat to my surprise, I managed to doze for three hours despite the spreadsheets and 3-D charts bouncing around inside my skull. I had finished putting together my presentation at four thirty in the morning. After a quick drive back to my now police-free house on Lincoln, I climbed into bed around five. My alarm went off at half past eight. I brought along a quart of Tropicana to quaff in the car. Since it was already 9:52, even the late-arriving software wonks were already in the building swallowing their first infusion of caffeine, and I had to park in the auxiliary lot across the street.

The thirty-minute commute with the windows open dispelled any grogginess. Now nearing the board room, my pounding heart pumped adrenaline to every nerve fiber in my body, and I felt sharp. Dressed in the Silicon Valley uniform of button-down shirt, khakis, and loafers, I strode into the room at precisely ten.

Half-full pitchers of juice and plates of pastries and bagels covered the credenza on my left. At the other end of the room, like a sheet dangling from the wash line, hung a white projector screen. Straight ahead through the picture window, the purple leaves and white bark of birch trees added a touch of nature to the ambience. I sat in the only unoccupied high-backed chair around the oblong conference table. Paul nodded at me, and I nodded in return.

"Let's call the meeting to order then," Paul intoned. The implication—which I didn't mind at all—was that they had been waiting for me. As Paul asked for comments on the minutes from February's meeting, I mouthed hellos to the others around the table. Bryce Smithwick, board member as well as corporate counsel, sat to Paul's right, leaning forward, an Armani-clad leopard.

Darwin Yancey, the technical genius behind Paul's previous company, Berk Technology, sat to Smithwick's right. As usual, Darwin's glasses had slipped down his nose so that he peered at Paul with his head cocked back. Darwin had worked eighteen-hour days at Berk, but to everyone's surprise had not followed Paul to Accelenet. Instead, he retired with his millions to the south of France. He piloted his eight-seat jet, an Astra, to San Jose Airport via Bangor, Maine, for each board meeting. He explained his decision to me once: "My wife told me that our first twenty years of marriage belonged to work and that the next twenty years belonged to her."

A rare representative of her gender in the macho world of top venture capitalists, Margot Fulbright had cofounded Chance and Fulbright, which managed close to two billion dollars in four funds and returned over thirty percent a year to investors, even after the dot-com crash. Seated next to me, she had her hands folded on the table like a prim schoolgirl. A sideways glance showed me that the short skirt of her expensive suit was designed to show off the thighs of a Parisian runway model, not a business executive. But Margot, approaching fifty, had a body toned as much as shiatsu, Bikram yoga, and two-thousand-dollar-a-day spas could achieve. Known for her ability to do complex calculations in her head, her mind was in even better shape.

The fifth board member, wearing his trademark bowtie, his crew-cut hair just beginning to show a few flecks of gray, was Leon Henderson, a Stanford professor. A handful of former students, including three Fortune 500 CEOs, had thrown him a sixty-fifth birthday party the previous January. I myself had taken his entrepreneurship course and now met him every month or two for breakfast at Stanford's Tresidder Union, where he offered me practical advice on management and product positioning. I had followed his suggestion to hold daily seven a.m. status meetings when put in charge of the Edison project. As he anticipated, that simple device showed the team how serious I was and, at the same time, helped us deal with any obstacles quickly and efficiently. Leon and I had talked through all the ideas that I would present this morning.

My head snapped up as I heard Paul call my name. The mundane business of approving board minutes and stock options had been completed. I stood and walked to the front of the table.

"Ian has been pushing to expand Accelenet's product offerings," Paul was saying. "He and I have batted around this idea for months, but before we decide on a course of action, I wanted to hear what you all think." Paul looked around the table. "Ian, it's all yours."

I sucked in a breath. Showtime. I clicked a remote-control mouse, and my first PowerPoint slide showed the company logo dissolving into a video clip of Barry Bonds bashing a baseball over the bleachers into San Francisco Bay.

"Our internal code name for this project is Bonds."

"Why Bonds?" Darwin asked.

"Ray Qi, the inventor, said it was a sure home run for Accelenet."

Corny, but everyone laughed except Paul.

I continued. "We knew when we started we might have something big—a patented algorithm that can encode information so data moves more than six times faster over any medium."

The shot on the screen dissolved into a board populated with ceramic-encased integrated circuits. "Bonds acts like a turbocharger for any information-carrying vehicle. Cable companies could sextuple the number of channels they bring to a home with the same wiring."

"Like Bruce Springsteen said, fifty-seven channels and nothing to watch," Darwin Yancey remarked.

"You would have enough bandwidth to plug a camcorder into your television and send high-quality live video of your darlings to grandma over a regular telephone line. And I'm not talking about a postage-stamp-sized picture either."

"I guess that counts as something to watch," Leon said, grinning at Yancey.

I let my voice reveal more of my excitement. "Manufacturers of computers, PDAs, and camcorders—and the phone companies themselves—are salivating at the prospect of regular telephone lines working as fast as today's fiber-optic connections. Every home could have superfast broadband with no additional cables to pull or install."

"So Bonds is supposed to work over copper wire. But aren't the phone and cable companies bringing fiber to the home anyway?" Yancey asked.

"Yes, about half a million homes are connected via fiber in the U.S. now. But there are 110 million homes and 1.5 billion miles of copper already laid in this country alone. Bonds can future-proof that huge investment and eliminate the expense of pulling all that fiber. We'd save a lot of lawns from being dug up."

"Let's get back to the here and now," said Yancey. "Does Bonds work?"

"Sure, with all the electronics on a thirty-centimeter square board and a lot of hand-tuning, we can get it to work," I said. "Our simulator says the current design, put in silicon, might work ten percent of the time. That means we have two technical hurdles to overcome."

"Getting it to work a lot closer to a hundred percent of the time and shrinking it to an integrated circuit the size of my thumbnail," interrupted Yancey.

"Yup, that's all." They laughed. The challenge was considerable.

Margot Fulbright broke in. "And how much time and money will that take?"

"Figure thirty engineers working for two years plus the fees for the foundry, support, and all."

"Fifteen million?" she asked.

"That's a likely outcome," I replied. "If it takes more than two turns to get the IC working, another year and another eight million. We reckon the chances of that at around twenty-five percent."

"So to be conservative we're looking at raising another twenty-five mil?"

"That's right, Margot." I skipped my next six slides and projected a list of potential partners. "And it's more than we could do on our own. I've met with representatives of the phone, cable, and consumer electronic companies you see here, and all are interested in strategic partnerships." The logos of Verizon, Time Warner, Deutsche Telecom, IBM, Sony, and Samsung lit up the screen. "We need companies who control communications in the home and business market as well as companies that can make low-cost, technically advanced products incorporating Bonds technology."

"So we're betting twenty-five mil that we can make billions?" Darwin asked.

"And we need to decide if the odds are in our favor," I responded.

I never returned to the presentation itself. The four outside members of the board continued peppering me with questions. The adrenaline more than made up for any lack of sleep. I explained how twin revenue streams would come from selling our Bonds chipsets to communications companies and from licensing the underlying technology to consumer electronics manufacturers. I answered Darwin's drill-down questions on technical risk, Margot's on the business model, and Bryce's on the strength of our patent applications. Leon did not keep his enthusiasm a secret from anyone. After ninety minutes of give-and-take, Leon applauded. "I guess Ian has thought of most everything. He's made a terrific case in favor of going for the gold."

Margot leaned forward, and Darwin started rocking in his chair. Leon's support was bringing them over to our side. But Bryce would not commit to anything until he heard from Paul.

"I can see where most everyone stands except for you, Paul," said Leon.

Paul spoke in measured tones. "First, I would like to thank Ian for that presentation. He has a vision of where Accelenet should be going, and he has made his case in his usual thorough and convincing manner. It's amazing to me that he could do such a high-quality job given what he's been through the past week."

Even as a general murmur of assent came from the other board members, my heart began to sink.

"Revenues here at Accelenet almost doubled last year. Frankly, we couldn't handle faster expansion. Our information systems are falling apart, customer support is deteriorating, it's tough to hire high-quality engineers, and the company has yet to put together two cash-flow-positive quarters in a row. We cannot gear up for the type of investment Ian's plan requires without raising more money, and who wants to do that now? The public markets are practically closed, and private investors are valuing companies like ours at a measly two times revenue. And what about the technical risks? Ian acknowledges that getting the chipset to work is a considerable challenge. Ian's outlined an innovative and brilliant plan. But a risky one."

Now Bryce saw which way the wind was blowing and chimed in. "What if the companies Ian has lined up are slow in implementing new products incorporating Bonds?"

"Then we'd need even more cash," Paul said. "Look at the networking and dot-com companies that overextended themselves and are now out of business. I have no intention of being responsible for one more dot-dead."

"But while we're studying the technology, Cisco or someone else could come up with their equivalent to Bonds," I interjected. "We need to go for it." Trying to muster enthusiasm, I knew instead my voice sounded forlorn.

Leon tried his best, but the die was cast. This was Paul's company, and nobody, including me, had ever gone wrong following his business judgment. Paul ended the discussion saying, "Fantastic work, Ian. We'll keep it under review for the right time."

I shook hands with the four outside members of the board. Leon clapped me on back and whispered, "I'll talk to him after the meeting."

"Thanks, Leon." I squeezed his bony shoulder. We gave each other a knowing look. Paul was not going to change his mind. He'd had plenty of time to think about Bonds.

I stumbled out the door and back to my desk. If Paul was going to put the kibosh on my idea, why have me go in front of the board? Why didn't he save me the embarrassment of being turned down in front of all of them? Had the time come for me to resign? I didn't know and was too drained to decide.

I noticed the blinking light indicating voicemail messages. I picked up the handset and started to roll through the twenty-two waiting messages. And for a second, I thought I heard Gwendolyn's voice again. But not quite. "Hello, Ian. This is Rowena. If it's not too much trouble, I'd like to take you up on your kind offer to pick me up from the airport. I'll be taking Southwest flight twenty-seventeen into San Jose. It arrives at twelve fifteen Sunday afternoon."

NINE

Rowena and I walked into the courtyard of a shingled three-story building in Menlo Park, a mile or two from the Stanford campus. I followed her up a wooden staircase. There was no yellow tape here, no outward sign that the police had entered Gwendolyn's last earthly abode—although they must have. Rowena fumbled with the lock a bit and then turned around.

"I am *so* clumsy." She shrugged her shoulders by way of apology. "Why don't you put my bag down? I know it's heavy."

She was right. While I had seen purses bigger than her overnight case, it pulled on my arm as if packed with lead bars.

"No problem," I replied.

I waited while Rowena's trembling hand tried to fit the key into the lock. Finally, she swung the apartment door open and slid into the gloom. With a quick flick, she opened the drapes in front of a wide picture window that overlooked the pink and white blossoms of cherry trees. Bolts of sunlight shot through the window, transforming

Rowena's long cotton skirt into diaphanous gauze. My eyes locked onto the outline of her legs.

When she started to turn around, I jerked my head up to meet her look. I gave her a hand-caught-in-the-cookie-jar smile, which, judging from her half smile in return, she took as a sign of awkward support. I berated myself. This was not the time for contemplation of the female form, and besides, in a strange way, I felt guilty of disloyalty to Gwendolyn.

Rowena sank into the wicker and cushion couch in front of the picture window. A tear dripped down her cheek. I wondered what to do, how I should comfort her. A hug seemed too open to misinterpretation, and I didn't know what to say. I swiveled my head to take in the room's other sights.

"Were Barnes and Noble your sister's interior designers?" I asked Rowena. Again a half smile in response.

Books, books, and more books. The walls were bedecked with every sort of volume—paperbacks and clothbound, tattered and new, thick and thin. Gwendolyn had even arranged shelves to go over the tops of doorways. Her books sent out tendrils of a library smell of paper, must, and ink that attracted me to them, just as her fresh-baked cookies had. I moved over to the nearest wall and started reading off the authors' names as my fingers caressed the bindings. "Margaret Drabble, Anita Brookner, Muriel Spark, Iris Murdoch . . . Barbara Pym, one of my favorites. Lots of these are British editions."

"She probably picked them up in Paris," Rowena said. I turned around and saw her wiping her eyes with a Kleenex. "Gwennie always had books. When she was in high school, her rule was one for me, one for them. She would read a book she chose herself for every one a teacher assigned." She looked down at her hands and then back up at me. "Do you really like Barbara Pym?"

"I confess. I get engrossed by every one of those lonely spinsters looking for love in drab London neighborhoods. I do really like her." When the corners of her lips twitched upward, I smiled back.

Gwendolyn had her own Dewey decimal system. One set of shelves housed American novelists, then came another crammed with volumes of history and philosophy. After passing the French section—stuffed with Proust, Camus, Yourcenar, and other immortals—I came to the doorway to Gwendolyn's bedroom. A white and yellow bedspread covered the double bed. A simple glass vase sat on the bedside table, and a pink rose drooped over the rim. Dead.

I continued my tour of the living room. Between the doorway and the corner came a shelf of English paperback mysteries. My eyes swept across a full series of Lord Peter Wimsey's as well as all the P. D. James titles I could think of. The other usual suspects—Antonia Fraser, Peter Dickinson, Robert Goddard—all made appearances.

"The mysteries make your sister seem more down-to-earth," I said.

"She read them for relaxation."

"But even there her tastes are highbrow—no Agatha Christies."

I had been hoping for another half smile, but instead her eyes began to well. Just as I resolved to go over to her, she wiped her eyes. "I'm sorry," she whispered.

The right words did not come. "For what?" I asked, and resumed circling the room, stopping at an old oak desk with a Mac on it.

"Go ahead. Turn it on," Rowena said. "I'd love to see what she was working on."

I pushed the power button. A few seconds later, a sense of déjà vu hit me—the same aborigines that inhabited the ersatz desert at my place pranced across Gwendolyn's monitor.

Rowena came over and pointed to the password box that had popped up amidst the digital Outback on the screen. "Let me try a few guesses."

She tapped out a couple of different phrases. None worked.

It became a game. I suggested her phone number, car license, address, favorite authors, and so on. Rowena knew her sister better than I did and had more ideas, ranging from the name of their old doll to the Torrey Pines High mascot.

After forty-five minutes, we ran out of ideas.

"I'll call Apple and see if they know a way to break in," I said. "People must forget their passwords all the time."

"Thanks. I'd really like to see what's in there."

"Maybe we'll find printouts in the apartment somewhere."

Rowena stood up and ran her hands across the bindings of the books. She stopped and pulled a large leather-bound album off the shelf.

She lugged it to the couch. Not knowing what else to do, I plumped myself down next to her. She opened the album without looking up and laid its front cover on my lap.

"Listen," she said. "If I start crying again, just don't mind me. Can't help it."

"Okay." Who could blame her?

I looked down at what had to be a picture of Gwendolyn at her high school prom. Her hair was swept up; she wore a white shawl that covered bare shoulders. Next to her stood a rangy teenaged boy in a midnight blue dinner jacket.

"That's Jason Blitzer, Gwennie's high school beau. He was class salutatorian and captain of the swim team."

"I saw him at the service, didn't I?"

Rowena nodded and then turned more pages. There was a casual photo of Gwendolyn reading in a contorted position no person over twenty-five could have ever considered comfortable. Next came a photo of her winning long jump at the state track meet. Her coach stood beside her, pointing at the gold medal around Gwendolyn's neck. There were pictures with her family, the kind that would be found in millions of such albums.

"Who took all these?" I asked.

"Mostly Dad or me until she gets to Stanford."

The Stanford pictures were just as typical. They showed Gwendolyn and her friends grinning goofily in her dorm and, again, her legs leading the way in the long-jump pit.

Rowena turned the pages, pausing to wipe away the occasional tear. After about ten minutes, she said, "Look. We've come to recent ones." I saw Gwendolyn leaning against her Toyota in front of her apartment building.

We came to a page where shards of tape seemed to indicate two photos had been removed. Of the two that remained, one showed Monica Hyde, her one-time freshman roommate, holding up a baby for the camera's inspection. In the other photograph, Gwendolyn stood alone in a backyard smiling at the photographer.

"Stop. What the hell?"

"What's wrong?"

"See, there's the apple tree and the Chinese elm, the ones in my backyard."

"But you said you didn't really know Gwennie."

"I did *not* take this picture."

"Who did, then?"

"I don't know. But I'd sure like to."

We sat without talking, but my mind was racing. The two missing pictures, were they of Gwendolyn in my backyard, too? Or, even worse, in my house? I did not make much progress before my cell phone began vibrating inside my pants pocket like a trapped bumblebee.

"Damn," I said, extracting the phone. "Probably just some crisis at the office. Hello?"

"Hello, Mr. Michaels? This is Ellen Ishiyama."

"Are you psychic? I was about to call you."

"I need to talk to you as well. I want you to come to my office. Do not stop anywhere. Drive within the speed limit. Turn off your cell. Where are you now?"

"At Gwendolyn's apartment in Menlo Park."

"Are you alone?" Ms. Ishiyama asked.

"Of course not. I'm with her sister. Did you think I'd broken in?"

"I'll see you in fifteen minutes." The phone clicked in my ear.

Ms. Ishiyama unlocked the door at Goodsell and Higgins and held it open. What she considered informal Sunday work attire—a creamy silk blouse, tailored black pants, pearls, and flat shoes—many women would have considered suitable for a Saturday night out in San Francisco.

"Thank you for coming so promptly. We have a situation here."

"What's that?" I asked with a falling sensation in my stomach.

"Come on. Let's sit down in my office." She relocked the door, and we padded down the hallway.

Once seated across from her massive desk, I asked, "So what is it?"

"The police have issued a warrant for your arrest."

It was what I had expected, but I still had to fight down a gagging reflex. "With what evidence?" I tried to make my tone normal.

"They have a witness who saw you go in the house just before the murder, and they have indications of a personal relationship. They think they have proof of premeditation."

I sat silently and thought. *Premeditated?* Then I grasped the point. "Because they think I faked the attack on Wednesday to set up the murder on Thursday." I rubbed the top of my head.

Ms. Ishiyama contemplated me with eight fingertips pressed together and her thumbs resting under her chin. She said nothing, so I went on.

"And the evidence of a personal relationship. That's the note on the refrigerator?"

"They have more. They have witnesses who saw you talking to Gwendolyn at Stanford."

"They must have heard that from Rowena." I winced as I spoke. She had not mentioned talking to the police. Why not? I wondered if she had suggested to them what she told me—that Gwendolyn and I had been in a relationship.

"Right. Plus they have photos."

"Like this one?" I reached in my pocket and pulled out the snapshot taken in my backyard.

"Yes. I saw two like this in the DA's office just an hour or two ago. Where did you get this one?"

"That's why I needed to see you. It's from an album Rowena and I were going through when you called." Just what I feared when I saw that pictures had been taken from the album—Officer Fletcher had them. She might sympathize with me, but that wouldn't make much difference now.

"Who took the pictures?" Ms. Ishiyama asked.

"Not me. It *looks* like I knew Gwendolyn. I did not." *Even if I wish I had*, I thought.

"Apparently, the DA's office does not place the same stock in your credibility as I do."

I wondered if she believed me because she could sense I was telling the truth, or was it that I paid her to believe me?

"She was meeting someone at my house. I have no idea who. She had some sort of secret life."

"Plenty of time to deal with that later. Right now we need to deal with the police—they're looking for you. I could call and ask, but I don't think they'll want to wait for you until tomorrow. This is murder one, and there's got to be a lot of pressure to make an arrest. I recommend we call and tell them you're coming in. You'll probably have to spend the night in jail."

I nodded.

"We can talk about how we'll make bail on the way over," she said.

TEN

"Sorry. Just routine," Fletcher said. For the second time in the last ten days, she rolled my fingers onto an inkpad and then rolled the ink off them.

The reception committee had included my old friends Mikulski and Fletcher and a pale, hunched man I didn't know. Ms. Ishiyama introduced him as Stan Jessup, the assistant DA who had pulled weekend duty. My manners made an unexpected appearance, and I stuck out my hand. I hoped he didn't feel it trembling.

"Let's get the formalities over with," Mikulski said. He pulled a small card from his pocket and began reading. "Ian Michaels, you are under arrest for the murder of Gwendolyn Goldberg. You have the right to remain silent. Anything you say can and will be used against you in a court of law. You are entitled to an attorney." Here he gave a deferential bob of the head to Ms. Ishiyama before continuing in the same monotone.

His words—which I had heard in countless movies and TV shows—turned my stomach queasy, my forehead clammy.

Finished, Mikulski turned to Ms. Ishiyama again. "This is where we say goodbye, counselor."

"It's okay," I said to her. "Don't worry. I'll be fine. I won't answer questions without you there."

"I'll get you out as soon as I can."

Fletcher gave me an embarrassed shrug as she led me over to take my prints and snap my photo. She leaned close and said, "My heart says you didn't do it."

"My mom always told me to follow my heart." That made her smile.

"Really, I hate to be the one taking you down."

"You're doing your job. I don't take it personally," I told her. "Of course, I might not feel the same after a night in a dank cell."

She smiled again and said, "Stand on the footprints." After the camera flashed, she said, "Now turn left . . . hold it . . . good. That's that."

Mikulski stepped forward with a pair of handcuffs dangling from his meaty fingers. Gunmetal gray, large and sturdy, these weren't the tin toys I had played with on the steps of the old police station as a kid. That friendly stone and brick building had been taken over by a senior center. We now stood in the back of the modernist, marble atrocity of a city hall the voters had approved in the name of progress.

Fletcher shook her head at Mikulski.

"Rules are rules, Sue," Mikulski said as he clamped steel jaws over my right wrist.

Lieutenant Tanner came around the corner, eyes panning between the two officers. "I don't think that's necessary," he told Mikulski. "You thinking of a mad dash for freedom, Ian?"

"I'm looking forward to a quiet night with friends," I answered.

A quick twist of a key, a click, and my wrist was unencumbered.

"Thanks, Officer," I said to Mikulski. "And thank *you*, Lieutenant."

"No problem," Tanner replied.

"I remember your saying that you wanted to catch up on old times. No need to have gone to this much trouble."

Tanner shook his head. "You haven't changed a bit in twenty years. Remember that story you wrote when you were a sophomore? About racism in Palo Alto high school sports? Showed guts. You still got 'em."

"Glad it looks that way to you."

"Our holding cell should be okay for the night. Come tomorrow, we'll take you down to the county jail in San Jose."

I followed the three police officers into purgatory.

———

All things considered, I was lucky to be locked up in Palo Alto and not a big-city jail. The walls of the cell were painted an off-white with nary a sign of a makeshift calendar to cross off the days. The white washbasin and toilet gleamed. The mattress was a bit lumpy and the door was made of steel, but, in all, the accommodations compared favorably with a Motel 6 I had stayed in once. Same smell, too: Pine-Sol. My reaction was different, though. I had never retched in a Motel 6.

I did make it to the toilet. Using my fingers, I washed the acrid taste from my mouth with the Ivory soap I found on the sink. I wasn't traveling with my toothbrush or a tube of Crest.

After about an hour, Fletcher stopped by to tell me she was heading over to a local deli and asked me if I wanted something to eat. My throat was raw and my stomach muscles sore, but purged and hungry, I accepted her offer. The taxpayers bought me a turkey, lettuce, and tomato on pumpernickel and a Dr. Pepper to wash it down.

I was innocent, I kept reminding myself. In second grade, a girl named Elaine told our teacher someone had stolen her brand-new pen. Miss Feldstein asked us all to open our desks. There sat the shiny pen on top of my papers. With no choice, I held it up and said, "Here it is."

Elaine sat right behind me and must have thrown her pen in my desk by mistake. Though innocent, I cringed under the suspicious stares of my classmates. I had the same sensation now. No court would hold me responsible for Gwendolyn's murder, but there had to be a reason for my abiding sense of guilt. Witnesses, photos, conversations, notes—all conspired to make me appear guilty, just as that pen had over a quarter-century before. What was my motive supposed to be? I wondered what they would come up with.

Who *did* kill Gwendolyn? Someone who had expected to find her at my house on that Wednesday. Someone who had been there before. Someone who had even taken pictures of her there—and now was making it look like I murdered her. And why had Gwendolyn called me just before she'd been stabbed?

Officers Fletcher and Mikulski weren't going to be any help to me. No matter what they thought, it was their job now to continue trying to build a case *against* me. And I sure as hell wasn't going to find the answer cooped up in Palo Alto's one-room suspect motel.

Around seven thirty, the bolt on the door clicked and Ms. Ishiyama entered the cell. I hoped the Pine-Sol scent masked any residual odor of vomit.

"Your bond was set at seven hundred fifty thousand," she said.

Holy shit! is what I thought, but what I said to Ms. Ishiyama was, "It's ten percent of that for a bail bondsman, right? I can sell stock or get a lien on my house."

"You don't have to."

"What do you mean?"

"You've got friends."

"Paul?"

"Yes. He and his wife are waiting out front. He's a good friend to have. I told Jessup I wanted to have bail set immediately. After we saw the judge—"

75

"How did you find a judge on a Sunday?" I interrupted.

"One's on call. Anyway, after the bail was set, I called Mr. Berk." She must have seen something in my expression and stopped. "Um, I hope that was okay. I thought I would line him up as a character witness to show that you wouldn't skip."

I nodded, and she went on. "Mr. Berk put up the bail, and now—poof!—you're out. And on a Sunday, too. Yes, a good friend to have."

"Let's get out of here, then," I said.

Tanner, Fletcher, and Mikulski stood shuffling their feet at the end of the hall.

"Glad to see you leaving," said Fletcher.

"Guess we won't catch up this time either," Tanner said.

Mikulski, arms crossed, said nothing.

"Until next time, then." I gave the three of them a little wave.

In the police station lobby, Kathy ran into my arms and hugged me. I shook her husband's hand.

"Thanks, Kathy. Thanks, Paul. I don't know how you managed this." Of course, I felt grateful to Paul for getting me out of jail. He had somehow come up with three-quarters of a million dollars on a Sunday afternoon. But I felt like a teenager who'd been caught by the police TP'ing a neighbor's house and whose parents had been called to come fetch him. At least, I might have liked to *try* to handle the situation myself. But I was out now. Enough of that.

Paul held up his free hand. "We'll talk about it later."

Kathy backed away and looked me over. "You don't look too much worse for wear."

"No chance for a police brutality claim, then, I guess."

We walked out the door of the station and across the street to Paul's BMW sedan.

I woke with a start. The glowing green numerals on my clock radio read two thirty. I rolled over and saw a figure standing motionless in the doorway. My fight-or-flight reaction kicked in. I hopped to the floor, ready to dive through the window.

"Who's there?"

I heard air drawn in through clenched teeth.

"It's me. Kathy."

"Kathy? You okay? What's the matter?" I rose from my crouch and took a step toward her. "How long have you been standing there?"

"A while."

"Where's Paul?"

"At home asleep. I'm worried about you. I needed to talk to you. You didn't answer when I knocked, so I let myself in."

I kept a spare key at the Berks' in case I locked myself out.

"Just a sec. Let me get a shirt." All I had on was a pair of light blue boxers. I headed for the big oak chest of drawers.

As I went by Kathy, I patted her arm. The contact galvanized her. For the second time that night, she put her arms around me. She bent her head and buried her face against my shoulder. I held her and stroked her hair a couple of times. Normally, she had it clipped and pinned, but now it hung free. I felt her nipples through her blouse against my bare chest. She was not wearing a bra. As the reaction of my own body started to betray me, I pulled away.

Two steps and I reached the dresser. I grabbed a T-shirt and slipped it over my head. The front began to soak up the tears Kathy had left on my chest.

The room was still dark, but I could see her sitting on the corner of the bed. Protected now by my shirt, I sat down next to her.

"What is it?" I asked in the kind of low voice one uses in the dark.

"I'm just so worried about you."

"I'm worried about me, too."

"I couldn't bear it if something happened to you."

"Shh. Nothing's going to happen. I didn't do it. I have a great attorney and good friends." I took her hand.

"Ian?"

She moved her face closer and brushed her lips against mine.

The kiss was a question. I released her hand. She was intelligent, supportive, and alluring. I had yet to find a woman who measured up to the standard she set. But she was the wife of my best friend and my boss; Paul had just proven how much he believed in me. I was gratified to discover I could say no to Kathy—but sorry I had to.

"Kathy, what's going on?"

"It's not working with Paul. Hasn't been. And then with you in jail . . . I lost it. I came here to tell you how I feel." She was gasping. "But I guess he and I are chained to each other. There's no getting away." Then she stood up, said, "Gotta go," and hurried into the hallway.

I chased after the squeaking pads of rubber soles on wood and caught her left wrist as her right hand opened the front door. Blinking at the light from the porch, I said, "Kathy, c'mon."

She shook her head, stray blond hairs forming a wispy veil over her face. "No, Ian. No pity, no apologies, no explanations. Don't make a bad night worse." Before any words came to me, the heel of her hand pushed hard against my chest. I let her wrist go and watched her half-run to the car. There was no look back, no wave over the shoulder as she drove away. Five minutes later, I was still staring out the doorway. Paul and Kathy had always been the perfect couple in the perfect marriage. Nothing was as it seemed.

ELEVEN

I PULLED ON A pair of jeans over the boxers and padded out the front door at eight the next morning. The automatic sprinklers raised their heads as I started down the brick walkway to rescue the newspaper from a soaking. As I started back to the house, I looked over my shoulder at Mrs. O'Flaherty's across the street. There she was, rocking in her living room. Despite my grubby attire, I turned and waved. Her face impassive, she dipped her head in reply. I wondered if she refrained from her normal vigorous wave because she thought me a murderer. Or was it because she felt guilty for helping build a case against me? Before I could pursue further nonverbal communication to find out, a rotating sprinkler took aim at me, and I ducked back inside.

The rubber band crackled as I rolled it off the morning's *Palo Alto Times*. Heart thumping, I looked down to see what Marion Sidwell had written about my arrest. Nothing above the fold. I held up the whole front page. Still nothing. An arrest in the murder that had been front-page news last week did not account for even a squib today? I crouched on my haunches, put the front section on the floor, and started turning pages. Nothing. Nothing. Nothing. Not even in the local news section.

What was going on? I had steeled myself against the screaming forty-eight-point headlines. But even without any sign of my arrest in the paper, I felt no sense of relief. The news was a monster lurking in the shadows; I might not be ready when it did pounce.

I walked into the kitchen. The holder for the cordless phone was empty. "Where is that goddamn phone?" I yelled. *Calm down*, I told myself. *Now's no time to lose it.* I took one deep breath and then another. Within a minute or two, my chest had stopped heaving, and I went to the study to use the phone there.

"Goodsell and Higgins."

"Good morning. This is Ian Michaels. Is Ms. Ishiyama in yet?"

Seconds later, I heard her familiar voice. "Hello, Mr. Michaels."

"Why isn't there anything in the paper this morning? I'm not complaining, but what's going on? What comes next?"

"Slow down, please, Mr. Michaels. The only way the press could have found out you had been arrested is if the Palo Alto police had told them. Nothing official goes on the record until the arraignment. Of course, the news would be splashed all over the front page had you gone straight to county jail. Everyone has sources there."

"So why wouldn't the police have had a press conference to tell the world that law and order has been reestablished in our fair city? They're clearly under pressure."

"I am not certain. I'd like to say they gave you a break, but it seems unlikely."

Maybe I owed Fletcher and Tanner big-time. "What next?" I asked.

"Arraignment will be set, probably for tomorrow or Wednesday. You won't have to appear in court. I can handle that. This morning I'm going to visit my old friends in the DA's office and talk to my ex-boss. Let me find out what the thinking is over there. Why don't you come by at four?"

———————

I left voicemails at work, saying I wasn't coming in. Paul would figure I was tending to legal matters; my staff would suspect I was licking wounds inflicted at Tuesday's board meeting. In fact, by nine thirty I was climbing the wooden stairway to Gwendolyn's apartment. I had told Rowena and her mother I'd help pack up Gwendolyn's things, and I meant to keep that commitment. Besides, I wanted to explain to Rowena—and at the same time dreaded explaining—why I had left yesterday in such a hurry. Better she should hear it from me than read it in the paper.

Rowena answered the door wearing a baggy UCLA T-shirt and a worn pair of double-knee painter's pants. No clandestine glances at diaphanous skirts this time.

She motioned me in. "Morning. Coffee? Uh, no, I mean, tea?"

"Please."

About a dozen sealed cartons were stacked along the far wall. Bald patches on the bookshelves told me what their contents were. I followed Rowena into the kitchen.

"This okay?" She held out a bag of Queen Anne Blend.

That damn tea again. "Perfect," I replied.

While I watched her move around the kitchen, I was trying to decide the best way to tell her I'd been arrested for her sister's murder. She set two mugs down on the butcher block table and with two short, graceful steps went to the cabinet over the range for the kettle.

"I tried to get into Gwennie's computer again last night," she said over her shoulder. "No luck."

I hit my palm against my forehead. "Sorry, I forgot to make that call to see how we can get in. Let me try now."

Five minutes later, Rowena came into the living room with my tea. "Milk?" she asked in a whisper. "No lemon here."

"You can talk. I'm just on hold. The recording tells me I have a five-minute wait. Milk is fine."

I took a sip and thanked her. Then, cradling the phone between my shoulder and ear, I started packing more of Gwendolyn's hundreds of books into the cartons. It seemed appropriate to start with the mysteries.

"How are you doing?" I asked.

She looked around the room before speaking. "It's sad staying here. I feel like Gwennie is so close. But it's not spooky like I expected."

"You're braver than I am. Since I've moved back to my place, I'm jumpy. Any noise wakes me right up."

Looking around the room again, Rowena said, "We have plenty of boxes, but we're running short on packing tape. I'll go to the 7-11 on the corner and get a couple more rolls."

As she went out the door, the automated attendant spoke in my ear, "Please be patient. All calls will be answered in the order received. We estimate that your call will be answered in fifteen minutes." I had moved backward in the queue ten minutes while I had been holding. Such were the miracles of modern technology.

I packed several more cartons and then picked up my mug and sat down in the Windsor chair in front of Gwendolyn's computer. A sip proved the tea still warm, and the Mozart playing on hold was soothing. Without thinking, I put down the mug and started fooling around with the keyboard. I typed the old exercise I had learned in Mr. Wilcox's seventh-grade typing class: "The quick brown fox jumps over the lazy dog." Of course, that didn't work. After every exercise, Mr. Wilcox required us to type in our names. So, almost without thinking, I did that.

The aborigines disappeared and the computer opened itself up to me. I leapt up and knocked over the tea. Goddammit. *My name* was the password.

A calendar of the current month took up the whole screen. I looked at the Thursday when Gwendolyn had died. "Clean, Ian's" was the only entry. The previous day read, "Row here 2PM."

The door opened, and I damn near jumped out of my skin.

Rowena flourished a few rolls of cellophane-encased packing tape and then saw the small puddle of milky tea on the desk. "Let me get you a paper towel."

She handed me a towel and peered at the screen. "Ah, they told you how to get in."

I did not correct her. Instead, I jabbed my finger at her name on the screen. "Gwendolyn's calendar says you were here the day before she died."

I turned in time to see her legs melt beneath her.

In an instant, she was sitting on the floor, sobbing. "I feel so guilty. If I hadn't left, Gwennie might still be alive."

My heart was thumping, but I tried to keep my voice calm. "Let's start at the beginning."

She took a slow breath and wiped her glistening eyes on her sleeve. "I've been trying to figure out how to tell you this . . ."

"It's all right. You can tell me now."

"Do you know what I do—for a living, I mean?" When I shook my head, she continued. "I'm a first-year associate at Tatum and Schulman, down south, a boutique firm specializing in entertainment law. Anyway, we'd just finished up on a revenue-sharing deal between two movie studios. We'd been working weekends to get it done, and the partner told me to take a few days off, so I came up to see Gwennie. It had been so long since the two of us had spent time alone, just Gwennie and I. Not at Mom and Dad's, I mean."

"So you were still here on Thursday?"

"Just in the morning. I was going to drop her off at your house at noon, go shopping, and pick her up at three. She never really told me she was your maid. She just said she had to go over to your house for a few hours."

"You assumed I was home?" A look at her expression made me understand. "You thought we were going to have some kind of afternoon tryst?"

She lowered her eyes, embarrassed.

"No wonder you reacted the way you did when I met you at the funeral," I said, nodding. "So what changed your plans?"

"I got a call from work, and the partner, well, he wanted me to come back for a breakfast meeting with our client on Friday. So I left, and Gwennie drove herself to your place. You think Gwennie would be alive if I had dropped her off, maybe gone in with her?"

"I don't know, but I do know what happened wasn't your fault."

"Thank you for saying that. I keep playing 'what if' with myself."

"Me, too. What time did you leave here?"

"Around ten thirty. I got back to Westwood by six."

"That's it?"

"Yes."

"You tell the police all this?"

"Susan, that nice woman officer, came down to Del Mar after the funeral and talked to me."

"She ask about me?"

"Nothing special. I told her I thought you were Gwennie's boyfriend, but it turns out you didn't really know her at all."

"Okay. What next?" I asked. "Why don't we see what's in the computer?"

We went through all Gwen's files. She was tidy and methodical, with an electronic checkbook and neatly categorized files for each of her classes. We opened folders and read her class assignments. One longish essay she'd written for a graduate English seminar—"Lonely Women, Fulfilled Lives: The Novels of Anita Brookner"—appealed to me; I printed out a copy to read later. We found an entry on the date she had come to hear Paul's speech at Stanford and heard me instead—the one time I had spoken to her.

We continued looking through computer files for a half hour or so and then finished packing up the books. I left at three forty-five to meet with Ms. Ishiyama.

I had not told Rowena I'd been arrested.

Ms. Ishiyama wasn't in, but she'd asked the receptionist to have me wait in her office. I had one of those you're-so-engrossed-that-you-forget-to-eat headaches I got at work a few times a month. The receptionist dug up a couple of Tylenol for me.

I was sifting through what I had learned from Rowena, and Ms. Ishiyama's return caught me off-guard.

"Sorry to keep you waiting, but I think you'll find it was worth it," she said. "I've been at the DA's office for the last three hours. I spent some time schmoozing, trying to figure out what they had that made them go for an arrest on a Sunday. Here's what happened. Mendoza—he's my old boss, the DA—and the deputy who does heavy felonies—that's Arlen now, he took my place—were at some DAs' convention in Aspen. They left Wednesday and just got back in the office this morning. Jessup was left to work with the cops who'd been urging the office to make a move on you for a few days."

"Boy, I must have made an impression on them," I said.

"Let me finish. Jessup's ambitious, and he went forward with the arrest to show Mendoza he was a take-charge kind of fellow. I sat down with them and reviewed what they have on you. It's not all that much, and they know it. I asked them, 'If Michaels and the victim were supposed to be lovers, what was he doing sending checks to Mindy's Maids every month? Why were they meeting clandestinely? They were both single. What was there to hide?'"

"What did they say?"

"Not a thing. Mendoza and Arlen are both very angry—Mendoza is 'royally pissed,' Arlen told me privately—and they think Jessup moved prematurely. When they heard that Paul Berk—*the* Paul Berk—went to bat for you, they realized what Jessup had bitten off. They're worried about bad publicity, and they're scared you'll sue for false arrest. I assured them that if charges were dropped, you had no such intention. Of course, they can come pick you up again, but for now they've dropped charges."

"I beg your pardon?"

"The charges are dropped. There will be no arraignment tomorrow or the next day. You are still the chief suspect. Of course, Jessup and the police will redouble their efforts to show they were right. But for now, you're a free man."

I put my hands on the desk to steady myself. I lowered my head and started taking deep, even breaths. Ms. Ishiyama reached across the desk and patted my hand with her long fingers.

Alone in my kitchen, I spread the paper out on the table, but after some time, I realized my eyes were not transmitting anything to my brain. I was used to spending time alone. From childhood, reading was the wall I erected between me and the outside world. But now my mind wandered. If, as Freud said, satisfying work and love led to happiness, I was light years from bliss. Work? I had my chance at the board meeting but couldn't carry the day. Love? Well, there was Kathy, married to my best friend, and Gwendolyn, murdered in my own bed. Happiness had to wait. For now, self-preservation was the name of the game. Next time the Palo Alto police arrested someone for Gwendolyn's murder, I wanted to make certain it was the murderer and not me.

But more than saving my own skin was at stake. If events had been allowed to follow their natural course, what would have happened that Thursday when I met Gwendolyn face to face? Someone had stolen her life and my chance to find out.

I looked down at my watch. Nine o'clock. I had been sitting at my kitchen table for almost an hour. What to do? Where to begin? I left the paper open, threw some clothes and toiletries in a bag, and strode out the front door.

TWELVE

I PULLED INTO THE Seawave Motel in San Clemente. My thigh muscles ached and my spine creaked as I stumbled out of the car. I managed to straighten out my hunched frame before entering the motel office. A grandmotherly, bespectacled woman pushed a registration card toward me. I started filling it out.

"How many nights?" she asked in a hospitable voice.

"Just one."

"You on vacation?"

"Sort of."

"You should stop by the Nixon Library. Open ten to five. It's only a twenty-minute drive from here. In Yorba Linda."

I looked up to see the smiling countenance of our thirty-seventh president jutting toward me, twelve inches from my face. The woman's right breast sported a 1960 "Pick Dick" campaign button, big as a compact disk.

"No, no. Never saw eye to eye with him." *As if I were old enough*, I added to myself, looking at the button again.

"Lots of people feel that way," she clucked with a glance back at a framed picture on her desk of Nixon with his wife and two daughters. "But a trip to the museum helps put all his accomplishments in perspective. He did more than flap his gums like Carter and Clinton. President Nixon opened up China, ended the Vietnam War."

What? No mention of Watergate, Spiro Agnew, Kent State, and enemy lists? "Good idea. I'll try to get over there." I handed over my American Express card.

As I headed toward Room 121, she called after me. "Don't miss the Pat Nixon exhibit. Been there thirty times and it still makes me cry like a baby."

I waved at her through the office window without breaking stride.

The room was clean, the shower was hot, the bed was hard. Nothing wrong with the motel if you ignored the politics of the proprietress. The lullaby of the surf had me asleep seconds after climbing under the covers.

On business for Paul, I had stayed in fancy hotels from the Carlyle in Manhattan to the Mandarin in Hong Kong. The eighty-nine dollars at the Seawave bought me a better night's sleep than what I got for five times more at those fancy caravansaries. Up with the sun, I pulled on a pair of shorts and ran barefoot for an hour on the hard sand by the water's edge. By eight, I was sitting on a stool at a coffee shop across the road from the motel, savoring the fresh-squeezed orange juice. By nine, I was back in the motel room dialing the phone. At ten, I was shaking the hand of Rabbi Sam Kahn at Congregation Sukkat Shalom in Del Mar.

"Thank you for seeing me on such short notice, Rabbi," I said.

"Nice to see you again. We didn't really get a chance to talk at the funeral," he said.

The rabbi escorted me into his office. Lined by chock-full bookshelves, it reminded me of Gwendolyn's apartment. Not only were there plenty of books in Hebrew and plenty more about Judaism, but the works of philosophers like Kierkegaard, Heidegger, and Jaspers were also sprinkled throughout. Open on his desk rested Marcus Aurelius's *Meditations* and Freud's *New Introductory Lectures on Psychoanalysis*.

"Rabbi, excuse me for the play on words, but you have catholic tastes in books."

"I'm doing research for a panel at UCLA next week on 'The Psychology of God.' I'm happy to talk about that, but that's not why you're here, is it, Mr. Michaels?"

Best to answer a direct question directly. "I'm trying to figure out who killed Gwendolyn Goldberg."

"Why not leave it to the police? Just last week an Officer, uh,"—he thumbed through an appointment book on his desk—"an Officer Fletcher was sitting where you are, asking me questions."

Her again.

"Three days ago, I was arrested for Gwendolyn's murder. They didn't have enough to hold me. Officer Fletcher isn't looking for the murderer. She's looking to build a case against me. I have to try to save myself."

"And just why would the police think you are the murderer, Mr. Michaels?" He showed no surprise at what I'd said.

I told the rabbi about the maid service, the notes, the photos, the meeting, and the voicemail. I even told him about the password to Gwendolyn's computer—something I had as yet told nobody else. Dark brows furrowed, he did not interrupt my fifteen-minute monologue.

"It sounds melodramatic," I said, coming to the end, "but the mystery of Gwendolyn's death is wrapped up in her life. I figured there was no better place to start unraveling it than in her hometown."

"You don't seem like a murderer to me, Mr. Michaels. But I believe what goes on in someone's mind is known only to God."

"And the person whose mind it is," I added.

"No, I don't believe that's always true. That's what Freud taught us. That we have a subconscious that can influence or even control what we do. You could be a murderer and not consciously know it."

I winced. The rabbi noticed and raised a brow in inquiry.

"No, no. I don't think I unconsciously killed anyone. But I still feel guilty. I could have done something to prevent her death. Just a little more perceptiveness, a better security system, even getting home a half hour earlier . . ."

"Uh-huh." The rabbi rubbed his chin. "I spent six years at NYU trying to become a psychotherapist. If I'd taken that route, I'd tell you that feeling responsible for Gwendolyn's death is normal. If you hadn't hired her, you might think, she would still be alive. She was murdered in your house, on your bed. That doesn't make you responsible in any objective sense, but your unconscious doesn't always think logically. I think the reason you're here is more that sense of responsibility than any effort you're making to save your own skin."

I felt uncomfortable and changed the subject. "Why did you give up psychotherapy?"

"I realized that after four thousand years, Judaism has more answers than a branch of science that's only a hundred years old. Take a look at the Bible. Talk about your dysfunctional families. A guy hears voices and decides to kill his only child. That's Abraham and Isaac. A younger brother tries to steal his brother's inheritance. That's Jacob and Esau. Jealous brothers sell their father's favorite into slavery. That's Joseph and his brethren. Judaism has been facing up to human impulses and imperfections and figuring out how to deal with them for a long time."

He paused, and we looked at each other. Of course, I recognized that the rabbi might be right in how he analyzed my motives. Perhaps he was even offering an alternative to hard work, ambition, and impressing Paul. But the timing was bad for a spiritual quest.

I broke the silence. "Makes sense, but what I need now is to find out what happened to Gwendolyn."

"You were at her funeral. You heard what people said. She was blessed with looks, brains, and talent. She intimidated people. And then maybe their high expectations intimidated her."

"Perhaps," I suggested, "she'd raised expectations so high she was afraid she couldn't live up to them. Maybe that's why she stayed in Paris and gave up the track scholarship."

"Could well be. It's a familiar problem among high achievers."

"Did Gwendolyn stay in touch with anyone around here other than her family?"

"I heard from her every now and again. Given her abilities as a writer, her e-mails were remarkable if only for being so unremarkable. Chitchat about her job and sightseeing trips when she was in Paris, about her classes and professors since she returned to Stanford in September."

"Did you save the e-mails?"

"No, sorry. Of course, the person she's closest to is her sister, but you've talked to her."

"Her parents told you I'd seen Rowena?"

He nodded. "Caroline asked me to call Abe Frankel at your congregation and check on you. She was a little worried about your helping Rowena. Abe thinks you're a *mensch*."

"He exaggerates." Rabbi Frankel, who had presided at my bar mitzvah, had always thought highly of me—even after I told him at age seventeen that I wasn't going to follow his advice and become a rabbi. "In any case, Rowena and I didn't talk much about Gwendolyn's past.

Kind of avoided it, in fact. I'll talk to her again. Anyone else stay in touch with her?"

"Jason Blitzer, her high school boyfriend. His parents are members here, too. All the adults cooed over them. She was valedictorian at Torrey Pines High, he was salutatorian. She was All-American in track, he was captain of the swim team. A golden couple. Everyone assumed they'd end up together. But he'd always dreamed of swimming for UCLA like his father had, and Gwen had her heart set on Stanford. The English department meant more to her than the track team. You know, I had the sense *she* cooled the romance off. She stayed in touch with him, though. I saw him last fall. He's working for a bank in LA."

"You know where I can find him?"

The rabbi rolled through a card file and gave me an address. "I don't have his phone number. Shall I call his parents and get it?"

"That's okay. I'll just call information. What do you think about my talking to Mr. and Mrs. Goldberg?" I asked.

"It wouldn't hurt if you waited a little longer. Jack is devastated. Caroline seems to be holding up better. I'm not sure what they could tell you that Rowena couldn't."

"Maybe I'll check back with you on that. Thanks." I rose.

"Please come again. And if you need someone to talk to . . ." He stood up, too.

"Then you'll hear from me," I said. "I enjoyed our conversation. Thanks again."

On the way back to the Seawave, I called information, but Jason's number wasn't listed. I packed and went to check out just before the one o'clock deadline. The superannuated Nixonette was still tending the motel office. I managed to settle the bill and buy an LA street map without hearing any mention of her hero. Just as I put my hand on the door to leave came the question I had been afraid of.

"You make it to the library?"

"Not yet. Had an appointment this morning."

"When you get over there, don't miss the Checkers speech. You'll see it on the monitor. It runs every half hour. Listen to the whole thing—doesn't take that long. Watch his face. You'll see a man who would never tell a lie to the American people."

"You have a wonderful motel here," I replied, and scuttled out the door.

Safe in the car, I studied the map. Having planned my route through the spaghetti plate of freeways, I aimed the Acura north toward an area of Westwood wedged between UCLA and Beverly Hills and arrived in front of a modern set of condominiums just after five. While it seemed early even for a banker to be home, I approached the cedar-clad building and rang Jason's doorbell. I heard footsteps inside shushing over a hardwood floor. Ah, for a banker's life. I had never been home by five in my entire working career.

I straightened as the steps came closer. My head was tilted upward to look into the face of a rangy swimmer, who, judging from the picture I had seen, stood a couple of inches taller than my six foot one. An eye inspected me through the peephole. I heard a gasp. The door swung open. I looked straight into the house; no blond athlete's head blocked my view. Lowering my eyes, I saw Rowena's familiar face, partly hidden by her hand over her mouth.

THIRTEEN

"May I come in?" I asked.

Rowena stood in the doorway dressed in the blue UCLA T-shirt I had seen the week before, white running shorts, and—of all things—a pair of pink, furry slippers. Damp wisps of hair, which had escaped from her ponytail, surrounded her face.

She dropped her hand and found the power of speech. "Sure. Sorry. Come in, come in." Rowena stepped aside. "I just got back from a run." A pair of white running shoes lay discarded on the polished oak floor behind her.

"So I gathered."

"How did you find me here?" And then, as if a new thought had just occurred to her, she asked, "Have you been following me?" Her tone wasn't accusing or frightened, more like embarrassed.

"This is just a happy coincidence. I wanted to talk to Jason."

"Oh." The single syllable was long and drawn out. "Why don't you sit down, and I'll make us both some tea."

She had me cast as a teaholic. "That would be great. May I use the bathroom? I've been in the car for three hours. I need to make room."

She laughed and looked back at me over her shoulder. The color was returning to her face. "Sure, go ahead. I'll get the water boiling." She pointed toward the hall.

Four rooms opened off the hall, and I peeked into them all. First was a study with a computer, lounge chair, television, stereo, and rowing machine. A headband and a pair of sweat socks were scattered on the floor in front of a futon-style couch. Next came a linen closet. I saw a queen-sized bed through the third doorway. Behind the fourth was the bathroom. I walked in and closed the door behind me.

I shook off my scruples and started to open the medicine cabinet. It creaked. I turned on the exhaust fan and finished opening the cabinet. In it were what a snoop would have found in my bathroom in Palo Alto—aspirin, toothpaste, toothbrushes, Band-Aids. On the bottom shelf also sat a box of tampons and a mascara brush. After emptying my bladder and washing my hands, I returned to the kitchen.

"Can I help?" I asked Rowena.

"You can wait in the living room. I'll just be a sec."

I sat on the couch. If a missing link existed in the evolution of interior decoration from dorm to condo, I had stumbled upon it. The modern couch I sat on still reeked of new leather; an oversized Sony flat-panel TV sat on cinder blocks and boards. The coffee table in front of the couch was smoked glass on verdigris-colored wrought iron; the dining-room table consisted of a door on two sawhorses. A vivid watercolor of a Parisian Left Bank scene graced one wall, while over the fireplace hung a giant UCLA pennant.

Rowena came in with the tea. I took a sip. Queen Anne Blend.

"My favorite again. Thank you."

"I remember. We drank it at my folks and at Gwennie's. It was delicious. Isn't that how it always is? You never notice something, then you start seeing it all over. I stopped at the Westwood Cheese Store today, and there it was."

"How long have you been living with Jason?" I knew I was being direct, even blunt, but I wanted to gauge her reaction.

"I don't live here. I have my own place."

"You spend time here, though."

She shrugged. "Sometimes, but last night was my first night here in a while. After the funeral, I stayed home. Then I came up to Gwennie's. The firm gave me personal leave." She wiped her eyes with the back of her hand as the tears started again.

"How long have you been seeing Jason?"

"Seeing him? I don't know. We've known each other forever. He was my little sister's friend. I was jogging past here one Saturday just as Jason was going out. We had coffee. I was a shoulder to cry on as he and Gwennie grew apart."

"After Gwendolyn came back from Europe?"

"Yeah."

"Did Gwendolyn know?" I asked.

"Know?"

"That you were seeing Jason."

"Seeing him? I think she was worried Jason was looking to me as a substitute for her." Now sobs supplemented the tears.

"What did you say to your sister?"

"I got mad. I told her how egotistical I thought she was."

"Is that why you really left her place early? Because you fought, because you were mad?"

"No, we would have worked it out. I told you, I had to leave because of work. I almost never fought with Gwennie, and then this time, we didn't have the chance to make up. And of course, she was right, and I knew it. He does see me as a substitute for her."

"If he does, he's nuts," I said.

She gave me her familiar half smile. She stood up. "I need a Kleenex."

She was halfway to the kitchen when a key clicked in the lock. She turned around as Jason came in, a figure straight out of *GQ*—tall, lean, broad-shouldered, blond, in a sharp Italian chalk-stripe. If I had to guess, the suit was Armani, the shoes Gucci, and the tie Hermes. My head swiveled to Rowena, who was not quite ready to join Jason in a modeling assignment—quite apart from her clothes, her eyes were red and her nose was dripping. Jason grinned when he saw her, put on a puzzled look when he took in her unhappy state, then frowned when he saw me. He turned to Rowena with raised eyebrows.

"Jason, this is Gwennie's friend, Ian Michaels."

I rose from the couch and stuck out my hand. "I hardly knew her at all, but . . ."

Jason's hands remained by his side, fingers clenched. "Rowena, I told you that I'm just not comfortable with you being alone with him." He pronounced the word "him" as though it were in capital letters.

"He's okay. I'm sure."

"What's he doing here, then?"

"He came to talk to you."

"I don't want to talk to him. The third degree from that policewoman was not pleasant." He swung toward me and said, "Please leave."

"I would really appreciate the chance to talk to you, Jason, but I can see this is a bad time."

I turned to say goodbye to Rowena and sensed Jason coming toward me. I slid to the side, and Jason's fist flew by my face as he tripped over my right leg. By the time he had used the back of the couch to pull himself up, I had my hand on the knob of the front door.

"What happened to Gwen?" he asked, his face displaying a mixture of frustration and anguish.

"Nobody wants to find out more than me. Goodbye, Jason. I hope to get a chance to talk to you again. So long, Rowena." I left.

Just as I reached the car, I heard the front door open and Rowena call my name. Doing Cinderella one better, when she started to run, *both* her slippers fell off. She scooped them up, and I watched her bare legs carry her toward me.

"I'm sorry for that," she said, breathing hard.

"It's okay. If I were Jason, I doubt I would have reacted any differently."

"He's been under a lot of stress, 'cause of work, 'cause of Gwennie. He's not really the person you saw back there. But I'm mad at how he handled things anyway. My car's at my place. I jogged over here. I told him I was going to get a ride home with you. Is that all right?"

"Sure. It's fine. But do you think it's smart? What will that be saying to him?"

Leaning against my car, I talked to Rowena while she calmed down. Jason, it turned out, was more than a bank clerk. After graduating from UCLA, he'd gone to work for an investment bank in Beverly Hills. He was going to apply to the business schools at Stanford and Harvard. I looked suitably impressed as Rowena told me what a great guy he was.

She gave my upper arm a tap and laughed. "Okay, okay. Ian the therapist. You got me going. Now I'm supposed to think, 'If he's such a great guy, I should go back in there and talk to him. He deserves that.' Well, it worked. I'll go back. Thanks anyway."

"I'll call you," I said. "I'd like to talk more."

"You know, maybe you're not the therapist after all. Maybe you're a patient like the rest of us. Finding out what happened, what Gwennie was like, is *your* therapy."

"Who's to say? Look, I'll wait here until you wave and let me know everything is okay."

"Thanks. Do call if you'd like." She kissed me on the cheek, and I watched her bare legs carry her back up to Jason's front door.

Leaning against the car, I thought about how Rowena hadn't bothered to tell me she was visiting her sister at the time of the murder. Now I find out she had taken up with her sister's ex. What next? How many more layers of the onion to peel? Then what about Jason? I didn't blame him for how he had just acted. Dumped by Gwen, taking up with her sister, he must have been at least a little confused.

Still, I counted three strikes against Jason. I had the natural Silicon Valley prejudice against investment bankers. We worked seventy-hour weeks to make a start-up successful. Then, when the payoff came, investment bankers got a six percent cut for a few weeks' effort. Strike one.

My second objection might have been a character flaw in me. I distrusted a man as good-looking as Jason. Strike two.

And finally, Jason had known Gwendolyn, been in some sort of romantic relationship with her. Even if what I felt was plain old envy, it was strike three and he was out.

Rowena waved through the front window. I waved back and drove off, wondering if Jason had told Fletcher where he'd been the Thursday Gwendolyn was killed.

At seven thirty the next morning, Kathy opened the Berks' front door looking as cool and elegant as ever. She wore a shimmering white blouse, tan slacks, and brown loafers with horse-bit decorations. She kissed my cheek, took my hand, and guided me into the kitchen. Beyond a little extra pressure on my hand—and that could have been my imagination—she gave no indication of our Sunday-night rendezvous.

I had shown up at Paul's bidding, conveyed via voicemail. Over breakfast, I recounted the events of my trip down south.

"Where do you think Jason stood on the two sisters? Do you think he was carrying a torch for Gwendolyn while he was seeing Rowena?" Kathy asked.

"Looks that way," I replied.

"So what's next?" asked Paul.

"I'm going to try to find out if Jason has an alibi for that Thursday. And if he was trying to take my head off yesterday, maybe he had tried before." I rubbed the top of my head, where a much-reduced bump still resided.

"Why are you so much more suspicious of him than Rowena? She hasn't told you the whole truth once," Kathy said. "She could have found out her boyfriend loved her sister more than her. That's motive. And she admits she was up here. That's opportunity."

"I reckon whoever killed Gwendolyn came looking for her at my place on Wednesday, her regular cleaning day. He—"

"*He?*" Kathy asked.

"You're right. It could've been a woman, but given where the bump on my head is, I'd say whoever hit me was at least as tall as I am. Now, that could be a woman, but Rowena's only five foot five or so. But Jason is a couple of inches taller than me." I brought my arm up slowly and lowered it with force. "The angle for him fits."

"Makes sense, dear," Paul said to Kathy.

"But don't worry," I said. "I won't take my eye off Rowena either."

"Shouldn't the police be doing the investigation?" Kathy asked.

"I know they're busy. I seem to be following in the tracks of Officers Fletcher and Mikulski. Maybe Ms. Ishiyama can find out more."

"I was impressed by her. Seems very competent," said Paul.

"Very competent" constituted high praise indeed from Paul.

Kathy rose from the table. "Don't get up. I have a ballet meeting in the city at nine thirty." A million-dollar donation to the San Francisco Ballet had been transformed into a board seat for Kathy. "I know you both need to talk about work, too." She leaned down and gave Paul a kiss goodbye, and then in a reprise of our parting on Sunday, she kissed me on the forehead and walked out.

I turned to my pancakes. Funny. Despite what Kathy had told me, I saw no sign she and Paul were anything but a loving couple. Just as I took my last bite, Roger appeared, as if by magic, to whisk my dishes away.

"Roger, you must have stolen your pancake recipe from the gods," I said.

Roger's round face lit up. Nobody appreciated his cooking like me. He looked at my clean plate. "Mr. Michaels," he said in his Cajun accent, "if you like to eat the food, I like to cook it."

After Roger's burly figure retreated through the swinging door, Paul said, "She didn't really show it, but Kathy is very concerned about you. After we dropped you off Sunday night, she didn't sleep a wink."

"I figured she was worried. That's why I didn't tell her the police are trying hard to build a case against me." I tried to keep my tone matter-of-fact. Did Paul know where Kathy went when she couldn't sleep?

"Some people must have been pretty embarrassed when the charges were dropped."

"That's what Ms. Ishiyama says. Paul, I am still so grateful to you and Kathy for bailing me out on Sunday."

"No biggie. Because I put up cash instead of buying a bond, there was no ten percent for a bail bondsman. And since you didn't run away and the charges were dropped, I got all my money back. Didn't cost me a penny."

"Thanks. Thanks a lot."

"Ian, I know this isn't the best time. I'm determined to be as supportive as I can. You make a big contribution at Accelenet. But now you have to worry about yourself. Your predicament has to come first, but we have a business to run. You already talked about leaving. And now it looks like you need to deal with your legal situation full time. If so, I need to make some management changes. Someone will have to take your place at least temporarily. Don't worry. We'll always have a place for you at Accelenet. Think over what you want to do. You don't have to tell me now."

I looked past Paul's youthful face. The only sound I heard was my own breathing. Then I plunged ahead. "Paul, I've worked for you for nine years. If not for you, I would be a miserable consultant squirreled away in some box up in the city. You've trusted me and given me more responsibility faster than I could have ever expected. But no matter what happens, I think it's best if I leave Accelenet for good."

"You sure? I'll hold your job if you say the word. You can think about it."

"I'm sure." I was breathing in short gulps.

"I'm not surprised. We're still friends?"

"No matter what."

As I left the Berks', I had a sense of déjà vu. I was seventeen again, getting on a plane to go to college. Cruising eastward at six hundred miles per hour, I had felt the tethers attaching me to my parents stretching and then breaking.

FOURTEEN

GWENDOLYN STARED AT ME from across the room. I sprawled on my bed, staring right back.

Rowena had let me take the photo I'd found in her album—the one where she stood in my backyard—and I had stuck it in an old photo frame. Her eyes, squinting from the sun, focused on me from her perch on the dresser. Shutting my own eyes, I could see her again on the very bed I rested on. Black hair contrasting with a pale face and bloodless pink lips.

A dagger of early morning sunshine sliced through the blinds and stabbed me through closed eyelids. I groaned and rolled away. Then came the electronic jangle of the phone.

"Hello?"

"Hello, Mr. Michaels. I didn't awaken you, did I?"

I peeked at the clock radio. "Not at eight thirty, Ms. Ishiyama. I'm an early riser. What is it?"

"May I ask you to come down to my office?"

Fortified by a bagel eaten on the way over, I entered Ms. Ishiyama's office at nine fifteen. My hair was still damp.

Ms. Ishiyama did not rise from behind her desk. Her lips formed two horizontal lines. "Mr. Michaels, representing you will be far more difficult if we are not candid with each other."

I frowned. "Yes, okay." Where was she going with this?

"Tell me again about your meetings with Gwendolyn Goldberg."

"Not 'meetings.' There was just one. I didn't think I'd met her at all, but apparently she came up to me after a speech I gave at Stanford."

"That's it?"

"That's it."

From behind her massive desk, Ms. Ishiyama pushed a piece of white paper toward me.

My eyes scanned the short paragraph of print.

Dearest Gwendolyn,

We need to talk. I still think we can make it work. The fact that we want different things doesn't make us incompatible. Can we meet for lunch at my place on Thursday?

Much Love,

"Why isn't this signed? Who is it from?"

"The police figure it was written on a computer, printed out, and then signed by hand," Ms. Ishiyama said.

"Whose computer?"

"Yours."

My mouth opened, but the words did not come out. I tried again. "I didn't write this."

"Nevertheless, the police found it on your home computer."

"What do you mean? I'd have seen it." I felt dizzy.

"I'm not certain how this works, but the police say this was written on your computer and then erased. I guess they can find it anyway. Do you know how they'd do that?"

I must not have answered right away, because I heard Ms. Ishiyama saying my name. I blinked, tried to get my brain going again. "Sorry. When you tell your computer to erase something, it isn't really gone. Whatever you've deleted stays there until it is overwritten."

"When does that happen?"

"It's random. Next time you save something, the computer might or might not overwrite what was there before. It's like dumping the kitchen garbage into the trash can in back. The garbage is out of sight, but it's still really there until the garbage truck takes it away."

"But when I drag something into the trash on my computer screen, I can't find it later."

"A couple of companies make tools to find files thrown away by accident. Most people don't know that, but it looks like Fletcher did. Bet she hasn't missed much." I looked up. "Where did you get this?"

"A colleague in the DA's office gave me a copy."

"This gives them motive and premeditation all wrapped together. So are they going to arrest me again?" My throat constricted at the memory of those hours in jail.

"Not yet is my guess. They were burned pretty bad last time. Jessup will be worried whether going through your computer was an illegal search. Now, you don't usually need a warrant at a crime scene, but I'd argue that searching the hard disk on a computer in another room isn't really a crime-scene search."

I nodded. "Then the note would be the product of an illegal search, and it couldn't be used in any trial."

"Good knowledge."

"Jessup's trying to show you that they have me dead to rights," I said. "He's hoping you'll urge me to cut a deal."

"A deal might make sense if I were defending the murderer."

"You're not. And I didn't write that note either."

"So who did?"

"I don't know. But we need to find out. We owe Gwendolyn that."

"Maybe. But right now my job is keeping you a free man."

Never certain when the opportunity for a jog would present itself, I kept a gym bag in the trunk of my car. I had decided to leave Accelenet, so there was no reason to head to the office. What I needed was a run.

Leaving Ms. Ishiyama's office, I turned west toward the hills instead of east toward town and my place. Riding in the back of my parents' Country Squire station wagon thirty years earlier, I would have been passing apricot orchards and horse trails. We didn't know it, but they had already been condemned when William Shockley opened a company in 1955 to exploit his invention of the transistor. In an almost biblical sense, Shockley Semiconductor was the progenitor of hundreds of the firms flourishing in the Valley, for people from Shockley begat Fairchild and people from Fairchild begat Intel and someone from Intel begat Apple, and so on. In a variation on the biblical theme, two of Shockley's most promising disciples, Gordon Moore and Robert Noyce, revolted against the founding father of the Valley to start that first competitor, Fairchild Semiconductor. Shockley was left claiming betrayal and ended his days using his Nobel Prize to defend his indefensible views on eugenics. This drama set the tone for Valley culture: young, brilliant technologists breaking away from companies run by the previous generation of entrepreneurs and founding their own.

Once a fellow named Gordon Teal discovered that Shockley's transistors could be built out of silicon—beach sand—it was inevitable that orchards would be replaced by semiconductor factories and then by tilt-up office buildings filled with software nerds. The world's best engineers and programmers were attracted like iron filings to the twin magnets of cutting-edge technology and low-priced stock options. What had once been known as the Valley of the Heart's Delight was now Silicon Valley, the high-tech capital of the world.

Grassroots environmentalists and farsighted politicians had combined to preserve the hills ringing Silicon Valley from the encroachments of expressways, parking lots, commercial buildings, and multi-acre estates. Each year, in a miracle of rebirth, the winter rains turned the sere brown hills lush green for a few months. Knowing the end of this annual Eden approached, I spent twenty minutes driving up a tortuous two-lane road that brought me to the entry gate. A ranger emerged from his shack, checked my driver's license, and waved me through. Foothills Park was open only to Palo Alto residents—to the resentment of those living in neighboring towns. At the first fork in the road, I went up and to the right and parked on Vista Hill.

The brisk breeze had chased away the normal haze. The deep blue background gave a sense of depth to the fleecy clouds scudding across the sky. Thirty miles north, I spotted the Transamerica Pyramid sprouting from the small thumb that was San Francisco. Turning east, I searched for my own house, but the trees that lined Palo Alto's streets hid it beneath a green parasol. Then I looked south and saw the three huge gray hangars at Moffet Field that had housed the Navy's dirigible fleet in the thirties. And running all the way from San Francisco to Moffet shimmered the blue of the bay.

On a weekday morning, there was nobody around to see me changing into my running togs. I stripped, pulled on a ragged T-shirt and nylon running shorts, then stretched. Hams, quads, calves, back. It felt good to be outside in the crystalline air of the hills, and I began loping down the trail. Muffled by a mat of clover and grass, my footsteps made no noise. I focused on my breathing. After thirty minutes, I was inhaling and exhaling rhythmically, and my mind turned malleable. What to do next? Having left Paul, my mentor, maybe I should follow the example set by Moore and Noyce and start my own company. I would be chasing my dream without the need for Paul's approval.

Running into a strong breeze, I started up another hill. Evaporating perspiration kept my face cool, but I felt splotches of sweat spreading across my shirt. Now, how had that note come to be on my computer? The police and DA would see it as proof that I had lured Gwendolyn to my house to kill her. Lying in wait counted as one of the special circumstances that justified the death penalty. I realized that when Ms. Ishiyama spoke of keeping me free, she was really talking about keeping me alive.

Enough thinking. I was trying to refocus on my breathing when I rounded a boulder and saw it. About thirty feet ahead of me. A crouching tawny coat amidst the dappling of the shadows. Coyote? No. I had come across coyotes in the hills before, but this was no coyote. The creature stretched out six feet, not counting the long, thick tail that slithered on the ground. It studied me through pale amber eyes. Even through the fur, I could see powerful muscles flexing. He had been trotting downhill just as I had been uphill. The wind blowing toward me meant he hadn't smelled me. The padding on the path meant he hadn't heard me. The twist in the trail meant he hadn't seen me. The mountain lion and I stared at each other in mutual surprise.

I turned to run. I looked back over my shoulder and saw him scraping a paw against the path like a bull before the charge. No way was I going to turn my back on that animal. So I stopped and faced him head-on. I looked right into the amber eyes, and he looked right back into my blue ones.

Ending the stalemate, I raised my arms, waved them, and took a step toward the animal. I yelled with all the power and fear inside me, "Get the hell out of here!" My words echoed off the hillsides.

I doubt the creature understood English, but after one last stare, he slinked back into the chaparral and golden poppies that bordered the path. I waited before turning my back on the spot where he disappeared. Then I headed back to the ranger station. It was only a half mile away, but my heart thumped as though I had just finished the Boston Marathon.

I entered the wooden building and found a tall, bulky blond fellow adjusting stuffed animals in the exhibit area. His green shirt and Smokey Bear hat marked him as a ranger. His nametag said "Roy." He and his colleague back at the entry gate were the only two people I'd seen at the park.

"May I help you, sir?"

"Yes, I was just running down the Toyon Trail by Wild Horse Canyon and came across a mountain lion."

"Just a sec." He went into his office and came out with a clipboard. He held it up. "Procedures," he said. He certainly was taking all this more calmly than I was. "Please describe the animal you saw."

"About six feet long, two or three feet high."

Ranger Roy was taking notes in a casual way. "And how close were you?"

"About twenty feet."

"Short little tail?" he asked.

"No. The tail was as thick as my arm. Two feet long or maybe three."

"Oh, shit." The ranger dropped his pencil. "Sounds like you saw a mountain lion."

"Yeah, that's what I just said."

"Well, a few people every month come down here to the station reporting a sighting. It always turns out to be a bobcat. Bobcats can get over three feet long, but they have short little tails."

"There aren't mountain lions here?"

"Must be. Now and then we come across deer they've killed. But in the last five years, we've only had two sightings. And you were a lot closer than either of them. What did you do?"

I raised my arms, took a step toward him, and shouted just as I had at the lion.

Roy whistled. "Smart. If you start running away, their reflexes can kick in. They like to kill from behind. Woman jogger near Lake Tahoe was killed that way. She ran away and the lion jumped on her back and ripped out her throat. They found her partly eaten under a pile of leaves. Mountain lions will leave you alone if you look big and intimidating."

"So will most humans," I said. "Anyway, I wasn't smart. I was lucky."

"Showed a helluva presence of mind either way. *I've* listened to lectures on what to do, and I figure *I'd* take off like a rabbit." He licked the tip of the pencil and scribbled on his form. Then he looked up. "If it's okay with you, I'll call the city naturalist. He'll want to walk out to where you saw the lion and take a full report. Procedures," he explained again, and went back to the office to make the call.

Two hours later, I drove out of the park. I was reveling in being alive, in surviving a primal danger. The time had come to take action, to step out from behind Paul, to make my life my own. Time, too, to confront that other predator who was trying to pull me down from behind. Whoever murdered Gwendolyn represented a bigger threat than any mountain lion. For that person killed not out of instinct, but out of cunning malice.

FIFTEEN

Baths have never made much sense to me. They take longer than showers and don't impart the same sense of squeaky cleanliness. Of course, in a small hotel overseas or even on a weekend stay at a friend's place, a bath might be the only alternative to body odor. Still, I didn't remember ever having taken a bath at home on a weekday afternoon, but here I was lowering myself inch by inch into scalding water. Within minutes, the steam had unfrozen my brain. My limbs floated limply on the water's surface, but my mind was running smoothly, and I resolved on my next step.

Just after four, legs still rubbery, I pulled in front of a wood-and-glass Eichler on Palo Alto's South Court. Named after the builder who had built a few thousand of them in the 1950s, Eichlers were meant to be affordable. Originally, they met that objective—my parents had purchased one for less than fifty thousand dollars—but now they cost at least twenty times as much.

A white Mazda minivan with a baby seat nestled in the narrow driveway. I rang the doorbell.

"Who's there?" a woman's voice called out.

"Ian Michaels. I wanted to talk to you about Gwendolyn."

"Just a minute." I heard a baby crying.

After about ten minutes of waiting, I knocked lightly again.

"Sorry. Just let me get the baby settled."

I started composing an apology for awakening him, but didn't get too far before a white Palo Alto police cruiser pulled up. Mikulski came out of the car and walked toward me.

"Hello, Officer," I said in a pleasant tone.

My attempt at hospitality went unreciprocated. Mikulski had screwed his surfer-boy countenance into an expression meant to look tough. But genetics had given him a round, open face, and he couldn't quite pull it off.

"We have a complaint. Are you harassing the homeowner here?"

I felt a pang of betrayal. The Monica Hyde with the squeaky voice I had liked so much at Gwendolyn's funeral did not trust me. No reason she should—we had not met. In any case, she was a cool customer. She had called the police and made sure I waited for them.

"No harassment, Officer. I just asked to talk to her. That's all."

"Why?"

"I wanted to ask her a few questions about Gwendolyn Goldberg."

"Why?"

"I'm trying to figure out what happened to her."

Mikulski pushed me against Monica's garage door and held me there with a meaty hand against my chest. "No, *I'm* the guy trying to figure out what happened. You're the asshole who keeps interfering."

Except during college, I had lived in Palo Alto since birth. I thought of the police as protectors against burglars and vandals. I waved at officers cruising by when I was out jogging. Even when I was arrested, I reckoned the police were just doing their job. They'd seemed polite, even apologetic. All that proved hard to remember now. My instinct was to swat his hand away. Mikulski must have known that, wanted that. Confronting the mountain lion head-on had made sense. Confronting Mikulski the same way did not.

"How so?" I was hoping I sounded calmer than I felt.

"You've been snooping around her apartment, talking to her sister. Now you're bothering her friends." He pressed his hand harder against my chest. "Go home. Stay out of our way. A woman was killed. This is real life, not some movie. In real life, it's the police who find the killer, not the prime suspect. Just stay out of our way."

"Thanks for the advice. I'll go home now. Give my best to Officer Fletcher."

On the way home, I wondered why Gwendolyn's old roommate wouldn't talk to me. How did she even know who I was? And why was she afraid? Had the police scared her?

Once home, I settled down to read the morning's *Palo Alto Times*. Right on the front page was the answer to my musings: "Police Narrow Search for Goldberg Murderer," by Marion Sidwell. My eyes scanned the story and then went back up to the first paragraph for a detailed reading.

> Palo Alto police are getting closer to an arrest in the Gwendolyn Goldberg murder. The *Times* has learned from police sources that the investigation is now focused on a single suspect.
>
> The suspect allegedly had a personal relationship with Ms. Goldberg that she had just called off. Police have recently reconstructed a note that the suspect wrote suggesting a rendezvous at the house of high-tech executive Ian Michaels. A witness saw the suspect go into the house close to the time of the murder.
>
> Ms. Goldberg, a Stanford senior, was working as a house cleaner when she was stabbed to death at Mr. Michaels's house on Lincoln Avenue on April 17. Ellen Ishiyama, the former lead felony prosecutor for the Santa Clara County District Attorney's

office, has reportedly been retained by Mr. Michaels. Neither she nor Mr. Michaels was available for comment.

Lieutenant Robert Tanner declined to comment on reports that an arrest was imminent.

With shaky hands, I turned to the continuation of the story on page eight. Sidwell never identified the suspect, but the *Times* had already reported I was the only person seen going into the house other than Gwendolyn. That, together with the sentence about Ellen Ishiyama, made the suspect's identity pretty clear to me. Apparently to Monica Hyde, too.

They meant to scare me, to try to make me confess. It was part of a campaign that included showing me the reconstructed note. The police and DA didn't have enough for an arrest, so they were hoping I would crack and make a deal. What next?

I began reading again, but the rest of the story was pretty much a rehash of what had run the day after the murder. The only news was that Mayor Frances Lister intended to put her plan for community policing before the city council—presumably to stop murderers like me. I snorted, and before the last of the air had left my nostrils, someone rapped at the front door.

I pulled myself away from my reflections on political grandstanding. Through the front window, I saw a white Ford Crown Victoria topped by a red siren. Mikulski coming back to push me around with his index finger again? *Stay calm*, I told myself, then swung open the front door. There stood the sturdy Officer Fletcher, this time wearing civilian clothes—a navy blue pantsuit and powder blue blouse.

"I mostly came to apologize," she began. "John told me what happened at Monica Hyde's. He shouldn't have pushed you around." She gave me an embarrassed grin.

"He gave me what he considered to be good advice," I said. "He thinks it's *his* job to be the detective. Anyway, I appreciate your apology." I hesitated. "My lawyer would shoot me for saying this, but why don't you come in?"

"Tanner wouldn't think it was such a good idea either," she said. But she stepped inside.

"Coffee, isn't it? Milk, no sugar?"

She nodded, and as she did so, the brown hair of her old-fashioned wedge haircut flapped up and down.

I loaded the coffee into the funnel of the Melitta and had a steaming cup of Peet's Dark Sumatra in Fletcher's hand in less than five minutes.

She took a small slurp. "I remember. You make about as good a cup as any non-coffee-drinker alive." She held up her mug in salute.

In business negotiations, the key to success is not talking. Make your counterpart uncomfortable. Make him—or her—come up with the first offer.

She took three or four more sips before speaking. "How are you doing?"

"Are we playing a game of 'good cop, bad cop'?"

"Maybe a little, but not intentionally. Mikulski just should not have come down on you like that."

I waited.

"Look. Tanner tells me I'm doing well. Finding the note on your computer, it blew the socks off everyone."

"It was good thinking to look. Most police officers wouldn't know about retrieving discarded files off a hard disk."

She acknowledged the compliment with a nod. "Now, Jessup and Mikulski, they smell blood. We don't get too many capital crimes in Palo Alto. It's their chance. Jessup wants to be head of the major felony prosecution unit. Mikulski wants to be a sergeant."

116

"And you?"

"I want to catch the murderer."

"Me, too."

She leaned forward. "That's it. We want the same thing. You must have suspicions, ideas of who did it. We could help each other."

"And if *I* did it?"

"I don't think you did. I've got a pretty good picture of you."

"How?"

"I've talked to your neighbors and coworkers." She looked down at a notebook. "About three dozen of them."

I winced.

"Give me credit for some discretion," she said. "I told them all it was just normal procedure. None of them figure you as a suspect. The picture they painted was of someone who was hardworking and hard-driving, but fair and honest. A couple of the women suggested you needed to settle down." Fletcher raised an eyebrow.

"That's embarrassing."

"One more thing. You don't panic. When you lost a big customer, the VP of sales wanted to fire the sales rep right on the spot. Not you. You were methodical. You flew out to Atlanta and talked to the customer, found out your product kept breaking."

"So?" I asked.

"So I don't think you killed anyone, but let's say you did. This isn't how you'd do it. You'd have planned it out. You would have made sure you weren't a suspect."

"Thanks. I'm probably not a killer, but if I am, I'm a cold-blooded one?"

"That's how I see it. I've done the checking."

"Everybody I've talked to seems to have spoken to you or Mikulski already. Can't see how I could help you much."

"There's a lot I don't know. Who took that picture of Gwendolyn? Who wrote that note on your computer? Who was she meeting here? What do you think?"

"I don't know. Objectively, I can see that I look like the odds-on suspect."

"My dad used to take me to the horse races every summer at the county fair in Santa Rosa. You know, he always did pretty well. 'The way to win,' he used to say, 'is by being right when most people aren't.'"

"Does that mean you're a little ambitious, too?"

She blushed. "If everyone thinks it's you, and I show it's not, I win. Tanner's fair. He'll notice."

"It's certainly in my interest to help you, and I will if I can. Now two of us want you promoted."

"You won't tell anyone about this conversation?"

"Why not? They'll compliment you on your creativeness in winning my confidence."

She laughed. "They would at that."

"The person who's going to get in trouble for this conversation is me. My lawyer warned me not talk to the police without her."

She laughed again and stood.

Walking to the door, I asked, "You like being a detective?"

"I love it. I like talking to people. I like trying to figure out what happened and why."

We shook hands to seal our battlefield alliance, and I shut the door behind the retreating blue figure.

So was this an act? Was Fletcher playing good cop? Maybe she just *was* a good cop. Didn't matter. When you're drowning, you don't question the motive of the person who throws you a life preserver.

SIXTEEN

JULIANA CALLED MY NAME. I turned. She stepped from behind the half-circular receptionist's desk in the Accelenet lobby. An oversized sweater hung to the tops of her thighs, where black leggings picked up the chore of covering her skin. That line about Cyd Charisse popped into my mind: "Her legs would have gone on forever if the floor hadn't stopped them."

"Ian, you're not even saying hello to me anymore." Juliana extended her lower lip into a pout.

"Juliana, good morning. I must be in a haze."

She looked right, then left, to make certain nobody was within earshot. Not likely at 7:35 in the morning.

"Because of the police?" she whispered.

"What about the police?"

Juliana took a step closer, and then the words spilled out. "A tall, blond fellow and a stocky lady cop were in here the day before yesterday."

"About the woman murdered at my house."

"Right. They asked if I'd met her."

"Had you?"

"No, but they asked to see my logs of who's in and who's out."

So that was the problem. She felt guilty for helping the police, who, she feared, were trying to build a case against me. "Helping the police is the right thing to do."

She let out a sigh of relief, then went on with her confession. "They asked about you, too. What time you come to work, what our working relationship was."

"Did you tell them innocent flirtation?"

A red flush spread from her neck to her cheeks. "Cut it out, Ian. This is serious. You're in trouble, aren't you?"

"No, not really. The police have to follow every lead till it peters out. Please just keep telling them the truth."

Oh yes, Officers Fletcher and Mikulski were paragons of discretion.

"Okay. When are you coming back to work, Ian?"

"Just going up to discuss that very question with Paul."

I had called Paul the previous afternoon after Fletcher left. I asked if I could come in and tell my staff I was leaving. All told, I had four direct reports and twenty people in my group, plus another ten on the Bonds team. I wanted them to hear that I was leaving from me, not in some company-wide e-mail. A few had left me messages asking when I would be back. Not wanting to meet up with any early birds, I went to Paul's office without stopping at my own.

Phone pressed against his ear, Paul signaled me to sit down.

"Okay. I'll see you in Milan on the sixth, and I need to be in London on the afternoon of the eighth." Paul traveled about half the time. The best way to understand our customers, he always said, was to talk to them. Our salespeople's entreaties fed Paul's wanderlust. Not many big deals closed at Accelenet without him.

"Listen, Ian just came in. Gotta go. See you on the sixth."

Paul hung up. "Roberto says hello." Paul walked over to the door and shut it.

"Sales look good in Europe this quarter?" I asked.

"So-so. Roberto thinks I can help close a couple of orders. But enough of that. You want to make an announcement you're leaving?"

"I'd appreciate telling my team myself. They wonder what's going on."

"Look, Ian, how anyone can survive the pressure you've been under, I don't know. Police skulking—"

"They talk to you, too?" I interrupted.

"Sure."

"What did they ask about?"

"About what you did here. About where you were on the day of the murder. About your reaction right after the murder. That kind of thing."

"Did they talk to Andrea, Barney, Deepak, and Grant?" They were my direct reports.

"Yup."

"They must wonder what the hell is going on. I need to talk to them."

"Maybe you should slow down. With what you have going on, you don't need to worry about unemployment, too. Take some more time to think about resigning. Take vacation. If you don't have any more, you can take a leave—with pay."

"I have about twelve weeks of vacation accrued." I hadn't had more than a few days off since I started at Accelenet.

Paul leaned across his desk and looked straight at me. "We need you here. I want you to come back. Take some time. Think about it."

"I have been. I'd like to start something myself, chase my own dream." I filled my lungs with air and then plunged ahead. "Here's what I want. I want to buy the Bonds technology from Accelenet. You don't want to develop it. I do." What had begun as a daydream on my jog through Foothills Park now flew out of my mouth as a fully formed conviction. Facing the mountain lion had catalyzed my desire.

"Where would you get the money?"

"I have some, thanks to you. And I'd go talk to some of our venture capital friends."

"The vulture capitalists?" Paul knew I would have to give up a far bigger piece of the company now than I would have at the height of the boom. He also knew Bonds was a bet some of the braver ones would make.

"What can you do?" I held my hands out, palms up. "I want to give this a shot."

"Right. You've got the police poking around your life, and you're going to start a company. I'll tell you what. We'll both think things over. I'll think about selling Bonds to you, and you think about coming back here."

"Deal," I said. So the tethers that connected my business career to Paul had been stretched, not broken.

Paul licked his lips and asked, "Could I talk to you about something else?"

"What is it?"

"Kathy and I have decided to live apart for a while."

"Oh, damn."

"What I said isn't quite right. She's decided to leave me." Paul sat back in his chair, arms folded across his chest.

"What is it? Why?" I was surprised, but much less than I would have been before Kathy came to see me the night of my arrest.

"She says we've been leading separate lives." Paul's teeth were clenched, as though trying to keep his emotions under control. "That we've grown apart. She wants to write poetry. I told her we can work it out."

"Not by going to London, Milan, and Cologne."

"You're right. I need to spend more time with her."

"You need a place to stay?"

"No, she's moving out. She's rented a cottage."

"Paul, I might be a little out of line, but I think you need to work this through. Isn't it more important than Accelenet? Throw yourself into it. Nobody I know has your powers of persuasion. *You* should take time off for personal reasons."

Paul's eyes glistened a little, but maybe it was just the way the early-morning light came through his office window. "Let me know what I can do," I finished.

"Thanks. It's nice to have friends at times like these."

"Ditto."

———

I turned to the last page of the book.

> So irrelevant did her death seem that I almost looked forward to discussing it with her. "What was it like?" I should have asked. The eyelids would have come down again as she considered. "Not all that bad," I can hear her say, in her famously throw-away tone. "You might give it a try one of these days."

I shook my head to escape the reverie and snapped shut Anita Brookner's *Brief Lives*. Reading Gwendolyn's essay had prompted me to pick up the book from the library on the way back from my talk with Paul. Once home, I had started leafing through it and, despite myself, had been drawn into the story of middle-aged Fay and her relationship with the superior and glamorous Julia. Absorbed, I had read how the scorned Fay had betrayed Julia—or perhaps just avenged herself—with a love affair with Julia's husband. Now, like a drunk awakening after a binge, I emerged into full consciousness and found myself with my legs draped over the arms of the paisley club chair in my living room. What in this book had appealed to a woman in her early twenties?

The title page of Gwendolyn's essay told me it was written for a class called "In the Footsteps of Jane Austen: English Women's Novels in the Twentieth Century." A Professor Woodward taught the class. I picked up the phone.

Ninety minutes later, I was crossing the Quad, which the robber baron Leland Stanford had built in memory of his son. The professor had given me explicit directions. I was to look up at the mosaic on Memorial Church and follow Jesus's outstretched hand to the right. "We're nestled in the bosom of the Lord," she'd said. I laughed when I looked up at the mosaic. It did appear that Jesus's arms were pointing to the buildings on either side. Trotting off, I came first to the Department of Judaic Studies. From a historical perspective, the proximity of Jesus and that department seemed appropriate. But then it occurred to me that I had followed Jesus's own right hand, which meant I had gone the wrong way. On the other side of the church, I found an entry door marked Department of English. I climbed the creaking set of wooden stairs that were surely the very ones Governor Stanford's entrepreneurial plunder had paid for. On the third floor, I rapped on a door made of translucent glass better suited to a shower stall than an academician's office.

"Come."

"Professor Woodward?" I was talking to a woman of around forty-five whose blond hair had been cut into a utilitarian bob and who wore glasses with oversized octagonal lenses. She looked like a stereotype of an English teacher, but when she stood up from behind the pile of papers on her desk, I saw she wore a basketball jersey and shorts. Neither short nor tall, heavy nor thin, she was in good shape. Healthy body, healthy mind, as the Greeks used to say. I lowered my estimate of her age to an even forty.

"Mr. Michaels? Sorry, I haven't changed from my lunchtime run. Please sit down." She wagged five fingers toward a chair in front of her desk. A direct, overland route would have brought me to the chair in three steps, but I had to navigate through an obstacle course of stacked books.

"Thank you for seeing me, Professor."

"Call me Nancy. I always figure if someone wants to climb those rickety stairs and find their way through this minefield of books, I ought to see them. Now, you said you want to know about Gwen Goldberg. Are you a detective? Hired by the family?"

"Not exactly. She was killed in my house."

"So?"

"I've been caught up in the case."

"Don't blame you. I certainly haven't gotten over her death. Did you ever teach—uh, was it Ira?"

"Ian. Just a few guest lectures at the B-school." Professors there had modern offices triple the size of Professor Woodward's. The business school was swimming in the donations of the great and grateful; somehow, I suspected, less money found its way to the English department.

"Let me tell you why a humanities professor teaches. First of all, it's to have the time to do what you love, and I love English literature. Reading it and writing about it and getting paid for it—now that's paradise. Teaching can just be the price you have to pay. Introducing Stanford students to the joys of literature is like being a nineteenth-century missionary in Africa. The local natives humor you but see no real need for what you're preaching. Students here look at learning as a means to an end. They want to be doctors or lawyers, journalists or entrepreneurs. But you know, every so often a student comes along who is just as enthusiastic about what you're teaching as you are. And you can see the potential—it makes my heart sing. That's why I really love teaching. I've had about a dozen students like that in twenty years of teaching. Gwen was one."

"And talented, too?" I asked.

"Yes. But she never believed it. She figured Stanford wanted her because she could jump farther than almost any other woman in the country. And the boys—she was astute enough to see they weren't swarming around her because of her critical faculties."

"Was there any boy in particular?"

"She was polite and she joked around with them, but I don't think so. Maybe when she was here the first time, but she's more focused now—or rather was. Since she returned this year, the only friend I know she had was a woman named Monica Hyde. Have you spoken to her?"

"Stopped by her place yesterday, but didn't get the chance."

"Monica's a grad student now. There was always a friendly rivalry between them. Monica's good, very good, but . . ."

"But no Gwendolyn?" I finished.

Her shrug said it all. "You should have read the piece she wrote on Anita Brookner," she said.

"I did."

"Really?"

"Her sister and I found a copy when we were packing up Gwendolyn's apartment."

"Terrific, wasn't it? I had her as a guest on my cable show to discuss it."

I leaned forward. "Is there a tape?"

"Sure. I'll show it to you now if you'd like."

"Yes, please." I held my breath.

She wended her way among the stacks, reached into a box in the corner, and snatched a videocassette. She had known just where to go; Nancy Woodward's filing system was more systematic than it appeared.

She shoved the tape into the maw of a small combination TV/VCR on her desk. It began to whir. "I have this to watch the lectures on the Stanford Instructional Network," she said with an embarrassed smile.

"Where did this play?"

"You don't watch my show?" Professor Woodward asked in mock horror. She pushed the fast-forward button. "Book Talk. It's on closed circuit on campus. It's also on the Palo Alto cable network. Channel 75."

"I'll look for it."

"Here you go." The professor swiveled the small screen so we could both see it, and I brought my face closer. There, tall and composed, her black hair pulled into a ponytail, sat Gwendolyn. Her pale face accentuated the blue eyes and dark smudges under them.

It was not a prince but a videotape cassette that brought Sleeping Beauty back to life. Gwendolyn was talking, and I stared without hearing. Only when she began gesturing with animation did I force myself to listen.

"Yes, *Hotel du Lac* is Brookner's most accessible book. It's about a woman who refuses to wither away after a disastrous love affair. She's going to try again. Brookner's protagonists are always looking for love." Gwendolyn showed no sign of nervousness. She spoke without "likes," "uhs," "ums," or "okays." This time her voice sounded lower than Rowena's, lower than I remembered from the voicemail—almost a throaty growl.

"And your favorite?"

"That has to be *Brief Lives*. Brookner explores the claustrophobic existence of one lonely woman, named Fay, and makes us understand how much humans need relationships. She seems to be telling us that even a flawed relationship is a better choice than solitude. She casts no moral aspersions at Fay's affair with a friend's husband. Fay also faces up to the consequences of death in the story." I shuddered at these words.

"Could you read us a passage?" the professor asked.

Gwendolyn began reading the ending of *Brief Lives*, the same paragraph that I had finished a couple of hours before. Two minutes more and the segment ended. I let out the breath I'd been holding.

The professor flicked a tear from her cheek. "That was just last month. She was getting over the flu. Made her sound a little like Lauren Bacall."

"Uh, do you have an extra copy of the tape?"

"Sorry. I just loaned it out."

"Oh?" I knew what was coming next.

"To a police officer investigating Gwendolyn's murder. An Officer, uh, Fleming?"

"Fletcher."

"Yes, that's it. You know her?"

"Getting to."

SEVENTEEN

"Got you." A long, bony hand grabbed my elbow from behind.

The black-haired beauty with the husky voice vanished from my mind's eye. "Leon!" I hadn't seen him since the board meeting.

"Were you in a trance?" he asked, chest heaving. "I chased after you for a hundred yards, bellowing your name the whole time."

"Sorry. The body was here, but the mind was elsewhere. Sure glad to see you, though."

"It's professors, not rising Silicon Valley stars, who are supposed to have their heads in the clouds."

Seeing Leon Henderson was always a morale booster. "Rising star? Me? You were at the last board meeting. I've moved into the right lane of the freeway of life."

"Slow down. We'll talk about it once I catch my breath."

His hand still on my elbow, Leon guided me through the sandstone walls and red tile roofs of the Quad. Jogging, biking, rollerblading, and walking, the students were pretending summer had already arrived. Shorts, T-shirts, and sandals made up the uniform of the day.

"I left a message on your machine this morning," Leon was saying. "Been wanting to talk to you. And you were right on campus. What are you doing here, anyway?" he asked.

"Discussing Anita Brookner with—"

"Who?"

"The Booker Prize winner from—"

"Is that the graduate engineering prize? Did I have Anita in my entrepreneurship seminar last year?" Impatient in everything, Leon had apparently resolved not to allow me to finish a sentence.

"I doubt it. She's an author. The Booker Prize is the British Pulitzer." Leon, I knew, belonged to the digerati, not the literati. I could imagine him leafing through an article on the latest breakthrough on silicon lithography, but the last novel he read was probably *Middlemarch* in freshman English a half-century before.

"What's going on at Accelenet?" he asked.

I recounted how I'd tried to resign. "I told Paul if Accelenet isn't doing anything with Bonds, I'd like to buy the technology from them."

"Figured you'd come to that conclusion," Leon said. He was no expert on the modern novel, but Leon *was* a perceptive scholar of Silicon Valley psychology.

"You figured that out right away? You could have saved me a lot of mental exertion."

Leon sighed. "I don't know what's up with Paul. Twenty years ago, he would have leapt at the chance. He started Berk Technology when he was under thirty."

"Don't rub it in."

"People told Paul he was too young. He went and proved them wrong. 'Big risk, big reward' is what he always said."

"I probably didn't make the case compelling enough."

"Baloney. The last presentation I saw *that* good was Paul's when he raised the original money for Berk Technology. The venture fellows said they'd see him as a favor to me. By the time he'd finished, they were making out seven-figure checks." Leon chuckled at the memory. "In fact, I closed my eyes when you were talking and felt like I was listening to Paul twenty years ago."

"Is *that* what you were doing? I didn't just put you to sleep?"

"What did Paul say?" Leon asked.

"He said he'd think about it if I would think about coming back to Accelenet."

"Paul knows you're the future of the company, and he knows you didn't kill the girl. For the last couple of years now, it's been your ideas that have fed the company."

"Not so, Leon. Paul's the one. You think we'd be on the cover of *Business Week* if not for him? You think we'd get in to see the head of Reuters if not for him?"

"Sure, he's got the reputation, but behind the scenes we both know who put together the network demo that dazzled Reuters. We know it's the development strategy you laid out that's got the best damned engineering team in the Valley so excited. I'm a board member, and it's my duty to do what's best for the company. If forced to choose, I'd put aside what I feel for Paul."

"Leon, stop," I said.

Leon was not stopping. He moved his hand from my elbow to grip my upper arm. His strength surprised me. It hurt.

"No, Ian. This should be said. Paul himself always told me that he expected an independent board of directors. Now, Paul's probably the best student I ever had, and my association with him has made me lots of money. If you are bound and determined to leave Accelenet and buy Bonds, I'll wish you well. I'm on the board, and I'll try to get you to pay as much as possible for it. But for Accelenet, I'd say the future is Ian Michaels, and I think the other board members might see it that way, too. Now, what I would like to do is get together with the board informally—"

Now it was my turn to interrupt. "Meaning, without Paul?"

"Right."

"There are only five board members, Leon, and Paul's one of them. You could never get a majority. Let's say you could convince Margot—she's a venture capitalist without personal loyalty to Paul. But Darwin is Paul's oldest friend. Forget it. And Bryce Smithwick—did you notice how he waited till he saw what Paul was going to do before he said anything? He'll do whatever Paul tells him." I did not mention that Bryce had recommended that Paul distance the company from me when first hearing of Gwendolyn's death.

"How naive this child is." He raised his face skyward.

"What do you mean?"

"It was Bryce who called me and suggested a little unofficial board meeting. He thinks Paul is getting—what did he call it—'mentally flabby.'"

I broke from Leon's hold on my arm and faced him.

"Okay, I *am* naive. But the answer is no."

"Loyalty can be carried too far."

"Maybe so, but I won't conspire against Paul. Paul knows I want to be chief operating officer, but he won't give me the job. He must have his reasons. So be it. Even if I want to leave the company, Paul's still my friend. He's made me what I am. I owe him too much to be his Brutus."

I had not meant to be playing to an audience, but I risked gathering one. Onlookers saw a man baying and gesturing in a pronounced, almost agitated fashion at the legendary Professor Henderson. Leon grabbed my elbow again and steered me down a path.

"I figured you'd say no." Leon shook his head. "And you might be doing what's right for you. Who's to say? But I doubt it's right for the company."

I grimaced, knowing that Paul would have counted sleeping with Kathy as less of a betrayal than what Leon had suggested.

What now? I sat at my kitchen table, munching on a sandwich. The portable phone rested on the table before me, tempting me. Why not call a few venture capitalists, maybe set up some meetings, see whether I could raise the money to buy the Bonds technology? Now was the time to look. Awash with money but afraid to put it to work, the VCs were searching for the Holy Grail—another Intel, Cisco, or Netscape. Bonds could be the philosopher's stone that turned raw ideas into gold for the VCs and a fulfilled dream for me. Yet my mind would not focus on business prospects.

I picked up the phone and found my fingers flying over the buttons. I had never even called the number before, just entered it in my Visor.

"Hi," I said, realizing that a live voice, not an answering machine, was at the end of the other line. "I'm surprised you're home."

"Ian," Rowena said in a matter-of-fact way, as though she had been expecting the call. "Not back in the office yet, but looking over some depositions from here."

I explained the situation to her, why I needed her help. She'd be up on Southwest the next morning at eight.

I picked Rowena up at the airport, and we headed down 101 to Monica Hyde's house.

"Rowena, I really appreciate this," I said. "You know, it's not just that she wouldn't speak to me. I *can* be persistent."

"You going to turn on the charm?" she asked.

"Whatever. But last time, she called the cops, and I don't want to count on Officer Mikulski's graciousness a second time."

"Don't worry. I talked to Monica. Can't blame her for her reaction. The guy who owned the house where her best friend was killed just shows up at her place. She was scared. What were you thinking, anyway?"

"I should have called before I went over."

"And she's got a baby. She's taking no chances. You ever read about mother bears?"

"You're sure that visiting her now is okay?"

"I told her you were okay and that I would come along."

Just as I had the day before, I marched up the driveway, sidling past the white minivan. This time, though, I had brought protection—a five-foot-five, 120-pound bodyguard.

Rowena pushed by me. "Let me go first." She pressed the buzzer, the door swung open, and Monica cried, "Rowena!" They hugged, then Rowena gestured toward me and said, "Monica, I don't think you've met Ian Michaels."

I pasted the friendliest smile I could muster across my face. "Glad to meet you. I hope I didn't frighten you the other day."

"And I hope I didn't cause you too much trouble. I saw you at the funeral, but better safe than sorry, I figured."

"Sure, I understand. No harm done."

"Could I see Celeste?" Rowena asked.

Monica led us down a short hallway to a room with Peter Rabbit, Jemima Puddle-Duck, and assorted other Beatrix Potter mice, squirrels, and kittens cavorting on the wallpaper. We tiptoed over to the crib and stared down at a baby breathing evenly, eyes closed. No expert at estimating children's ages, I could only guess she was somewhere between birth and her first steps.

"Gwennie was her godmother," Rowena whispered to me.

A few minutes later, we were seated in Monica's living room, sipping from steaming mugs of coffee—it would have been pressing my luck to ask for tea. Monica showed no signs of excess flesh remaining from her pregnancy; she couldn't have weighed much more than a hundred pounds.

"What can I do for you, Ian?" Monica asked.

"I was hoping you could tell me something about Gwendolyn."

"Why?"

I thought about the photo of Gwendolyn that sat on my dresser. "Not sure. Maybe I just want to find out what happened to her."

"Can't the police do that? The two officers who interviewed me seemed pretty thorough."

"I think they're looking in the wrong places."

Monica looked at me. "Did you kill her?"

"Monica!" Rowena started to stand.

"It's a reasonable question," I said. I gestured for Rowena to sit down. She slid back onto the couch. "No, I didn't." I looked straight back into Monica's eyes. Gutsy woman. "You see her much this past year?" I asked.

"It wasn't like when we were roommates. But we'd get together about once a week for a meal or coffee. Gwen was pretty focused this time through. She didn't have track anymore. Her old undergraduate friends have jobs or they're in grad school. I knew she was working a few hours a week, but except for that she spent all her time studying. Straight As. She was awfully smart."

"I hear you are, too."

"I always tried to do better than Gwen. I was so competitive, but she didn't even notice. In a race, there are two kinds of runners—the kind who tries to beat everyone else and the kind who just tries to do her best. Gwen was the second kind."

"You were the first kind?"

"I have five brothers. In our family, you learned to compete."

"Was Gwendolyn seeing anyone?"

"I don't know if she had much of a social life. She wanted to go to grad school in English. She was working on a novel, but . . ."

"What?"

"I don't know if I should say. It's personal." She looked at Rowena. Rowena nodded.

Monica took a deep breath. "A few weeks ago, we went for coffee. I asked for some Kleenex—to wipe off Celeste's mouth. She'd spit up. Gwen fumbled around in her purse." She looked at Rowena. "You know how she could never find what she wanted in those big bags of hers. I saw birth control pills in there. She saw that I saw. I asked if she was dating someone."

I held my breath and prayed that Monica found out who the guy was. Jason, maybe?

"What did she say?" Rowena asked in a strained voice. Maybe she guessed we'd hear Jason's name as well.

"Celeste started crying. Gwen had to get back to school. She said she'd tell me about it when we had more time. She said she wasn't sure how it was going to turn out."

"Did you ever talk about it again?"

"No. I just saw her once more, when she was here for dinner. We had other guests and no time to really talk." Monica fought back tears. "I'd just brought a life into the world. Everything was perfect. Why couldn't God just leave well enough alone?"

"Want to come in?" I asked as I turned into my driveway.

"I don't think so." Rowena's head vibrated from side to side as if shivering.

"Let me just grab my sunglasses." I sprung from the car and trotted into the house.

Who could blame her for not wanting to come in—into the house where her sister was murdered? My place was only a two-block detour on the way from Monica's to the airport. A morning breeze had whisked away the fog shrouding the city, so I had asked if I could stop at home for my sunglasses. She hesitated, but when I told her I didn't need them after all, she told me not to be silly.

Needless to say, my glasses weren't on the bedroom dresser, where I remembered leaving them. After a flurry of rummaging, I found them in the pocket of the sports coat I had worn when I went to see Paul.

When I came out my front door, I saw Rowena standing next to the car in animated conversation with a tall woman whose back was to me. Of course, I recognized the woman right away. Her sense of timing was as flawless as ever.

"Mom?"

EIGHTEEN

"YES, DEAR." MY MOTHER turned and held out her arms.

With a sense of foreboding, I walked into her embrace. She must have found out about the fix I was in and resolved to come to my rescue. Even from Eastern Europe, her sensitive antennae could detect distress in her only son, her firstborn. In my mother's loving grasp, I steeled myself against the onslaught of questions.

The top of her head came up to my forehead. She stood five-nine. Her high school friends told me she looked just the same now as she had four decades before. And it was true that her face remained smooth and that her hair had only an occasional gray strand, even in her sixty-second year. Exasperating and opinionated, she looked at the world from a different perspective than me, different from all the technophiles and gadget freaks who populated Silicon Valley. Where I withdrew cash from an ATM on weekends or late at night, she withdrew money only after a long Friday chat with a bank teller. Where I delighted in watching a DVD in my pajamas, she insisted on watching Hollywood's latest in a crowded theater. She was the Leaning Tower of

Palo Alto; she tilted away from the modern age more each year but, in the end, would outlast any new skyscraper.

Gently pulling her arms down after what was—for her—a short, thirty-second clinch, I asked, "Mother, I take it you and Rowena have met?" I inclined my head toward my companion, who stood leaning against my car, looking wickedly amused.

My mother saw no reason to hurry in answering my question, though I knew she would get around to it. "I called you at work and got your infernal voicemail. I'm not leaving a message on one of those things. How would I know if you ever got it? So I called that nice receptionist, Juliana, and told her to get Paul for me. Paul told me you were taking care of personal business." It was Wednesday. Mom had pulled Paul right out of his weekly staff meeting. Ah well. Paul knew Mom.

I tried to explain, but a parting of the lips was as far as I got before her waterfall of words washed away anything I was about to say.

"Personal business? I told Paul that he works you too hard and it was about time he gave you some time off. I tried your cell phone. Then I called you at home, but there was no way I was leaving a message on your machine either. So I just decided to walk over and leave you a note." She waved a piece of paper filled with her florid writing toward Rowena. "You made a good decision. This personal business is worth taking time away from your precious Accelenet."

In my mother's value system, a thirty-five-year-old unmarried son constituted a crime against nature. By my age, my mother had told me on my last birthday, my father—may his memory be a blessing—had two children and would have had more if God had permitted. Mom had been waiting so long for me to get married that she would have been reasonably satisfied if I brought home a voodoo priestess—as long as she proved fertile. The attractive lawyer she saw before her was reason for celebration. In her mind, she was picking out a florist and a band. This time, I didn't mind her misinterpretation of what she saw—with each word my mother uttered, I became more relieved. Neither Juliana nor Paul nor Rowena had told Mom about Gwendolyn. Of course, she probably hadn't given them the opportunity to.

Canute-like, I held up my hand to stop the onrushing tide. I had more luck than that ancient Dane. My hand and words stopped the force of nature, or at least redirected it. "Mother, I thought you weren't coming home for two more weeks."

"The guide knew nothing. Most of the good stuff I'd seen at the American Craft Museum in New York already. The people on the tour were mostly German. They were polite and even complimented my German. Can you imagine?" Mother smiled at the joke she knew I would understand. Modern-day Germans took the Yiddish she'd learned from her grandparents to be some local dialect. "They stuck pretty much to themselves. Everyone on the tour was paired off but me. I couldn't even get a bridge game going." She sighed. "Oh, how I miss your father." Then, in a bit of play-acting, she looked down at her watch. "Now, don't you need to take Miss Goldberg to the airport? You don't want to be late." She started bustling us into the car.

"Mom, you want a ride back home?"

"No, no. I'm going to the downtown library to pick up the Carol Shields book my book group is reading. You kids move along."

Rowena took my mother by the hand. "I can't tell you how glad I am that Ian forgot his sunglasses and gave us the chance to meet."

"Yes, we can always count on a certain degree of absentmindedness from my boy. It was a pleasure meeting you, too, dear, and hope we'll meet again." By now, her thoughts had probably moved on to the caterer.

Driving off, Rowena and I waved back at her.

Rowena laughed. "What a wonderful woman. What a shame she had to cut her trip short."

"All in all, it's a minor miracle she lasted two weeks," I said. "What did you two talk about?"

"I answered questions mostly. She now knows who my parents are, where I'm from." Her voice trailed off.

"She must have asked more than that. The Constitution doesn't apply to my mother. You can't plead the Fifth. She'll just wear you down till she wheedles an answer out of you."

"She knows my parents' names, where I grew up, that I'm Jewish, that I went to UVA for law school, that I'm working in entertainment law, that I'm not married."

"Yup. Mom can find out a lot in five minutes." But the moment of truth had been postponed: she hadn't yet found out about Gwendolyn.

"Thanks for helping with Monica," I said. Rowena and I were walking toward the security checkpoint at San Jose Airport.

"All things considered, was it better than being thrown against her garage door again?" she asked.

I laughed. "Yes. I'll pick hospitality over hostility anytime."

Rowena took her driver's license and boarding pass out of her purse as we reached the security check-in line. Then she blurted out, "After Jason's performance the other day, I thought it best not to stay there anymore."

Was she telling me they'd broken up? But before I could respond, Rowena reached up a long-fingered hand and placed it on the back of my neck. She was pulling my head down to hers. My lips were dissolving against her lips. I was keeping my eyes open and seeing that hers were closed. I was closing my eyes.

It could be that the security officer was a romantic soul and held the line up so that we could have a little extra time. In any case, when I

141

felt a little tap on the shoulder, I took my arms off Rowena's back, and she let my hair run through her fingers as she withdrew her hand.

"Sorry, sir," the officer said from over my shoulder.

"Thanks for waiting as long as you did."

Rowena showed the guard her ID and then drew me toward her again. Speaking in a low tone, looking into my eyes, she said, "I want you to make sure the person who killed my sister is caught." Then she walked through the checkpoint and waved her hand back at me without turning around. She knew I was watching.

"So what do you think about it all, Paul?" I asked.

I needed an antidote to the drug of Rowena's kiss. I needed the slap across the face that could only be provided by talking with Paul—despite our conflicts at work, despite what I knew from Kathy. I reached him by cell phone on the way back from the airport, and he told me to meet him at his house at five. Now we'd gone through the facts as I knew them, and it was approaching six.

"You sound lucky. From what you've said, Rowena is intelligent, she's good-looking, you're attracted to her, and she's attracted to you. Maybe something good will come out of all this."

"Out of Gwendolyn's murder?" I asked, my voice rising.

"Why not?"

Paul took a sip of his thirty-year-old Laphroaig single-malt Scotch from a cut-crystal tumbler. I took a gulp and felt the liquid smoke burning toward my belly. We could have been in a London men's club. We faced each other from matching leather armchairs. Walnut bookshelves encircled the room. Volumes on the top shelf could be reached by a brass ladder that ran on railings some ten feet above the Oriental-carpeted floor. We heard nothing of the outside world; the books themselves seemed to deaden sound. We sat in what Kathy called the library.

"It's too good to be true. I'm the logical—if incorrect—suspect in Gwendolyn's murder. Gwendolyn's best friend called the police when I showed up. I understood that. Her reaction made sense. But Rowena's never shown a single sign of distrust. She's never minded being alone with me. She asked me to help pack up her sister's apartment. Now she's told me to go find her sister's murderer."

"And you figure maybe she knows that you can be trusted because she knows who did kill her sister. You figure it was either her or she's covering up for someone. How about Jason? Maybe you figure Jason's not really her *ex*-boyfriend at all. And she's using her not-inconsiderable charms to divert you."

As I had known he would, Paul had shot an arrow into the bull's-eye of my fears. I grimaced.

"If that's her plan, it seems to be working," he continued. "But what you really hope is that she intuitively trusted you because she fell in love with you when she saw you for the first time."

"Yes, if I have to choose, I guess the second explanation would be my preferred choice," I said.

"Mine, too." He looked down into his drink. "Even with what's happened between me and Kathy, I'm still a romantic."

I pulled up short. I had been so focused on my own problems that I had not even asked Paul about his. A friend deserved better. "What *is* happening?"

He waved his hand as if shooing something away. "Later. One crisis at a time. What do you think you ought to do?"

"Just what Rowena said. Find the murderer. The police aren't going to do it. They're spending all their time building a case against me."

Paul rubbed his hand up and down his face. I could hear the friction between his palm and the late-afternoon whiskers. I leaned forward as he said, "What you're proposing is the offensive strategy, proving someone else did it. It doesn't seem to be getting you anywhere.

You're bound to keep tripping over the police. How about a defensive strategy, proving *you didn't* do it. Work with your lawyer. Make sure you can knock down any of the DA's arguments. Have expert witnesses standing by ready to testify that the head blow could not have been self-inflicted. That kind of thing."

"And leave Gwendolyn's murderer walking around free?"

"Are you worried about the murderer going free? Or clearing your name?"

I didn't answer right away; when I did, I spoke slowly. "Both. I want to know who did this to Gwendolyn. I want to know who's setting me up. And Rowena asked me. I don't want to let her down. Probably doesn't really matter why I'm going to look for him. I just am." I paused. "Did I tell you Gwendolyn was seeing someone? The birth control pills, the pictures taken in my backyard—she was definitely seeing someone at my house." I had put Gwendolyn up on a pedestal. Thinking of her—of either Goldberg sister—in a sexual liaison irritated me, even disturbed me. "I just wish I knew who."

NINETEEN

IT HAD MADE SENSE when it had occurred to me driving back from Paul's the night before. It had even made sense as my mind played over the possibilities in Seat 23C on the flight to LA. I rehearsed just what I was going to say as I steered the Hertz rental on the 405 toward Beverly Hills. But as I walked off the elevator on the sixteenth floor of the building on Sunset and confronted the raised mahogany reception desk, I wondered what the heck I had been thinking.

A woman with a cocoa complexion and a cool demeanor asked, "May I help you?" in a posh English accent.

"Jason Blitzer, please. Tell him Ian Michaels would like to speak to him."

"Is he expecting you?" she asked.

"Perhaps not right now, but I think he would be expecting me sooner or later." I gave her what I hoped was a confident smile.

The receptionist raised her right eyebrow and opened her mouth. I prepared for her to tell me in a dramatic tone that the investment firm of Douglass, Rogers & Wilson was not the sort of establishment one could barge into without an appointment. But she closed her mouth, looked me over, turned aside, and picked up the phone. The way she looked at me with narrowed, appraising eyes made me think that my gray suit, white shirt, tassel loafers, and harness-bit tie had tilted her decision in my favor.

She twirled her chair and faced me again. "Mr. Blitzer is busy, but he can see you around eleven thirty." I looked down at my watch. I would have to wait thirty-five minutes—a period of time long enough to let me know that he was a busy man but short enough to ensure I would wait.

"That's fine. Thank you."

She smiled back at me, reached for a ringing phone, and pointed toward the couch and chairs that constituted the waiting area. I sat down on the couch and looked over a smorgasbord of a dozen newspapers spread before me on a marble-topped coffee table—everything from the morning's *Wall Street Journal* to *Variety*. I found the *LA Times* sports section, a joy for a fan like me. My eyes skipped from the baseball box scores to local qualifying rounds for the U.S. Open to the "will he/won't he re-sign" soap opera of an overpaid NBA star whose free-throw percentage was bested by any decent high school player. Peering over the top of the paper, I surveyed what I could see of Douglass, Rogers & Wilson. The fancy address, the lithographs of America's Cup races that graced the walls, the aristocratic accent of the receptionist—all were meant to reflect conservative taste and quiet money.

"Mr. Michaels?" My musings were interrupted as I looked up—and up farther—to find the source of the female voice that had called my name. Once standing, I still had to look up to meet her green-eyed gaze. She had the advantage of three-inch heels on her black pumps, but even without them she would have been close to six feet.

"Hello."

"I'm Louise, Mr. Blitzer's assistant. Please follow me."

I said, "Glad to meet you" to her retreating back and then scurried to catch up. In most respects, her attire appeared to meet the firm's leitmotif. Her blond hair was pulled back and tied with a black velvet ribbon. She wore a gray pinstriped suit whose fabric could well have come from the same bolt as my own did. However, the cuffs of my suit trousers broke over my loafers in a traditional full break; her skirt hung only to mid-thigh.

"Thank you," I said as she shepherded me into Jason's office. Phone receiver cocked by his ear, he waved me into the single chair in front of his desk. Following the tradition of the nearby movie back lots, Douglass, Rogers & Wilson spent the big bucks on a facade. Jason's office was neither paneled in wood nor carpeted with the best of Persia; it was nothing special, a ten-by-twelve room with a utilitarian wooden desk and gray wall-to-wall carpeting. The only two frames on the wall contained a college diploma and a certificate proclaiming that Jason G. Blitzer had been admitted to the UCLA chapter of Phi Beta Kappa. No surprise. I hadn't expected that the Goldberg sisters would hang around with a dummy.

Mounds of research reports and prospectuses hid most of Jason's torso. Rather than glaring at me while on the phone, Jason had turned his chair toward the window behind him. Evidently, a view out to the beach at Santa Monica and to the sparkling ocean beyond held more allure than exchanging stares with me. I checked my watch—eleven forty-five. He had kept me waiting a little longer in what I guessed was an effort to keep me in my place.

"Amy, not every company can be rated a 'Strong Buy,'" Jason was saying. "After that inventory surprise last year, I've got to be careful. How do I know it won't happen again?" Jason listened to her response and then decided that I had waited long enough. "Look, Amy, Ian Michaels—he's the VP of marketing from Accelenet—just walked in

". . . Oh, you do? . . . Okay, so let's talk again next week." I had the sense he was using me to show Amy how important he was.

With a final goodbye, Jason hung up and whirled his chair around to face me. I gripped the arms of my chair, my fight-or-flight reflex on standby.

"You a little nervous about what I might try here?" he asked, his long swimmer's frame leaning over the desk between us.

"Should I be?" I extended my hand.

He shook his head and grasped my outstretched hand with a strong grip. Then, still standing, he gestured toward the phone. "Amy Kroll says hello," he said.

"She's one tough customer," I said. After taking over the Edison project, I had sat across the table from her for the better part of two days, negotiating a volume purchase agreement with her company, Strait Semiconductor. Only Strait's gate-array chips could give us a shot at meeting our insanely aggressive schedule, and Amy knew it. But we could have settled for a short delay and paid their main competitor thirty-five percent less, and Amy knew that, too. She had been firm but reasonable, and we ended up with a deal that Accelenet could live with.

"Tell me about it," Jason said, rolling his eyes. "Like every CFO, she figures her company is the best buy on NASDAQ, and she calls me every week or two to tell me so. She must have been on her high school debating team." He sighed.

"Want me to close the door?" I asked.

"No. Let's just sit down. The room gets stuffy."

The air conditioning was whooshing over my head. Was Jason afraid of being in a closed room with me? Because of what I might do or what he might do? "How long have you been at Douglass, Rogers?" I asked.

"A year now. Since I finished at UCLA."

"And you're a semiconductor analyst?"

"Assistant analyst. That means George gets Intel and the other big boys. I take the smaller ones like Strait. What can I do for you, Mr. Michaels?"

"Sounds like your job is more fun," I said, ignoring his question.

His head bobbed up and down like a kewpie doll. "You've got it. I've got the highfliers. Big risk, big reward."

"Aren't you kind of young to be an analyst?" If he was Gwendolyn's age, that made him all of twenty-three.

"George's name goes on the report, but they've cut me some slack since I made some lucky recommendations."

"Like?" I asked.

"Belfil."

I whistled. "Not bad. What did it go up last year? Seventy percent? And in this market?" I wondered if the big-money guys knew who really made the calls that moved those stock prices.

"Thanks." He stopped, trying to switch gears like a sixteen-year-old driving a manual transmission for the first time. You could almost hear the grinding. "Listen," he resumed, with an All-American grin that would have done better at winning a lass's heart than my trust, "I'm glad you're here. Back at my place, you caught me off-guard. I was kind of out of control."

"Why did seeing me set you off?"

"First Gwen chooses you over me, and then I see you at my place with Rowena. What did you expect?"

"Gwendolyn chose me? What do you mean?" My mouth turned dry.

"I didn't know it was you until after she died—was killed."

"Know what was me?"

He gestured in a shy, almost embarrassed way. "You know, that you and Gwen were starting something."

I felt the blood draining from my face. Like Alice, I felt I was falling down a hole. "Why would you think that?"

"Gwen told me."

"Could you tell me what she said when?"

"Why should I? I already told all this to the Palo Alto police."

"Listen, I'm just like you. I'm trying to make sense of what happened to Gwendolyn. Help me out." What I said was the truth, and the pleading in my eyes was not simulated either.

He scrutinized my face for a long time, then plunged ahead. "Last fall, I called Gwen and told her I wanted to come up for a weekend. She said she was too busy. Now, that wasn't a good sign, but I asked if I could come up for a day anyway. She met me at the airport. When I leaned over to kiss her, she gave me her cheek. Like my grandmother would've. Anyway, we walked around the Stanford campus for a while, then sat down in the Quad and began to talk. I asked if there was someone else, and she said that wasn't the point. She told me she loved me and that I'd always have a special place in her heart. She started to cry and apologized for hurting me. She was breaking my heart, and I ended up comforting her. On the way back to the airport, I asked her again if she was seeing someone else. 'Sort of,' she said. I asked if she'd met someone at school. She told me that it was someone who was already working but that the relationship was precarious. She wasn't sure where it was going. I asked her when she last saw this guy. It was a Thursday, and she told me the day before."

"On a Wednesday, then," I said.

"Right. Well, I read in the paper that she cleaned your house on Wednesdays."

"So?"

"Well, it didn't mean anything at the time, but I went up and saw her a couple weeks ago."

"When?"

"The Monday of the week she died."

A day before Rowena made the same pilgrimage. "How come?" I asked. "It sounds like you two had broken up."

"Well, I wanted to tell her that I had a thing for Rowena. Kind of embarrassing, huh?"

"Did you tell her?"

"Yes."

"And how did she take it?"

"She put me through the third degree, kept asking if I really cared for her sister. She was ready to protect her sister's virtue. In the end, she said if two of her favorite people in the world ended up together, that could only be a good thing."

"That was it?"

"I asked if she was seeing anyone. She told me that this guy didn't know how she felt, but that maybe it was time to tell him, 'tell Ian,' she said. Now do you understand why I reacted that way when I met you? Starting up with you led to . . ." Jason's eyes were shining. "It led to her dying."

"I didn't kill Gwendolyn, Jason. But it might be true that if she hadn't been cleaning my house she would still be alive." Now I stopped. Telling him that I had not embarked on a relationship with Gwendolyn seemed futile. Everyone but me seemed to think we had, even Gwendolyn. Why had she mentioned me to Jason? For that matter, why had she used my name as a computer password? Why did she call me on the day she died? Was she delusional? Was I?

I wrenched my mind back to Jason and asked him, "Did Rowena know you went up to see Gwendolyn?"

"No. The night I got home, she told me that she was thinking of driving up to see Gwen on Wednesday. I couldn't say, 'Don't worry. You thought I was at work, but I just got back from seeing her.' So I let her go up without saying a thing." He stopped. "You won't tell Rowena I was up there, will you?"

"Gwendolyn didn't give you away?"

"No. She wouldn't." Jason stopped, took a Kleenex from his pocket, and wiped his nose. "Anyway, I don't have a shot with Rowena anymore. Probably never did. It's for the best." He gave a helpless shrug.

The poor schlemiel.

TWENTY

BACK FROM BEVERLY HILLS, I turned on the oven to reheat the cashew chicken and beef with broccoli that I had picked up at the Mandarin Gourmet the night before. For two hours, the oven stayed warm but empty as I sat staring at my kitchen table, trying to fit invisible puzzle pieces together. In the end, it was not pangs of hunger that caused me to set aside the puzzle. It was the urgent peal of the phone.

"Hello," I said into the handset.

"Did I tell you when the doctor told me your father had cancer, or did I keep it from you?"

"Mom."

"Did I tell you when Cousin Selma's daughter got an abortion?"

Indeed, she had entrusted me with the deepest secret in our family history. "Yes, Mom." I scrunched up my face in anticipation of what was coming.

"So you're arrested, and you don't tell me?"

"How did you find out?" I asked. I expected that my mother would find out about the murder in my house, but the arrest? That hadn't even been in the paper. Of course, my mother had a network of informants that would have done the CIA proud.

"That's not the point," she said.

"I didn't want to worry you." Of course, now it was easy to see the inevitability of her discovery. I had taken the coward's way out by not telling her myself.

"I'm a mother. Worrying is my job."

"Someone broke into my house and murdered my maid."

My mother gasped. "Not that nice Gwendolyn you were so fond of? I thought it was someone you didn't know."

"Mom, I didn't know her."

"Oh? You talked about her. And I even tasted cookies she baked for you."

"We exchanged notes. But Mother, listen to me. I didn't know her."

My mother detected stress. "Shall I come over now? You can tell me the whole story."

I wasn't too excited about going through the whole story with my mother right then. She would demand—and get—every detail. "How about tomorrow night?"

"I'm going over to your sister's tomorrow for Friday night dinner. You come, too. Allison says she hasn't seen you since I left."

"Okay, Mom. I'll be there. But one last thing. How *did* you find out?"

"About an hour ago I ran into Kathy Berk in the poetry section at Kepler's. She's taking a course at Stanford, and I was looking for some Elizabeth Bishop. Anyway, I saw the circles under her eyes, and it didn't take long to find out what was going on with you. You know how fond of you she and Paul are. You've got them plenty worried."

———

My thighs were holding up remarkably well under the strain of the jumping and squirming. My ears were doing worse. My two nieces, five-year-old Sophie and three-year-old Charlotte, were nestled on my lap singing the pre-meal blessing. "We give thanks to God for bread . . ." They made up in enthusiasm what they lacked in melody.

"Now, girls, it's time to sit in your own seats, and then we can begin eating," Allison told them when we finished singing.

Sophie slid down the slide that I called my right leg, but Charlotte didn't budge. "I want to sit with Uncle Ian." She locked her arms around my waist; if she could have handcuffed herself to me, she would have. I didn't know how to respond to being wanted so much. I put my arms around her and squeezed. She hugged back, her body trembling with effort, her eyes closed. This was pure love with no hidden motives. In the best spirits since being clobbered on the head, I kissed the top of Charlotte's head. I basked in the embrace for a few more seconds and then looked around.

The dining table was draped with a special Sabbath blue and white tablecloth that had silver threads running through it. At the right end of the table stood Allison's husband, Harold, a pediatrician, carving a huge roasted capon. Harold, though no older than me, was stooped and graying and wore thick glasses. I found talking to him awkward; we had nothing in common. But he was a nice guy. Before him, Allison lived her life as a tortured poet à la Sylvia Plath and had gone through a series of self-destructive relationships with narcissistic rock musicians, artists, and writers. During my last year of business school, Allison had run away to London with Laurence, a guitarist in a heavy metal band. Two months later, she called me, and I was on the next plane winging to Heathrow. She'd been abandoned with a cocaine habit and without cash in a dingy South London walk-up that smelled of rotting cabbage and dead mice. Even my mother didn't know about that episode. If she had, Cousin Selma's daughter's abortion would have sunk to second place on the hit list of Michaels family scandals.

Somehow, Allison had come to her senses and ended up with this Woody Allen of a guy with no talent for the arts but with the ability to make her happy and give her wonderful kids. He was Jewish, which in my circle of acquaintances was not unusual, but he took his religion seriously, which was. He looked at his two girls and said, *"Baruch Ata, Adonai, m'kor ha-chayim, m'sameach horim im yaldayhem."* It had been over twenty years since my last Hebrew lesson, but I did a rough mental translation of what Harold said: "Blessed are You, God, the source of life, who causes parents to rejoice in their children."

At the other end of the table from Harold sat Allison, the only woman I had ever felt completely at ease with. She was only eleven months younger than me, and that made us virtual twins. We used to joke that Mom and Dad must have done the deed while Mom lay in the hospital recovering from my birth. Eight or nine years ago, after London but before Harold, I stayed with Allison in her San Francisco apartment while my house was being painted. She cooked dinner for me, and I cooked breakfast for her. In the evenings, we read or went to the movies. For ten days, we lived compatibly and contentedly. We each knew the other's eccentricities and could divine the other's mood. Our great aunt Leah and her brother, Uncle Ben, had shared a house on the Near North Side of Chicago for over a half century. As I left, we half-humorously resolved that if no one else would have us, we could always end up like them. I was still looking, but Allison had a loving husband and family. She caught me smiling at her and winked back as though she knew what I was thinking.

Then her expression turned stern. "Charlotte, off Uncle Ian's lap." The child squeezed tighter before peering up at her mother from under long, thick lashes. Charlotte met an unyielding glare that she knew meant defeat. She climbed down my leg headfirst and went to her own setting between me and her father. Sophie had settled in on my other side. The elongated flames of the white Sabbath candles framed my mother's face across from me. "That's a good girl, Charlotte," she said. Her tone indicated how impressed she was that Allison could handle the situation with a single look and a single sentence. Neither Allison nor I had been so tractable—not close.

My plate arrived heaping with succulent capon, steamed asparagus, and my favorite, potato kugel. My fork hoisted the first bite of kugel into my mouth. My teeth crunched through the crispy topping and into the peppery grated potatoes underneath. Allison had explained to me that the Sabbath was a vacation in time. For most people, vacation meant going somewhere—to a cabin or to Disneyland or wherever to "get away." But Allison and Harold, every week starting at sundown Friday, left the workaday world for twenty-four hours without leaving town at all. They enjoyed a family dinner on Friday nights. Saturdays they would go to synagogue and then take a walk, read stories together, or visit with friends. While I had set becoming COO of Accelenet as my goal, Allison had found a different route to happiness.

After dinner, I yielded to the girls' demand for a bedtime story. "This is what we read from on Friday nights," Allison said, handing me a children's Bible with a bookmark indicating where to begin. I had just missed the excitement of the plagues in Egypt, the parting of the Red Sea, and the giving of the Ten Commandments. Sprawled on the floor of their room, I read to my two pajama-clad nieces about the forty years the Israelites had wandered in the desert. Sophie looked down on me from the top bunk; Charlotte rested her head on her pillow with eyes unfocused, trying to draw mental pictures of the hardships that Moses, Miriam, and their compatriots had endured.

Fifteen minutes later, Allison stuck her head back in. "Let's finish up, Ian. Time for bed." She disappeared back down the hall.

Charlotte ran out of bed and plopped herself in my lap. "Why did they wander around the desert?" she asked.

"Because they were on a quest," Sophie answered from on high, in her bunk.

"What's a quest?" Charlotte asked.

"It's a journey where you look for something," her sister replied with a superior air.

"You ever been on a quest, Uncle Ian?"

"Sure, honey. Life is a quest where we look for what we're missing."

"Like Dorothy trying to get back to Kansas?"

"That's it."

Allison stuck her head back in the room. "Uh, Ian. It's your cellular phone. It started ringing and mom found it in your jacket pocket and answered it. A Ms. Ishiyama?"

"Ask her to wait just a second, please." I carried Charlotte back to her bed and received a hug and kiss for my trouble. Her sister reached down from her bunk and gave me the same.

"May God bless and protect you, girls."

I dimmed the lights and walked back to the living room. I knew Harold and Allison didn't answer the phone on Friday nights. I felt like the character in *Lost Horizon* who had let others follow him into Shangri-la and disturb the monks' tranquility. Yet, all I said was, "Sorry. I forgot to turn that darn phone off."

Mother must have been bursting to ask me what was going on, who Ms. Ishiyama was, and a myriad of other questions, but she passed me the phone without comment.

"Hello?"

"Ellen Ishiyama here." Her soft voice floated into my ear.

"What's up?"

"I'm not going to sugarcoat this for you. Are you ready?"

I almost gagged. Dammit, I didn't want to vomit. The dinner had tasted better going down than it would coming up. I steeled myself. "Ready," I said.

"It appears that you'll be arrested again soon."

TWENTY-ONE

Two yellow, malevolent eyes sped toward me. I stared back at them until they stopped a scant ten feet from where I stood. Their luminance dimmed, and I saw behind them the outline of a snazzy BMW two-seater. Ms. Ishiyama stepped out and asked, "Have you been waiting long?"

"Just a minute or two."

She nodded. Pursing her lips, she reached in her handbag and pulled out a card that she waved at a blinking brown box. The door unlocked with a click. I reached for the handle and swung open the door to the offices of Goodsell and Higgins. The card must have sent a message to a building automation system to light the path to Ms. Ishiyama's office. After we walked a few feet past a ceiling fixture, it would turn itself off. We were being pursued by darkness.

Again, I sat across from Ms. Ishiyama's huge heirloom of a desk.

"I hope I didn't pull you away from anything important," she said.

Because she'd reached me on my cellular phone, Ms. Ishiyama had no idea where I had been. Her call had plucked me from a refuge of warmth and love and returned me to an arena of suspicion and murder, but I spared her the details. She was doing her best by me.

"What's up?" I asked. I wanted to ask if Fletcher and Mikulski had found more evidence against me, but they couldn't have, could they? New evidence would point to someone else, not to me.

"I was over at the DA's office. It was Arlen's fortieth birthday, and they were having a party for him. You know, black balloons, licorice icing on the cake, that sort of thing. Anyway, I was invited." As always, Ms. Ishiyama spoke in her precise, almost prim voice.

I meant to nod with understanding, but some impatience might have escaped to the surface of my face.

"So Stan Jessup came up to say hello," she continued evenly. "Well, actually, he came over to boast a little. The way the DA dropped charges against you last time? Well, we know Jessup was humiliated, and he's determined to show that he was right about you."

"So what more does he have? Why does he want to make a move now?"

"First of all, he's got Mikulski, who wants you out of the way. He says you've been intimidating witnesses." She gave me a reproachful look.

"The police don't seem to be doing much to find the real killer . . ." My voice trailed off.

"So you're playing amateur detective?"

"A little," I admitted.

"Not advisable, but it's the results that count. You find anything out?"

For the next ten minutes, I told her about going through Gwendolyn's things, about how Rowena and Jason had visited Gwendolyn in the last week she'd been alive, about the birth control pills Monica had seen, about Gwendolyn seeing someone.

161

"Lots of what you found out fits perfectly with you and Gwendolyn having a relationship. Or at least that's the way Jessup will see it."

"But I have an advantage over him. I know I didn't do it, no matter how it looks."

"Does anyone else know about the computer password being your name or the voicemail Gwendolyn left?"

"Just you and me and her rabbi."

"Communications with clergy are privileged. So we're okay there."

"What about me being arrested?"

"Jessup was oozing confidence. He obviously knew something and knew I didn't know. He should not have said anything to me, but he couldn't resist."

"And it was?"

"The knife, the murder weapon. Jessup had just talked to the state lab in Sacramento. Their tests take a while."

"What tests?" I asked.

"The murderer had wiped the knife clean, but there were still traces of Gwendolyn's blood on it."

"Wouldn't that be expected?"

"Yes, it would. But there was also a trace of your blood."

I felt a steel band tightening around my chest. "Can they tell how old the blood on the knife was?" I asked.

"No, they can't tell that."

"Then what's that worth? They could go in my bathroom and get my razor. It would have my blood on it, too," I said. "So the murder weapon was my knife. I must have cut myself on it sometime or other. Look." I knew I sounded desperate, but I showed Ms. Ishiyama my left hand. The webbing between my thumb and index finger was cross-hatched with scars. "I'm the worst bagel cutter ever."

"Did you have a cut on your hand at the time Gwendolyn was killed?"

162

"I don't know."

"But you would have had an open wound from the assault the day before the murder?"

"Yeah, on the back of my head. I could have had shaving cuts, too. Who knows?" I paused. "Does the knife really matter that much?"

"Not in itself. It's everything together. The indications that you two were having an affair, the computer note, the eyewitness who says you were the only one who went into your house, and now the knife with your blood on it."

"So why wait for the arrest?"

"Jessup won't get the official lab report till Wednesday. He's had a call from the technician, but the written report takes a few more days. Until then, Jessup's putting everything together so that he can get Mendoza's okay for the arrest the instant they get the report. He's crossing all the t's this time. He said that if it were up to the police, you would have been arrested already. Mikulski's not used to a suspect conducting his own investigation. He keeps telling Jessup to get you out of his way. Plus, he thinks you're dangerous."

"Dangerous? How?"

"Mikulski says you had a secret relationship with Gwendolyn and now you're starting one up with her sister."

How the hell would Mikulski know about that? I felt like Ms. Ishiyama was cross-examining me. "I just told you Rowena went with me to talk to Monica, Gwendolyn's old roommate."

"Right. After you and Rowena left, Monica called Mikulski and told him you'd been back. Mikulski spotted you at your house and followed you to the airport."

I flushed with embarrassment. "Then he saw us saying goodbye?"

She nodded. "He told Jessup you were up to something with Rowena. Maybe trying to make sure she wouldn't testify against you. Maybe winning her trust before . . ."

"Before what? Before I get rid of her?" Paranoia, I reminded my-self, was the *imaginary* sense that everyone was out to get you.

"It doesn't matter. Mikulski wants you off the street. Jessup wants to try for no bail this time. It's a capital offense. If he can convince the judge that you're a danger . . ."

I lowered my head into the cradle of my hands. I heard Ms. Ishi-yama stand up and walk out of the room. She returned. "Would you like some water, Mr. Michaels?"

I looked up and saw her long, fragile fingers wrapped around a tumbler.

"Yes, thank you." I took a quick drink. "Tell me, is Officer Fletcher pushing for my arrest, too?"

"Funny you should wonder about that. Jessup said that she had been given enough time to come up with alternative explanations. She's come up empty."

I found it comforting that Fletcher did not have me pegged as the killer.

While I drank, she said, "Mr. Michaels, you seem to be resourceful and intelligent. I am, too. We *will* be able to show that you did not murder Ms. Goldberg."

"God, I hope so." I sighed and asked, "What now?"

"Jessup is not going to move prematurely this time. The DA will see that—sorry, but this is how it is—that there's plenty for a grand jury indictment."

"So I just twiddle my thumbs till they come get me on Wednesday?"

"Jessup agreed not to have you picked up. I promised to bring you in again when asked."

Turning myself in at the station accompanied by Ms. Ishiyama held little appeal, but I preferred it to being shepherded from my house in handcuffs. "Thank you. I appreciate that." I wondered what that small concession had cost Ms. Ishiyama in the quid pro quo trading game that defense attorneys and DAs played.

"Just keep that cellular phone on so I can reach you."

"I will."

"Shall I talk to a bail bondsman so we can get you out right away?"

"Please." I didn't want to depend on Paul and Kathy this time.

As if hallucinating, I saw Gwendolyn sitting on the steps to my house. I was pulling into my driveway on the way back from Goodsell and Higgins. I shook my head and looked again. The specter floated to her feet and moved into a ring of brightness cast by the porch light. It was Kathy Berk; she had the same lanky build as Gwendolyn, but her hair was as blond as Gwendolyn's had been dark. I turned off the ignition and opened my car door.

Kathy was dressed in white—white jeans, white polo shirt, and white sneakers. She waited for me with her head tilted and her eyes alternating focus between me and the ground. I had not seen her alone since the nocturnal visit to my bedroom, and she must have been wondering how I would react, whether she'd be welcome. I should have phoned her when I heard that she and Paul were separating. Some friend I was.

"Kathy, so good to see you," I said, my arms wrapped around her in a hug.

"Oh, Ian, I should have called you to see how you were doing." Her chin pressed against my shoulder.

"Me, too." I held her away from me. "I mean, when I heard about you and Paul, I should have called. Come in."

A few minutes later, we were ensconced in my living room holding steaming mugs, mine of tea, Kathy's of cocoa. We sat and sipped but said nothing. Kathy squirmed in her chair—embarrassed, I guessed, at having shown up again past normal visiting hours. It was close to ten thirty.

"So?" Again my unerring instinct for just the right words to put someone at her ease.

She took another sip, and when she looked back at me, I could see that the liquid chocolate had coated the down of her upper lip. Kathy might have been forty-seven, but right then, in my living room, lit only by a single lamp, she looked twenty years younger.

"So," she said, "I needed someone to talk to. You know people tell me I have a lot of friends, but I have friends I serve on committees with, friends I golf with, friends I go shopping with, friends I discuss my poetry with, but I'm not sure I have friends to talk over my problems with. You're part of the problem, but . . . remember—when was it?—maybe six or seven years ago, when we talked about Paul and me not having children?"

She and Paul had seen countless infertility specialists. The curse of money was the unwillingness to take any no as final, to always keep looking for one more expert—at Johns Hopkins or some clinic in Zurich or wherever—who would have the answer. They had had no luck anywhere. After all the probing of her organs, after all the invasive tests, not one of the specialists could tell them why Kathy didn't get pregnant. Her plumbing appeared in order, and Paul's sperm count, if a little low, registered in the normal range. Kathy, of course, blamed herself. Paul told her he didn't mind not having kids, but Kathy couldn't be convinced. I'd held her hand while she cried in her kitchen.

"Yes, I remember," I said.

"You're a good listener and a good friend."

"I'll listen." I leaned forward on my armchair. Kathy kicked off her shoes and curled her feet under her thighs on the couch.

"Paul and I were so happy at the beginning. I worked as a research assistant at the Huntington Library. He did his graduate work at Cal Tech. We didn't have a dime. But it was phenomenal. All that mattered was that we had each other. Paul had the idea of Berk Technology, and I told him to go for it, that we could make it." She looked across at me. "You know, I wish Berk hadn't been so successful, at least not so quickly. It was the rocket-ship ride up that was so much fun. I don't like where we landed."

"Where's that?" I asked.

"On different planets, where he goes his way and I go mine. We haven't slept together in over a year. I mean, that's not literally true. We did share a bed until last week."

She was fumbling a little, and I tried to help. "I understand."

"He offered to be the one who left, but I needed to get out of there."

I started to say something. Kathy held up her hand.

"Hush. I'm talking. You're supposed to be listening. I told Paul that I'd always had feelings for you—"

"You said that to Paul?"

Kathy continued. "I told him that you'd never given me any sign or encouragement, that all you'd been is a friend I could talk to. But I told him I was going to find out if there was anything more there."

"What did he say?"

"He said to do what I needed to do."

Astonishment swept over me. She told this to Paul? As the initial wave ebbed, another wave began to crest: Paul had not said a thing. He had bailed me out of jail and listened to my problems knowing all this. Class.

"Did you tell him about coming over that night?"

"No, that was no longer his business. You just don't feel about me how I feel about you. That doesn't matter. I still needed to talk to you as a friend."

A relationship with Paul's wife? I couldn't tell her it would feel Oedipal. "Kathy, I do love you, you know. You're the warmest, sweetest woman—"

"I'm sorry," she said. "I found out what I wanted to know that night in your room. I don't want to discuss that again. I want to tell you what's happened to me and Paul. I also want to make sure you're all right. I still worry about you and that horrible murder. I saw your mother—"

"She told me."

"How are you doing? How are you bearing up?"

"Everything is going to be fine."

She put her head down, and I got up and sat next to her on the couch. I held her hand while she cried.

Then, for the third time that day, the electronic ring of a telephone interrupted me.

Kathy raised her head with a start.

"I'm not going to get it," I said.

"Go ahead. I'm okay."

I trotted into the kitchen and picked up the receiver. "Hello?"

"It's Paul. We need to talk."

TWENTY-TWO

"OH, HI, PAUL. How's it going?" How could he know Kathy was here? Not that I was doing anything wrong. In fact, what I was doing was Paul's job—giving his wife no-strings support. Still, I felt as though I had been caught in *flagrante delicto*. Guilt came easy to me; a life as my mother's son had ensured that.

"Is it too late?" Paul asked.

For what? To give me the job I want? To keep me from leaving Accelenet? To interrupt Kathy and me before something happened? To save Gwendolyn?

"No problem. I'm still awake," I answered. I looked through the doorway out to the living room and saw Kathy leafing through an *Economist*, doing her best to appear oblivious to my conversation with her husband. She looked up, and I made a gesture indicating that I would be done soon.

"Listen, I'm having trouble with our board. I need your support."

I wondered what Leon and his co-conspirators had been up to. "You don't have to ask. You know you've got it," I said.

169

"It's nice to hear it anyway." I heard the strain in Paul's voice. His wife was gone, and now his baby—Accelenet—was slipping away.

"Paul, you're right. We should talk. I want to know what I can do to help. I need you to fill me in on what's going on."

"Is now too late? I could be there in five minutes."

"No, it's not too late," I said slowly. I had a brief fantasy of playing marriage counselor, of having Paul and Kathy reconcile right in my living room. A moment's reflection and I realized that it was best to deal with one Berk at a time. "But if it's okay with you, how about first thing tomorrow?" I asked. "You know I do my best thinking early. Come on over at eight."

I looked out at Kathy again and saw her still studying the magazine. At first, she had me fooled. She seemed absorbed. But then I saw her fingernails—white, bloodless. She wasn't reading the magazine, she was squeezing it.

"That's fine," Paul was saying.

"Don't worry, Paul. We'll take care of this. Just get a good night's sleep."

Kathy didn't look up right away when I came back through the doorway. "Did you hear that?" I asked.

She might've pretended that she wasn't listening, but she wouldn't lie about it.

"I couldn't help it." She shrugged. "But tell me why you're helping Paul out. You deserve a shot at chief operating officer, and he won't give it to you. Isn't it time to get out of there and go someplace that will give you what you want?"

"Maybe. I've told Paul that I do want to leave Accelenet. But now, maybe for the first time ever, he has to have help from me, and I'm going to give it to him."

———

My heart pounded. Sweat dripped in my eyes. The endorphins had kicked in, and I broke through an imaginary tape at the foot of my driveway. I had gone to bed around midnight, but thoughts of what awaited me on Wednesday condemned me to a sleepless night. Now, sweat and physical exertion were flushing out not just bodily toxins but also fears of impending arrest. I had run nine miles—up to "the Dish," the radio telescope on a hill behind Stanford, and back. Normally, on a Saturday morning the Dish run teemed with runners and ramblers, but I had been up there before seven and passed only a portly, ponytailed man with a walking stick and a lean, short-haired woman whose bare, muscled midsection resembled a Kit Kat bar.

After a quick shower, I brewed the coffee and tea. Promptly at eight, the doorbell rang. Paul did not look good. Judging by appearance, Kathy seemed to be handling their separation better. Then again, it could have been the Accelenet situation, not his dissolving marriage, that had given him the puffy eyes and sallow complexion.

Paul settled onto the couch, where his wife had been curled up ten hours before. Could Kathy's scent still be detected? I took a discreet sniff but could smell only Paul's coffee. So I leaned forward in my chair to hear Paul's woes, just as I had Kathy's.

"The company can't afford Bonds," Paul opened.

"We've been through this. You know I don't agree, Paul, but you're in charge, and you have good reasons for your decision."

"I need you to tell the board that you've reconsidered what you put forward at the board meeting."

"I can't do that."

"Listen, Leon has been up to mischief. He's telling people I don't have the drive—'that buccaneer instinct,' he calls it—that I used to have. Who does he want to have running Accelenet, Errol Flynn?"

"How can you really be worried about the board, Paul? It's your company. Literally, almost. You own about twenty-five percent, and other employees, including me, own another fifteen percent, and none of us want you going anywhere. Are you really worried?"

"It's arithmetic. Forty percent is not a majority. And the last thing we need is some sort of fight for control of the company. How would employees react to that?"

"Given your reputation, I can't imagine any kind of fight."

"Directors read the papers. They keep hearing they should get involved in how a company is being run. They're taking all that stuff seriously, damn them."

"But you've never let any of them down."

Before Paul could answer, the phone began to ring. We stared at each other. After only three rings, before the machine could pick it up, the ringing stopped. It took a few more seconds before Paul picked up the thread of the conversation again.

"I didn't want to go public when the market was hot. That didn't endear me to Margot or Bryce."

Paul had resisted pressure to go public. He wanted to make certain that Accelenet stock would not double or triple on the first day only to dwindle below the offering price within twelve months. "I want to see a future of steady growth in revenues and profits that will ensure our stockholders a successful investment," he had told the board. The reward for this principled stand was resentment from two directors who would have rather taken a quick profit. Perversely, Margot and Bryce now seemed willing to wait for an IPO until Bonds was ready.

"Leon's got them thinking the company could be bigger than Cisco if we exploit Bonds. Your presentation wowed them."

"Didn't seem like it at the time."

"They didn't want to contradict me publicly. But within a few days, they all called me."

"I'm surprised," I said.

"Now that they heard you might be leaving . . ."

"That's my plan, Paul."

"And I'm being second-guessed from here to Kalamazoo. If you told them that you'd changed your mind about Bonds—"

"I can't do that. The board knows I was Bonds's biggest proponent, and I still believe in it."

"Then if you'd just agree to stay, for six months at least, this can all blow over." Paul's lips turned upward in a poor imitation of a smile. A muscle under his left eye twitched.

What could I say? A corporate chess player would have moved in for the mate by telling Paul that he would stay if promoted. But even if Paul yielded, it wouldn't mean I had earned the promotion. If I wasn't going to get it, I wanted to leave and build something, show Paul what I could do on my own. "Of course I'll stay," I said.

"I knew I could count on you." Paul let loose a sigh of relief. "Thanks, Ian. You made that easy for me."

"Are you certain you'll want me to stay? What about the Gwendolyn situation?"

"Are you in trouble again?" Paul frowned.

"My lawyer tells me I could be arrested again."

"I know you didn't do it. You stand by me, and I'll stand by you."

If I were arrested, that couldn't be good for Accelenet. "I think I'd better stay out of the office another week and see what develops."

"Sure, sure," he said. "Take another week. It's been grueling." The wave of Paul's hand showed that he believed—or that he wanted me to believe—that I had nothing to worry about.

"How about you, Paul? What's going on with you and Kathy?"

He quivered at the mention of her name. Then, with a shake of his brown-haired head, he leaned back on the couch. "I need to call her."

"When did you talk to her last?"

"It's been a few days."

"Don't you want to get back together?"

"There are ties between us that will never be broken, but I don't think we're going to reconcile." Paul's tone indicated that he would brook no more questions concerning Kathy. She had been equally reticent to speak of him. I wanted to help with a reconciliation; their separation represented one more pillar of my once-stable world that had crumbled.

I walked Paul to the door and swung it open for him. I looked for his BMW at the end of my walkway.

"I walked," he said. "It helped me think."

We said our goodbyes, and I walked back in and dropped onto the couch. It still emanated Paul's warmth. The balance of power between us had shifted. He'd had a wonderful wife, and I'd served at his pleasure. Now Kathy had left, and he needed me at Accelenet to keep his job. I closed my eyes, and my thoughts skipped like a stone over a pond—from imminent arrest to work to Rowena—each splash making widening ripples.

Then came a clang. The mail chute on the front door opened, and a single page of paper wafted onto the floor. Not the postman. I threw my arms forward to give my body the momentum necessary to escape from the gravity of the couch. I opened the front door and saw the familiar back retreating down my walkway, Birkenstocks creaking.

"Mother, you could knock."

She whirled around at the sound of my voice. "Sorry, dear. I called half an hour ago, and you didn't answer. I figured you weren't home. You're not screening your calls again?" Mother didn't like the idea that I could hear who it was on my answering machine and decide not to pick up. It seemed un-American. In fact, I often did listen to who was calling, but if I heard her voice, I always answered.

"Paul was here. It would have been rude to pick up." I hoped good manners constituted an acceptable excuse.

"I was out for a walk and thought I'd see what last night's emergency was all about. I saw Mrs. O'Flaherty across the street. She told me she'd seen you leave just a few minutes ago. So I left a note."

I looked at the Lincoln Avenue sentinel. Slightly stooped, wearing a yellow shirtwaist, her blue-white hair reflecting the sun, Mrs. O'Flaherty was spraying her flower beds by hand. My grandfather had watered the same way. What was it about people over seventy that made them distrust automatic sprinklers? The light spray from the nozzle bathed a dazzling bed of red tulips and golden daisies. You could argue with Mrs. O'Flaherty's gardening technique, but not with her results.

"That must have been Paul," I said. "Come on in, Mother." I didn't want to worry her unnecessarily, but I also didn't want her to be shocked on Wednesday.

She pecked me on the cheek and looked at me expectantly. I steeled myself for the third degree.

TWENTY-THREE

I PACED. I PLOPPED down. I stood up. I wandered into the backyard and gazed up at the apple tree I'd seen in Gwendolyn's photo album. I inspected the small green orbs that would be filling pies come September. It was Tuesday. Twenty-four hours before Ms. Ishiyama picked me up for another date with the booking officer at the station. And this time my picture would be on the front page of every paper. Friends and acquaintances would wonder if Ian, who would never do such a thing, had. Images knocked on the door of my consciousness and entered uninvited. I flashed to the glowering face of Rabbi Kahn. I saw tears rolling down my sister's cheeks. My mother shaking her head disbelievingly. Kathy staring at me with wide-open eyes. The shock draining the blood from Rowena's face.

I hit my right palm—purposely and hard—against the wall along the driveway. An electric shock pulsed up my arm. "Sonuvabitch." Breathing hard, I bent over, holding my right elbow. Whatever the answer might be, it was not a couple of rounds with a brick wall. I sat down, crossed my legs, and focused on taking long, even breaths. A fellow pushing a baby in one of those jogger contraptions loped by. He looked startled when he saw me sitting in the middle of my drive- way looking like some leftover from a 1960s transcendental medita- tion class.

Dammit. I needed to do something. I shook myself to escape the nightmarish reverie and realized my phone was ringing. When I jumped up, I stumbled forward—my leg had fallen asleep. Dragging the tingling appendage after me, I picked up the receiver in the kitchen before the answering machine cut in.

"Hello?" My voice wavered a little in the greeting.

"Ian, is that you?"

I recognized the deep voice. "Who else, Leon?"

"Don't know. You sound funny. Anyway, we're going to have an informal board meeting this afternoon. And we want you there."

"Have you asked Paul?"

"Um, no. We thought it might be best to have a frank discussion without Paul." Leon took a deep breath, then rushed on. "Paul domi- nates any meeting he's at. We want to have an open discussion of where Accelenet is and where it's going. And for that to happen, Paul cannot be there."

"I can't stop you from meeting, Leon. And I understand that you're doing what you think is best for the company. Well and good. But I cannot go if Paul isn't going to be there." Leon started to interrupt. "Cannot. Period," I finished.

Leon sighed loud and long. "I told them that's what you'd say." He paused. "You still quitting?"

"No. I told Paul on Saturday I'd stick around at least six months more."

Another sigh. "Paul's smarter than all of us, isn't he? There's no al- ternative to him but you, and now he's foreclosed that option. Did he appeal to your loyalty?"

"Didn't have to. He's got it."

Sigh number three. "Okay, we'll still have the meeting at my office at four. I'll call Paul and make sure he's there, too."

At four fifteen, eighty percent of the board of Accelenet and one invited guest sat around a glass table in Leon's office making nervous conversation. Leon's office was to Professor Woodward's as the Taj Mahal was to a Tobacco Road shack. We five sat in maroon leather chairs around a thick piece of glass about six feet long supported by two intricately carved elephants. A Shiraz rug covered the floor between us and Leon's walnut desk. A rogues' gallery of photos lining the near wall reminded us of Leon's role in the history of the Valley. Paul and other mythic figures, like Bill Hewlett, Steve Jobs, Andy Grove, and Bill Gates, posed with the hardworking pachyderms currently crouched at my feet.

We were waiting for Paul, who was never late. Margot Fulbright, seated to my right, was complaining about what the "bubble rubble"—the dot-com crash—had done to venture capitalists. "VCs are still awash in money from a few years ago, but there aren't enough good deals to invest in anymore. That means one of three things: you don't invest at all, you put money in lousy deals, or you pay too much to get into good deals." Margot looked around the table, her eyes asking for sympathy. Twisting to see each of us required her to overcome the resistance of jeans that appeared to be spray-painted onto her legs.

"The screw turns," Darwin Yancey laughed. "After Paul and I started Berk Technology, we had to go on our knees to you venture capitalists. We managed to get three million in financing. We heard all the lectures about how it was the VCs taking the real risk with real money. Right." Yancey snorted. "It was our lives, and the VCs were investing other people's money."

"Paul shared the entrepreneur of the year award with Michael Dell," recalled Bryce Smithwick. "Darwin, you must take some pleasure in how the VCs who said no kicked themselves." Looking smooth and feline even in his Bobby Jones polo shirt and crisp khakis, Bryce whipped a pocket calculator out of his briefcase and punched in a few numbers. "If a VC had invested a measly million in Berk and sat on it until the company was sold, they would have had 217 million."

No one said anything. We were all thinking about the missing progenitor of such wealth. Paul's absence dominated a meeting almost as much as his presence.

"I left messages for Paul at home, at work, and on his cell," Leon said.

"Let me try him again." I dialed his cell. One ring, two rings, three rings. When voicemail came on after eight rings, I hung up.

"We might as well get started," Leon said. "I think we all know why we're here. Accelenet has come to a crossroads, and it's our job as directors to make certain that the correct strategic decisions are made and that the right leadership is making them. Now I'm happy to report that despite his disagreement with Paul over the Bonds technology, Ian has agreed to stay on at the company. What I'd like to do now is hear from Ian what ideas he has for the future of the company and what role he'd like to play in it."

"Leon invited me to this meeting," I said, "and I very much appreciate that. But there are two things that I need to convey to you. First, I've told Paul I'd stay at Accelenet at least another six months working for *him*. That's the role I anticipate playing." I looked around. My small audience was hard to read, but their heads leaned toward me. "I am uncomfortable discussing the company's strategy without Paul here. In any case, there's one more factor that must be brought to your attention. As you all know, a woman was found murdered in my house several weeks ago. I fear the police mistakenly believe I had a role in her death."

"Be serious," Leon said. "You're a suspect in that girl's death? Come on. I'd stake my life on you having nothing to do with it. Wouldn't you?" He glared at Margot and Darwin through his thick lenses until they nodded.

When his head swiveled to Bryce, Bryce ignored him and asked, "Ian, have you obtained legal counsel as I advised?"

I met each board member's eyes. "Thanks for those words, Leon. They mean a lot to me. Next, to answer Bryce's question, yes, I have retained Ellen Ishiyama of Goodsell and Higgins."

"And what does she say?" Bryce asked.

"That I could very well be arrested for murder, perhaps as soon as tomorrow."

Margot gasped. Darwin and Leon looked at me goggle-eyed. Bryce turned to his fellow board members. "That throws a spanner in the works, doesn't it?" And then Bryce turned to me. "And what should we do?" he asked.

I reached into my notebook. "I brought this letter for Paul. It's my resignation. Although I promised Paul I'd stick around, I wanted him to have this to use at his discretion." I gave the letter to Bryce. "When Paul does arrive, please give him the letter. I think it best for me to go."

I shook Bryce's hand and then Darwin's. Margot started to extend her arms for an embrace, thought better of it, and gave my right hand a two-handed shake. Leon felt no such inhibitions and hugged me. He whispered in my ear. "You got class. Let me know what I can do to help."

Approaching the door, I looked back. "I appreciate your faith in me." Whether I was speaking of their belief in me as an executive or as an innocent man, I did not know myself. "Oh, and one more thing. What works did I throw a spanner in?"

Leon pointed to a pile of press folders bearing the winged Accelenet logo that sat on the credenza just to my right. I picked one up, waved, and departed.

I opened the folder on the hood of my car. On the left side was a color photo of me; behind it was one of Paul. On the right side was tucked a press release marked "Draft" and dated Wednesday. "Accelenet Names Ian Michaels CEO; Paul Berk Moves Up to Chairman." So that's what the plotters had in mind. The Fates had conspired to make certain that the press release remained a draft.

———————

As I pulled the Acura into my driveway, I spotted Mrs. O'Flaherty spraying her front-yard Eden. I grabbed the press folder and hopped out of the car. She saw me coming. Her eyes narrowed a mite, but she did not back away. Her strong, blue-veined right arm continued to cast the waters on her thirsty plants. I stopped on the sidewalk some twenty feet away from her but only inches away from the splatter of water.

"Afternoon, Mrs. O."

"What can I do for you, Ian?" she asked. Her eyes, swimming behind thick lenses, followed the arcing loops of water rather than meeting mine.

"I have something I'd like to ask you. It would be a tremendous favor."

She turned off the nozzle, and the last splash of water wet my shoes as I took a step forward. She looked up, and this time her eyes did meet mine. "Just a minute, Ian." She retreated, hauling her hose. Watching me still, she knelt down and wound it into a coil that looked like a sleeping dog at his mistress's feet. As she straightened up, she asked, "Would it be satisfactory if we talked here on the sidewalk?"

I admired her coolness. Neighborliness was an ingrained trait. It required that she talk to me, but her sense of prudence was just as strong. It prevented her from asking me in for brownies as she would have done a few weeks ago.

"Yes, that's fine. I just have a question to ask you."

A voice came from behind me. "What do you want to ask her?" I jumped a bit and then whirled around to see Officer Susan Fletcher crossing the street.

"You keep catching me off-guard, Officer," I said.

Under her arm, she carried a brown folder with black ribbon ties. Over her left shoulder, I spied her patrol car parked at the end of the block.

"I'll take that as a compliment." She looked at Mrs. O'Flaherty. "Any problem, ma'am?"

This time Mrs. O stood up for me. "I don't think so. Ian just wanted to ask me something."

"Go ahead, ask," Fletcher told me.

I turned back toward Mrs. O. "I know you said you saw me going into the house at quarter past twelve on the day that woman was murdered. But I didn't go in until after one."

"I know what I saw," she said with compressed lips.

"What was that?" I asked.

"Well, you came home for lunch. The maid's Toyota was in the driveway."

"Right. Do you remember what I was wearing?"

She closed her eyes. "Yes. A dark suit."

"I had jury duty that day and was wearing khakis and a sweater."

"I know what I saw." Her head was bobbing up and down.

"Are you sure it was me? Could it have been him?" I handed her a photo.

For the full thirty seconds that she peered at it, my heart pounded as if trying to break through my ribcage.

"Maybe." She shook her head. "I don't know." She brought the photo closer to her face. "Could have been, I guess. Picture's not you, but looks a lot like you."

Fletcher took two steps forward and grabbed the picture from Mrs. O's hand. She looked down at the photo of Paul Berk that I had taken from the publicity folder.

TWENTY-FOUR

"Yessss!" Fletcher raised two clenched fists over her head, doing a respectable imitation of Steve Young just after hooking up with Jerry Rice for a touchdown. I was leaning against her black-and-white, my mind spinning right along with the car's cherry red light. Paul—boss, friend, mentor, rival, and now murderer? Across the street, Mrs. O had gone back to casting loops of water on her flora. She had her back to me but peeked over her shoulder every few seconds.

I was trying to tune in Fletcher's voice.

"She can't identify you. I win," she was saying.

The reception still was not good. "You win? Win what?"

Her right arm thrust out, she grabbed my hand and started pumping it with a grip as firm as any football player's. "Thank you for not doing it. They all said you did it. Just Tanner and I said no. He kept saying people don't change after high school." She grinned and then veered off on another tack. "How did you know it was Paul she'd seen coming out of your place?"

"I wasn't sure, but Mrs. O'Flaherty told my mother she saw me leaving my house Saturday. But it was Paul, not me. Figured the same thing could have happened on the day of the murder."

"I knew you didn't do it. It was too cute. Someone figuring the police would gratefully grab onto the scraps they were tossed." Her head kept time with her handshaking as though the faster she nodded and pumped, the more convincing she would be.

"Selling *me* on the theory that I'm innocent is not hard. But the game's not over, Officer. Mrs. O'Flaherty wasn't certain it was Paul."

"That's just it. She wasn't certain it was *you* either."

"I don't think the whole case hinges on her. There's the knife, the notes, the letter on my computer, the fact that it happened in my house. I don't think Jessup in the DA's office will give up the hunt based on doubt from one witness."

Fletcher's emphatic nodding ceased, she let my hand drop, and I asked her, "What did I say to Mrs. O after she said she might have seen Paul instead of me?"

"Nothing," Fletcher said. "You just turned around, walked away, and came over here to the car."

"Just a minute."

I marched back across the street. Now holding the hose less like a weapon, Mrs. O'Flaherty saw me coming during one of her over-the-shoulder glances and turned to face me. I stopped on the sidewalk a dozen feet from her and said, "Thank you, Mrs. O. I'm sure it wasn't easy to say that in front of Officer Fletcher."

More staring, then she dropped the hose and stepped toward me. Precariously balanced on the ground, the nozzle was squirting water straight up, Old Faithful–style. The spray caught the sun, and a shining rainbow rose behind her. She extended her hand, and I took it into mine and squeezed it. "It couldn't have been you, could it? I'm sorry for what I did to you." Then she lowered her head and muttered, "Silly old lady." Looking up at me again, she said, "I don't know what I could believe in if you had done such a thing." She withdrew her hand, emitted a dry sob, and threw her arms around me.

"It's okay, Mrs. O. You did what was right by coming forward. And others have made the same mistake. People always say Paul and I look alike." I patted her back.

Then the nozzle started to tip. The hose whipped like a striking snake and shot one last jet before the pressure came off the handle and the water stopped. The rainbow disappeared.

A free man, I sat in the front seat of Fletcher's police cruiser as we drove by houses with Moorish tile roofs and stucco facades. We traveled down Waverley Street, leopard-spotted by the late afternoon sunlight shining through tree boughs. She slid the car in front of the Berks'—or, more accurately now, Paul's.

Up the brick-lined walk and then I reached for the doorbell. Fletcher grabbed my wrist and shook her head. "This isn't a friendly call," she said. She pushed the button with her left index finger while her right hand flexed over her holstered gun. Through the glass porthole in the door, I had a distorted view into the foyer. I waited as I often had before for the tread of Paul or Kathy or Roger across the kaleidoscope of Oriental carpets.

Two more pushes on the buzzer and still nothing. We went back to her car the way we had come.

"What kind of car does Paul drive?" she asked. "You know the license plate?"

"Sure. A newish gray seven-series BMW. License is PAULK. Why?"

Instead of answering, Fletcher opened her car door and reached in for the microphone. "Hello, Bernie, you there?"

"As ever. What can I do you for?"

"Listen, I got a car I want found. BMW, gray, seven-series, license P-A-U-L-K. That's Papa, Alpha, Uniform, Lima, Kilo. Registered to Paul Berk. Check out the details with the DMV."

"Stolen, was it?"

"That's not it. What we need is to find Mr. Berk. He's fifty"—she turned and looked at me—"brown hair, thinning a little, about six feet, probably a hundred seventy pounds. Anyway, I'll bet you can get a color photo off Accelenet's website." She looked at me to confirm or deny. She had supposed correctly, but I wasn't helping anymore. Fletcher watched me turn my head and gaze out the windshield. Inside, I tried to make sense of the jumble of fear, betrayal, and repulsion coursing through me. But I had not murdered Gwendolyn, even though the spotlight of police suspicion had focused on me; I wanted to hear Paul's story before I reached any conclusions about him.

After a few seconds, Bernie's voice asked, "You want to bring in Paul Berk. Like *the* Paul Berk?"

"Yup."

"What for?"

"Material witness in the Goldberg murder."

"C'mon, Susan. That one's wrapped up. Mikulski's been boasting that he has—what's his name—Michaels trussed up like a Thanksgiving turkey." I continued to look straight ahead through the windshield.

"Just do it," Fletcher said. "Count him dangerous. I'll explain. Find Mikulski and Lieutenant Tanner. They're going to want to hear what I have to say."

"Right," Bernie said. Fletcher's tone had brooked no equivocation.

"Thanks. Ten-four." Fletcher turned to me again. "You got this whole thing figured out?"

"We'll see." I opened the passenger door. "I appreciate your letting me ride along. I think I can use a walk home. To clear my head."

As the door swung closed, I caught Fletcher's parting "We'll talk soon." I walked toward my place as she accelerated down Waverley. Once Fletcher's squad car disappeared, I turned back to the Berks' red brick walkway. I reached in my pocket and looked at the key ring. No, I had returned the key to Kathy after staying at their house. So I walked up the driveway to the standalone garage and lifted the side door up by the knob and pushed. Paul got into the garage this way when he forgot his keys, a not-uncommon occurrence. Shutting the door behind me, I stood waiting for my eyes to become accustomed to the darkness.

My nose detected motor oil seasoned with a hint of dried grass. I could see through the gloaming that only the Range Rover and John Deere tractor mower were in the garage. The BMW, Paul's everyday car, was gone, as was Kathy's two-seat Mercedes. I walked over to the neatly arrayed boxes of nails and screws in the tool area. I counted over three boxes from the left on the second shelf, thrust my hand into a box of twelvepenny nails, fished around, and plucked out the house key from its hiding place. As a cop, Fletcher had to ring the doorbell and ask permission before entering, but Ian Michaels, private citizen, was bound by no such strictures.

I unlocked the back door and was greeted by ominous beeping. 11-21—I pressed the keypad with the date of the initial public offering of Berk Technology, and the silence returned. I meandered from room to room. Perhaps the only remarkable thing I noticed—like the failure of the dog to bark in the Sherlock Holmes story—was the lack of anything remarkable. It looked like Kathy and Paul had just stepped out and could return at any time. The shining stainless steel of the kitchen's built-in dishwasher and refrigerator showed fingerprints overlaying gleaming surfaces. The family room, with its glass tables and immense theater-style television screen, had been dusted in the past week but not in the past day or two. I snapped the lights on in the living room. Built-in spotlights shone on the wall that displayed their renowned new-glass collection, but my eyes focused on an empty space. Missing was my favorite piece, a mix of black glass, crystal, and jade-green glass by the Hungarian artist Maria Lugosy. Kathy had loaned the piece to the Corning Museum, whose patrons would now be studying a young man's bust that could be transformed, with a tilt of the head, into his death mask.

Padding up the red, green, and beige Esfahan-style runner, I passed a wall of photographs. There was Kathy as a little girl, laughing with delight as she came down a slide into her mother's arms. Her blond beauty radiated from her wedding portrait. A younger Paul held a ticker printout from a Quotron machine. I didn't stop my ascent but knew that with a close look I would see the initials BKTK printed on the scrap of paper; they represented the very first shares of Berk Technology traded on the NASDAQ. At the top of the flight, in a black metal frame, Paul stood, supported by crutches and my arm, in Beijing's Forbidden City; Paul had broken his leg in a fall on the Great Wall, where we had been whisked by our hosts from the Chinese Ministry of Technology.

The house was empty, but I moved with caution nevertheless, anxious not to disturb . . . what? I didn't know. I just had a sense I didn't belong here. Then, outside Paul's home office, his sanctum sanctorum, I heard something. Was it someone sighing? I breathed once, put my hand on the knob, and swung it open. There before me swam three fish. They looked at me from inside an aquarium that measured ten feet long and four high, built into the bookshelves. Bubbles gurgled up to the surface at both ends, and a hidden electric motor hummed. I laughed out loud, embarrassed by the knot of fear that was just untying itself in my belly.

Fright would have been a legitimate response if I came across these lionfish on a dive in the Red Sea; their dorsal fins were venomous. Paul had told me of the steel supports between the floors that had been added to support the three thousand pounds of water in which they swam. I tiptoed over to the fish flapping their striped fins, picked up the box of food, and sprinkled some over the aquarium's surface. They took their time getting to their floating dinner. Their sluggishness showed they had not been fed for some time.

I moved to Paul's antique Chinese desk and sat down in a Mandarin chair whose backrest displayed the character for good fortune. I pressed the power button of the computer on Paul's desk and watched a series of screens each spend a minute or so on the monitor before giving way to the Windows logo. I wondered if the folks in Redmond had ever figured how many person years were spent every day waiting for that logo to disappear. Finally, I logged into the calendar, running on a server back at the office, which all of us at Accelenet shared. With millions of bits racing back and forth over the T-1 line, I leafed through browser screens, each containing one day of the last six months of Paul's life. Everything was there. Board meetings, one-on-ones with me, symphony performances on Saturdays that he attended with Kathy. I procrastinated, then focused on Wednesdays. The entries indicated he was at the barber's, at the gym, or at lunch with people whose names I did not recognize. But I knew where he'd really been.

Angry at myself, at Paul, at Gwendolyn, I started opening the desk drawers. I didn't know what I was looking for until I found it, a sheaf of double-sided laser printing with the words "Gaseous Body by Gwendolyn Goldberg" on top of the first page. The story began, "Tranh fell in love with someone she had never met."

I leafed through the two hundred pages. The novel opened with Tranh, a Vietnamese woman, picking up the phone. Through flashbacks, the reader learns that Tranh was raised in privilege in Hue by progressive parents who straddled the culture of the Vietnamese aristocracy they had inherited and of the French intellectuals they had become. While paying obeisance to half their heritage by sending Tranh to the Sorbonne, they follow the other side by arranging an appropriate but unfortunate match. Her husband and parents are killed in the Tet offensive of 1973, and Tranh flees to France. Accepted to medical school in Paris, she works as a maid to support herself. She cleans the house of a doctor named Charles but never meets him. Over time, what she learns about him—from the art he displays, the books he reads, the summer trips to Africa with *Médecins Sans Frontières*—starts to feed an obsession. She leaves him notes in the old-fashioned handwriting the nuns in Hue taught her. His responses show that he thinks of her as an older woman. With each exchange of letters, she is more enthralled, but at the same time more afraid of meeting him. After all, she is his maid. Without revealing who she is, she meets him at the university after a lecture. A Vietnamese in Paris, a housemaid, a woman who does not exist to the man she loves, she wonders if she is invisible, made of vapor. The story ended where it started, with Tranh picking up the phone— with the clear implication that she is calling Charles to arrange a face-to-face meeting.

I put the manuscript down. I wondered what Tranh would think of Charles once she met him. I knew he could never live up to her expectations. Or was the novel unfinished?

I untucked my shirt and used the front tail to wipe my forehead. Time to finish up. I walked to Paul and Kathy's bedroom. Nothing out of place in there. I opened the door to the huge walk-in closet. Kathy's side had lots of empty space. On Paul's side hung rows of custom suits organized into grays, navies, browns, checks, and tweeds. No sign of anything missing.

Back in Paul's office, I found a manila envelope, slipped Gwendolyn's manuscript in, tucked it into the back of my khakis, and covered it with my loose shirt. I reset the security system and closed the back door. As I turned down the driveway, there in the dusk stood Fletcher, hands on her hips. A primitive part of my brain, the part that told my forebears what to do when a saber-toothed tiger approached, screamed that I should turn and run. More civilized neurons exerted supremacy, though. I'd half-expected to be picked up, which is why I'd hidden away the manuscript. I mustered a confident grin. "You figured I would go in on my own, and you could just wait for me to come out. Smart move." I gave her a half bow.

"So what did you find?"

"Thin layer of dust. Fish hadn't been fed for a few days." I could feel the sweat forming between my back and the manila envelope.

"Nice work. We'll talk about a job on the force once this is over."

"I fed the fish."

"The Berks give you access to the premises regularly?"

"Yup."

She gave me a mock salute, got in her cruiser, and pulled away again. At the first mailbox I came across on the way home, I took out the envelope, sealed it, and addressed it to myself at work. I found the stamps in my wallet, pressed them on, and dropped the envelope through the slot.

TWENTY-FIVE

INSTEAD OF SPENDING WEDNESDAY as a guest of the county, I went to the office. No one realized Paul had gone AWOL. Monday he was supposed to be flying. On Tuesday, his calendar said he would be in Milan with Roberto. When I called Roberto at home—it was one in the morning in Milan—he reported that Paul had left him a message on Saturday canceling the trip. While Roberto assumed Paul had remained in California, employees in the main office thought Paul was in Europe. They figured he must be following his typical breakneck schedule, so they were irritated but not concerned about his failure to respond to voicemails or e-mails.

I knew Fletcher was hunting for Paul. No one knew Paul better than I did. In my bed that evening, I tried to think like him, be him. I stayed there for hours—head resting on my hands, eyes staring upward—trying again to fit together the pieces of the puzzle of Gwendolyn's murder. Where the hell was he? I think the phone rang, but I wasn't paying attention. Retreating into myself was a habit from childhood.

What bothered me most about being sick as a child was not a stuffy nose or a stomachache. It was my mother hovering over me, sticking a thermometer in my mouth, and carrying bowls of chicken soup to my bedside. It worked best for me to distance myself from the external world. If I could lose myself in a book or just in my own thoughts, I could make bodily woes seem far away. This withdrawal drove my mother nuts. The sicker I became, the more hot liquid got dumped down my gullet, and the more I retreated into myself.

My adult relations with women followed the same arc. That desire to retreat cost me Cindy, my roommate in my second year of business school, the year my father died. During that last semester, I told myself I was just focusing on my studies, but I felt like a hermit crab retreating deep into its shell. "You don't need me or anyone," Cindy told me the night we graduated. "I know you must be grieving for your dad, and I've been here for you, but you're somewhere else and I can't get through. I'm tired of trying. Have a great life." I had followed her career since and rooted for her with a sense of fondness—but not of regret—as she moved from her first job at Goldman Sachs to assistant professorship at Columbia to deputy assistant secretary in the Commerce Department.

Since then, I had enjoyed the company of women and listened with patience and interest to the intricacies of their lives and aspirations. I won points as a good audience, but after a few months of seeing each other, they would want tit for tat. When they started probing my insides, I started a mental game of hide-and-seek. "Fear of intimacy" is what one redheaded amateur psychologist had diagnosed— accurately, I guess—as we broke up.

After a couple of hours of ceiling gazing, I solved the mystery of what was missing for me. I knew what I wanted, or rather whom I wanted. I hadn't felt such a compulsion since . . . well, ever. My watch dial read ten o'clock—not too late to call. I reached for my handheld, then stopped. My fingers knew which buttons to push.

One ring and then Rowena's voice. "Ian?"

"How did you know?"

"I was lying here thinking of you."

"Me, too."

"Are you in trouble?"

"Don't know. I'm just trying to figure things out."

"Maybe we can see each other," she said, and then added, "soon."

"I'd like that."

"Okay, let me get back to you," she said, her voice businesslike now.

"Good." Then I tacked on, "I miss you."

"Good," she said, and hung up.

In my dream, Rowena leaned over and kissed my cheek. The sense of her presence overflowed the vessel of my unconscious, and I blinked my eyes open. Outlined by a light from the hall, a woman's shadow straightened up. Kathy again?

"Who's that?" I asked.

"It's me, Rowena."

"What? How . . ." I looked at the luminous numerals of my clock radio. 3:25. I was clad in my version of pajamas: T-shirt and boxers.

"After we hung up, I didn't think, just jumped in the car and drove up. Not much more than five hours door-to-door. Pretty good time, don't you think?" She was trying to sound cheery, but her words trailed off into an awkward pause before she started in again. "I thought you wanted to see me. It's okay, isn't it? Should I leave?"

"It's okay." Damn, I could do better than that. "No, it's great. Thanks for coming." I held my arms out. She knelt by the bed and laid her head on my chest.

After a minute of feeling her long hair, cool cheek, and hot breath through the thin cotton material, I put my hand under her chin, lifted her head, and kissed her. I closed my eyes as if to go back to dreaming. Her lips were soft as our tongues began a duel of tentative exploration and grew harder as the sparring became more urgent. Following a rhythm set by an unseen conductor, we inhaled and exhaled together, and I pressed a soft "ah" from her as my arms snaked around her back. In turn, she placed her fingers into the concave spaces between my ribs and pressed. I reached down to her legs on the floor and scooped them up; our mouths stayed together and I rolled on top of her. On the verge of being swallowed by what was happening, I opened my eyes and saw hers pressed shut.

Our mouths separated, and we looked at each other. I read in her shy smile an interplay of conscious desire and primal drive. She knew what was happening and with whom and was glad. I hoped my returning smile sent the same message as I reached down to the bottom of her shirt. She arched her back as I pulled it over her head.

———————

I opened my eyes, squinted, and then shielded them with my raised hand. Sunbeams were slicing through the slats of the blinds. Rowena's head, nestled on my chest, faced away from the window. The light marked her naked back with tiger stripes. In the dimple at the bottom of her spine, I saw the sparkle of blondish down.

I dozed off until awakened again by a kiss.

"Good morning."

I hugged her and found myself responding to the feel of her against me. "I hope you have another of those little foil packages somewhere," she said. Last night, it had taken me a minute or two and some fumbling through drawers to find some protection; I hadn't needed any in quite a while.

This time went slower than the last. In the light, my eyes, mouth, and hands explored her soft breasts, firm stomach, long back, and muscular legs. She purred as I nuzzled her neck. We had more time to enjoy what was happening and took more time to build to a climax.

Afterward, sticky with our combined perspiration, we pulled apart. I rolled to my side with my arm propping up my head.

"So that's what everyone's been talking about all these years," I said.

She smiled back at me. "I don't think they have a clue."

She saw me looking at her body and brought her free arm over her chest in an instinctive, protective gesture. Then she looked back at me, laughed, and moved it away.

"I'm hungry. Let's eat. What do you want for breakfast?" I asked. As I swung my legs onto the floor, I looked down and saw her clothes strewn on the rug—navy T-shirt, nylon shorts, plain white cotton underpants and bra, and a pair of fancy running shoes. I liked the fact that she didn't try to hide her body this time as I looked at her over my shoulder. "Did you bring a bag or something?" I asked.

She shook her head. "I know it's kind of dumb, but I just hopped in the car. You sounded like you needed company. Any thinking I did was in the car on the way up. Had a full tank, so I never stopped. Almost turned back coming over Pacheco Pass, but . . ." She shrugged.

I leaned toward her and brushed her lips with mine. "That's okay. I'm sure I can find a shirt for you and probably a new toothbrush, too. My dentist loads me with them." I leaned the other way, reached down, and picked up her clothes. "For underwear, though, unless you like boxers . . ."

"If you can loan me a robe, I'll throw the panties in the washer."

As she took the clothes from my outstretched hand, a brass key with a little tag fell from a pocket in the shorts. I raised my eyebrows.

"Your key," she said.

"My key?" I snatched it off the sheets. "That's how you got in. Where did you get it?"

The quick motion and urgency in my voice made Rowena's blue eyes open wider. "It was with Gwennie's stuff. I came across it when I was unpacking. I kept it."

"Why?"

"Did it without thinking. Maybe my subconscious was at work." She lowered her head and scrunched her eyes and nose.

I looked down at the key and saw my own name in my own handwriting on the tag. Gwendolyn must have picked it up from the maid service the previous September.

My mind started working again for the first time since 3:25. Too many people were ending up in my house without a formal invitation.

"Ian, what's the matter?"

I started pulling clothes on. "Robe's in the closet. New toothbrush in the medicine cabinet. The washer and dryer are off the kitchen. Gotta go."

"Wait. Where are you going?"

I was already heading toward the door. "I'll be back soon. Maybe the key to figuring out what happened to Gwendolyn has something to do with my house key."

TWENTY-SIX

"Don't know where he is. Don't care." Kathy stood with her back to me, leaning over the espresso machine. The cords in her neck, tight above the collar of her T-shirt, belied her indifference. After a few seconds of tinkering, she whirled around, standing with her fists on her hips. "I haven't seen him in over a week."

"C'mon, Kathy. He's not in Europe, where he should be. I can't find him. Where's he gone?"

"I don't know. I don't care." She pirouetted toward the coffee machine, a gleaming brass number that bubbled, spritzed, and steamed. It was my first visit to Kathy's pied-à-terre. In the thirties, a woman might move to a cottage on a ranch near Reno to await her divorce; Kathy had a better idea, having migrated to a cottage near Stanford. The neighborhood was called College Terrace, because its streets were named Williams, Yale, Harvard, Princeton, and so on. Coincidentally—or perhaps not—Kathy now lived on a street with the same name as her alma mater, Wellesley.

"Latté?" she asked with a quick look over her shoulder.

I shook my head and watched her busy herself with assorted knobs and gauges. "Kathy?"

"Hmm?" She didn't look up.

"Where's your copy of the key to my place?"

"Shit." She was waving her right hand and blowing on it as a spray of steam whirled upward. "Can't figure the damn machine out." She held her hand under cold water.

She went back to the contrivance and held up her coffee cup in triumph. "Home-brewed latté. You sure you don't want one?"

Even if I had been a coffee drinker, it wouldn't be worth the risk of causing her additional bodily harm. "No thanks."

"Okay. Let's sit down."

We sat across from each other at a rough-hewn pine table. Kathy's hands encircled the cup on the table in front of her.

"The key?" I asked again.

"It should be in the top drawer of the desk in the kitchen—where it always is. Isn't it there? I haven't seen it in months."

"What about the night you came to see me? Didn't you use my key to get in?" It was hardly gallant to mention that occasion, but I could find no alternative.

"Oh, yes. Except that time." Kathy turned her head away.

"And did Paul know where the key was?"

"I don't know. It was labeled. He went into that drawer all the time. It had the calendar in it, too. Probably."

"Look, Kathy. The police are going to be after him."

She took another sip, then put the cup down quickly, too quickly. Hot, milky brown liquid splashed on the table. I started to move back, but Kathy grabbed my wrists, her nails digging into flesh.

"Because he was using the key to get into your place, to meet her?"

"To meet Gwendolyn? Yeah, I think so."

"He must have taken some satisfaction in playing afternoon delight at your place every Wednesday." Her voice was calm; the emotion was in the tight grip of her hands.

"What difference did it make if they met at my place?"

"He was so jealous of you."

"Of me? Be serious."

"You made him feel old."

"What do you mean?"

"Look. You're on the rise. He's on the down side of the hill. You've got the drive and the passion he's lost. He knows the board will turn to you." She held up her hand to forestall the interruption she saw coming. "He's trapped in a marriage that's sterile, both literally and figuratively. Look at the contrast. Every married woman in Palo Alto is trying to set you up with single friends and daughters. He's looking for what you have—youth and promise. And I guess he tried to recapture some of that with that girl."

Did she believe that the man she had lived with—slept next to—all those years could commit murder? "But Gwendolyn's dead," I said.

She let go of my arms to take a drink from her cup. Then she raised her eyes to focus on mine.

I shook my head and said, "No, Paul could not have killed her."

She sipped more latté.

On the way out, I saw four red crescents smiling up at me from each wrist. Kathy's nails had drawn blood.

———————

Parked in my driveway, I slumped in the seat. Okay, for the sake of argument only, say Paul did do it. Gwendolyn's death could have been an accident, a flare of passion. But the forged computer note had to be a cold-blooded attempt to frame me for the murder, to send me to prison or even on my way to a lethal injection. Its goal was to take my life away. Could Paul want that? Would the envy that Kathy described have led him to that? Did he find out that Gwendolyn had called me? No, no, no. Everything I had attained in the past nine years had been because of him. He redeemed me from a tedious career as a consultant, introduced me to high-tech management, kept promoting me. He served as my role model and mentor. I never saw him do anything unethical—not even once.

I wanted that promotion to COO, and he wouldn't give it to me. Was that because he was envious or because he thought I was unready? I didn't know. Perhaps he didn't either. Paul had not believed that I killed Gwendolyn. Whether his assurance came from knowing me for nine years or from knowing I was innocent because he was guilty, I didn't know that either. I needed to talk to him.

So where could he be? Even if I wanted to talk to him, did he want to talk to me? I knew that if Paul didn't want to be found, he would stay missing. Probably the smartest man I had ever met and one with plenty of resources, too, Paul could arrange to vanish. But if innocent, why would he disappear? I ceased this circular reasoning and went in the house.

An odor of sugar and cinnamon tickled my nose as I went through the front door. Gwendolyn had been a baker, and my sense of smell told me her sister was, too. Rowena came out of the kitchen, barefoot, now wearing her own clothes. I had been gone longer than a washer and dryer cycle.

"Hi," she said, arms outstretched. I accepted the invitation. She laid her head against my chest, and I pressed my cheek against the top of her head. Her hair glistened with water and smelled of my own woodsy shampoo. She sighed and broke away. Then she swept her hand across my forehead. "You're wet," she said with some surprise.

"Perspiration, I guess. Nervousness. Too much thinking."

"That hug was awful nice, but now listen." Her finger pressed against my breastbone, and her eyebrows pressed together to form a small bump atop her nose. "I'm going to just tell you what I think. No beating around the bush. I didn't much care for the way you left this morning. I'm not meant to be Della Street, filing briefs back in the office while Perry Mason runs down the murderer. Gwendolyn is my sister. I want to know what's going on, and I don't want to be left like that again."

My initial reaction was to clam up. Good thinking, Boy Wonder! You've managed to come up with the perfect way to drive Rowena away. Just last night, I had felt alone. I had needed her. I had called her. She had driven up here because she thought I needed her. She'd been right. Why think of pushing her away now? Fear? Cowardice? Habit?

"Fair enough," I said. "I don't understand why Della didn't make partner." I kissed her forehead. "Let me tell you what's going on."

The bump disappeared as her expression relaxed. "Good. Come sit down. I've made a coffeecake and brewed some tea." I sat across the table from Rowena just as I had sat across from Kathy a few minutes earlier. I looked right at her as I went through what I had found and when I had found it. I loved the way she listened, head tilted, a look of fierce concentration on her face.

When I told her about finding the manuscript of Gwendolyn's novel at Paul's, she said, "So a copy was at Paul's and not at her apartment?"

I nodded.

"But why did you mail it? Why not turn it over to the police? It's exculpatory." She stopped. "Whoops, sorry. That's the lawyer in me talking. I mean it makes you look innocent, doesn't it? It shows that you really didn't know her."

"You're right. But that story seemed kind of private to me. What if the newspapers got hold of it? What if it were introduced in evidence in a trial?"

"So why not just carry the manuscript home with you?"

"I had a feeling the police would get their hands on it one way or another."

"Would they have?"

"Yeah."

"Were you worried about being arrested?"

"Maybe."

"I figured."

"You did? Then why are you here?"

"Because you didn't kill Gwennie. I'm sure of that. But you knew that it's standard practice to search the scene of arrest." Her eyes welled up. "Thank you for what you're doing for Gwennie."

"Look," I said. "It's not that noble or anything. If I need the manuscript, I know where to get it. I just didn't want to use it unless I needed to." She had known all along I was a suspect? What had I done to deserve the faith she had in me? I took a bite of the coffeecake and returned to my narrative, finishing up with the meeting I had just had with Kathy.

"It sure looks like Paul," she said. "He had means, motive, and opportunity. His wife won't even stick by him."

"I'm not willing to count him guilty until I talk to him. I'm not the police. They might figure they have probable cause. But what's good enough for them isn't for me."

"Innocent until proven guilty beyond a reasonable doubt," she recited, the lawyer again.

"My presumption of innocence is about all he has left." Paul had seemed to possess what I wanted: success in starting new companies, wealth, and a wife like Kathy. And all the time, did I have what he craved? A chance to do it over again—to fall in love, to start a company, to make a fortune, all for the first time. Now what of his life remained, with his wife gone, his mistress dead, the board rebelling, the police investigating?

Rowena picked up the morning's *Palo Alto Times*. "Want some?"

"Sure. I'll start with the sports." She spread the front page out on the table in front of her.

"Eww."

I looked up from the latest dispatch from Florida, where the Warriors had been thumped by the Magic. "What?"

"This." She slid the paper across the table and pointed to a headline: "Remains Found in Foothills, Mountain Lion Attack Suspected."

I shivered.

"What is it?" Rowena asked.

"I came across a mountain lion last week when I was jogging up there."

I could hear the sudden intake of her breath. "Could it be the same one?"

"Who knows?" I read the story aloud. It began, "Human remains were found in the hills above Foothills Park last night by a hiker. Police suspect a mountain lion attack."

In a delayed reaction, a thrust of fear penetrated deeper now than when I had been face to face with the cat. I shivered again. I had been lucky; someone else had not.

Before I could scan the sidebar about "Living with California Mountain Lions," the phone rang. Rowena reached behind her and handed me the receiver. "Thanks," I told her. "Hello?"

"Mr. Michaels."

"Yes. Hello, Ms. Ishiyama. I was going to call you this morning and—"

She cut me off. "Listen, I've heard about Mrs. O'Flaherty tentatively identifying Paul. And now the police are looking high and low for him. You should have called me right away. A friend in the DA's office told me Jessup still thinks you are the man. So there's no arrest, but Jessup and a couple of cops are coming to question you further. Now, pay attention.

You have the right to have me there. The first words out of your mouth should be, 'I want my lawyer with me.' They cannot ask you anything until I get there. No matter what, answer nothing until I get there. I'm coming right over."

"Okay."

"I heard you talking to someone before you said hello. Who's with you?"

"Rowena Goldberg."

"Gwendolyn's sister?"

"Right."

"Did she spend the night there?"

"Part of it."

"Damn," she whispered to herself. And then to me, she said, "It would be better if she weren't there when Jessup arrives. Send her away."

I heard two car doors slam outside.

"Too late," I told her.

TWENTY-SEVEN

"JUST WHO DID HAVE keys to your house, Mr. Michaels?" asked Jessup. *If you hadn't been so promiscuous with your keys,* his disapproving tone seemed to say, *you would not have been knocked out on that Wednesday afternoon last month.*

For over an hour, we had been gathered around the glass and copper coffee table in my living room. On my side, in a club chair that matched my own, perched the prim Ms. Ishiyama, back erect, hands folded. On the other side, enveloped by the couch, sat Assistant District Attorney Jessup and Officer Fletcher of the Palo Alto Police Department. Each time Jessup leaned forward to make a point, he was pulled back by the clutch of overstuffed cushions.

I looked at Ms. Ishiyama, who gave the slightest of nods.

"Let's count. Paul and Kathy Berk had one key."

"Why did you give them a key?"

I didn't need to look toward my lawyer; her clacking pearls told me that I could answer. "That's for my convenience. I locked myself out a couple of times and could just pick up the key from them."

He nodded. "Do you know where that key is now?"

"No."

"Did your mother have a key?"

"Where are you going with that? Is my mother a suspect? That's a pretty wide net you're casting." I was getting fed up and realized I was halfway out of my chair. Jessup didn't reply, but his pursed lips told me that his intent had been to get a rise out of me. I settled back, took a deep breath, and said, "My mother does not have a key. By the way, she was out of the country at the time of the murder."

He nodded again. "And other keys?"

"Just one. I sent it to the maid service last September. Gwendolyn used it to let herself in on Wednesdays."

"Do you know who has that key now?"

I did not answer right away. Through my living-room window, I could see Rowena sitting on the grass, her back against the pepper tree, with a book on her lap. Officer Mikulski paced back and forth on the sidewalk in front of her. Jessup had arrived with both Fletcher and Mikulski in tow but had asked Mikulski to take Rowena outside. Mikulski's reaction was a glower, Fletcher's a hint of a smile. The balance of power between the police officers had changed. With a shake of my head, I returned to the matter at hand. What to do? Answering Jessup might lead to Rowena getting the third degree. But not answering would make her a suspect once Jessup and the police found out that she did have Gwendolyn's key.

"Yes, I do." I took the key out of my pocket and dangled it from my thumb.

"And where did you get it?"

"Her sister found it among Gwendolyn's effects and returned it to me."

"When?"

"When did she find it, or when did she return it?"

Jessup narrowed his eyes and raised his voice. "I want both answers, please, Mr. Michaels."

Good to know that I could get a rise out of him as well. "I don't know precisely when she found the key among Gwendolyn's things," I said. "She returned it to me this morning."

"When did you meet Rowena Goldberg? What's your relationship?" Jessup asked.

It was as if the workings of Jessup's brain could be seen through a transparent skull. He had known Rowena had a key and had heard from Fletcher that Rowena was visiting her sister the day of the murder. No matter what the truth, his evidence indicated that I knew Gwendolyn. The prosecutor's cerebral machinery would settle on the proposition that Rowena had murdered her sister out of some sort of sibling jealousy. And maybe, in a noirish twist, the murder was done with my complicity.

Thanks to Mrs. O'Flaherty's tentative identification of Paul, I had just begun to climb out of the dungeon of suspicion. I was not about to send Rowena down into it—with or without me. For better or for worse, one makes bets in life. Going to work for Paul was one. Betting on the future of Rowena and me was another.

I looked toward Ms. Ishiyama. She, too, had looked through Jessup's skull and did not want him to find out where Rowena had spent last night. "That's enough, Stan," she said. "Mr. Michaels is, of course, happy to help you out in your investigation. But that's different than prying into his private life for no good reason." Jessup started to interrupt. Ms. Ishiyama held up her hand. "Let me finish. If you think Mr. Michaels is guilty, then arrest him again. If not, then he'd be glad to help you with your investigation. But no more about his personal life."

I wouldn't want to play poker with my attorney. The slight bite in her voice when she said "arrest him again" reminded Jessup how prematurely he had moved last time. She knew he dared not make a move until he had me bound in a straitjacket of incontrovertible evidence.

"Okay, then, with your permission?" he said, nodding at her. He had folded. "Let's jump straight to the end. Mr. Michaels, you've been doing a little investigation of your own?" I shrugged. He continued, "Tell me, then, do you have any idea of who killed Gwendolyn Goldberg?"

Jessup and I stared at each other in a petty battle of wills that I did not plan to lose. I wasn't going to answer. Then our heads swiveled toward the front door as Mikulski's big frame hurtled into the living room. "Can we talk? I need to talk to you privately." He was speaking to Jessup and Fletcher.

"Go ahead. Use the kitchen," I offered. Fletcher led the way through the swinging door. I glanced at Ms. Ishiyama, and she gave me an approving thumbs-up that said I had done okay. Less than a minute later, the three marched out of the kitchen.

"Thank you for your help, Mr. Michaels. Time for us to go." Jessup nodded a goodbye. "Ms. Ishiyama."

Mikulski and Jessup led the way through the door. Before she could follow, I grabbed Fletcher's arm. She didn't pull away. "What is it?" I whispered.

"They found the remains of a body above Foothills Park."

"Yeah. Saw that in the paper. Mountain lion, maybe."

"They think it's Paul Berk."

Fist curled, I pounded on Kathy's front door. My chest heaved with each thump. "Where could she be?" I muttered to Rowena. It wouldn't take long for Jessup and the police to home in on Kathy. Better Kathy should hear the news from me than them. Or was I impelled by a desire to see her reaction firsthand? Where the hell could she be?

"Let's look in back." We trotted across her front lawn, and I opened the white picket gate to the side yard. Before us extended a garden plot, roughly six feet wide and sixteen feet long, that bore witness to Kathy's meticulous nature. In her cottage only a few weeks, she had already laid out plants in little squares like postage stamps on an album page. We hurried along the brick path between the plot and fence. No horticulturist, I could identify only the yellow and red of a flock of marigolds and a tomato plant beginning to reach up along a stake. The other stamps in the multicolored collection were an assortment of mysterious green herbs, yellow squashes, and red flowers. Not a single weed marred the miniature perfection. I knew this did not represent a professional gardener's work, but Kathy's. I had seen her many times at her old place, trowel in hand, knees on ground, floppy hat on head, tending her botanical progeny. I expected to see her just like that as I turned the house's corner. But no Kathy.

"A swing set?" Rowena pointed toward the back fence, where a wooden play platform including swings and a tower stood in a sandy pit.

"Must be from the previous owners," I said as Rowena started toward the other side of the house.

I watched her and then started toward the swings. I wiped the back of my hand across my cheek. I was crying. My best friend might be dead. Paul had done more to make me who I was than any person besides my parents. Over the nine years I had worked for him, his values had become mine. Separated from him or not, Kathy was the other person whose world would be turned upside down, whose gut would be turned into a black hole if Paul were really dead.

I heard Rowena shriek "Ian" and whirled around in time to see two gleaming blades thrusting toward her neck. She took one quick step back and then another to move out of their reach. Running now, I saw a woman's body fly into view from around the corner of the house, followed by an aluminum ladder tottering on two legs. The body hit the walkway headfirst with a cracking sound. Moving past Rowena, I reached my arm out and thrust the now-falling ladder away from the prostrate body. It clattered on the lawn with a sound like the crash of cymbals. Rowena stood, out of breath, her feet inches from the tips of the blades.

I grabbed her hand. "You okay?"

She nodded.

I looked down to see Kathy, her head resting on red bricks, face in repose, eyes closed. A pair of pruning shears with the two long, lethal blades lay open just above her outstretched right arm. By her left arm rested a set of headphones and the shattered case of a Walkman. The roots of her blond hair were turning crimson.

"Rowena, there's a cell phone in my car under the driver's seat. Call 911."

She turned and ran out through the gate.

I put my ear against Kathy's chest. I felt it move up and down in a ragged rhythm and heard the thump-thump of her heart. I touched the back of her head and she moaned. Her eyes fluttered open and she looked at me. "Paul?" she whispered, and then her eyes closed again.

I heard footsteps at the entry to the side yard. Without looking up, I called, "How long till the ambulance gets here?"

"Five minutes." But it wasn't Rowena's voice. Officer Mikulski stood at the gate, resplendent in blue, hand on his holster.

TWENTY-EIGHT

"Didn't take Mikulski long to get here," Rowena said. "It's like he had ESP."

"Just coincidence, I think. He must have come by to talk to Kathy himself." I snorted. "And what does he stumble in on? Shears lying open, Kathy's head gushing blood, my ear on her chest. It was one helluva tableau."

We were leaning against my Acura in front of Kathy's College Terrace cottage. The ambulance, Kathy, and Mikulski had gone. I had started to climb into the ambulance with Kathy, but Mikulski blocked my way and got in himself. I reached around him and squeezed Kathy's hand, whispering that I was sorry. But, cocooned in the ambulance, only semiconscious at best, she didn't understand the apology and wouldn't have understood the news about Paul either. But Mikulski would be telling her soon enough.

"She'll be okay?" Rowena asked. "I mean, a little woozy, but okay?"

"A concussion and a few stitches, like the paramedic said."

"I should have caught her. At least broken her fall."

"Don't be silly. That would have meant moving toward the shears instead of away from them. From where I stood, it almost looked as though those blades were being aimed for your neck."

"I don't think they were aimed. I just startled her. She was clipping the hedgerow. She didn't hear us because she had her Walkman on. And then she just fell off the ladder. Except . . ." She stopped.

"Except what?"

"She cares for you, doesn't she?"

"Yeah, I guess." I had never said anything to Rowena about Kathy's feelings toward me. "I care for her, too."

"Not the same way, I bet. Still, as for her aiming the shears at me . . . no, I think I just surprised her."

I held Rowena close to me. If the shears had struck Rowena's neck, for the second time I would have been just too late to stop a Goldberg sister from being stabbed to death. The very thought made my guts contract. I let go and tilted her chin up toward me and brushed her lips with mine.

Shot with regret for what coming to Kathy's had led to, shuddering at the memory of the blades pointed at Rowena's neck, horrified about the news of Paul, I said, "Let's go home."

Fletcher found me sitting on the back patio with Rowena. "Ian, I want to ask you a favor."

"You let yourself in through the gate?" I asked.

"No answer when I rang. Thought I'd come around."

"You and Rowena are acquainted." Fletcher had gone down south to interview her just a few days after Gwendolyn's murder. "Sit down," I invited her.

Fletcher shook off the offer. "Mrs. Berk has a concussion and is dizzy. I can't really ask her, and so I'm here to ask you."

"To identify Paul?" I asked. Until I saw Paul's body with my own eyes, I resolved to figure him alive.

"As best you can."

"Okay. Want to come?" I asked Rowena. A promise was a promise. She nodded.

"Wait, I don't know if she—"

I raised my hand to deflect Fletcher's objections. "It'll be fine," I said. "Let's go."

We hiked up the trail from the valley floor of Foothills Park. I had figured bodies were identified in the county morgue. A sallow, balding guy would pull a steel drawer out of a refrigerated cabinet, and then he'd peel the sheet off the face of the corpse. But once in the car, Fletcher had explained that the body was still *in situ*. Except that she did not call it a body. She used the word "remains."

Ducking under branches, we walked single file past the mossy logs and delicate ferns. We left the pellucid clarity and warmth of the valley and entered a cooler, shady realm with an odor of vegetable decay. Through the branches, I could see patches of sunlight below, but the contrast only emphasized the dankness of the world we were traversing.

Fletcher held a walkie-talkie up to her mouth. "Where are you guys?" I heard Mikulski's voice, but the words themselves were lost in static. Fletcher looked at us. "A few hundred yards more, I think." The trail began to level off, oaks replaced ferns, the dappling of light and shade disappeared, and we were blinking in the sunlight again. Rowena pointed down at some animal scat. It wasn't dog, cat, or deer. Was it mountain lion?

Two more twists in the serpentine trail and we came upon Jessup standing under an oak tree. He was still dressed in a white shirt and suit pants, his feet still encased in brown wingtips.

"Why did you bring *her*?" he asked, indicating Rowena with a gesture of his head.

I answered before Fletcher could. "Because I wouldn't come without her."

Jessup hesitated and then went on. "We have two regular officers and two park rangers combing the area, along with Doherty from the coroner's office. Mikulski is down there"—again a head gesture—"taking a look, too. We'll have more help from auxiliary officers in the next hour or two."

"What have you found?" I asked Jessup.

"Some personal effects. Bones."

"Why do you think they're Paul's?"

Jessup's smile exposed his straight yellow teeth. He reached into a rucksack over his shoulder and pulled out two glassine bags. He handed me the first one. "Go ahead and open it."

I plucked a mud-encrusted crocodile billfold out of the first bag. Some forest creature had chewed its edges. But inside were half a dozen credit cards; $463 in currency, also sampled by a rodent; and then Paul smiling up at me from his driver's license. It expired on January 14, his birthday, next year. "Sure, this is Paul's wallet. It's got his license and credit cards in there. You don't need me for that. You find it up here?"

"A hiker did. Well off the beaten trail. Turned it in at the ranger station." Jessup reached into the other bag and pulled out a gold ring. He rolled it between his left index finger and thumb. "Is this Berk's wedding band?"

Despite the separation, Paul had not stopped wearing his ring. Bringing it close to my face, I peered at the inside perimeter. After rubbing against Paul's finger for twenty-two years, the faint indentation of the letters "PILY" could just be seen. "It's his," I said.

"Who's Pily?" Jessup asked, pronouncing the word with a long *i* sound. He had looked closely, too.

"It's an abbreviation for 'Paul, I Love You.'" Behind me, Rowena gasped.

Another tramping sound, and a man wearing a plaid flannel shirt, jeans, and a red windbreaker emerged from the grass below.

"Hey. Ranger Steve Alvarez." He extended his hand first to me and then Rowena.

"Steve is an expert on mountain lions," Jessup said.

"I saw one here in the park a few weeks ago," I said. "Reported it to the ranger."

"Oh, okay," he said. "You must be the guy who had the last visual. But we know there're lots of them around. They've left their spoor. Deer carcasses, scat, tracks."

"And the human remains?"

"Mr. Jessup told us to leave them. D'ya wanna see what we've got so far?"

"Please." I turned to Rowena. "You want to come?" She nodded.

"Why doesn't she stay here with Officer Fletcher?" Jessup asked.

"I'd like to go along," Rowena said.

We left Fletcher behind on the path to guard the area. Rowena and I followed Alvarez, and Jessup followed us. Holding hands, Rowena and I leaned backward to keep control as we edged down the steep slope. Jessup stumbled against me on the way down. I took a quick half step, dug in my right heel, and used Rowena's hand for support until Jessup regained his balance. He said nothing, nor did I.

Past a clump of grass, we saw a triangular orange flag waving atop a flexible stick. As we drew closer, I spotted a grayish bone half-hidden by a fern next to the bottom of the stick. Rowena must have spotted it, too, because I felt her legs starting to buckle. I put my arm around her waist and hoisted her up. The blood had drained from her face. Then I felt her own muscles taking over again. "I'll be okay now," she whispered.

"Do you know what kind of bone this is?" I asked Alvarez.

"Doherty, one of the assistant coroners, who's around here some-place, said he thought it was a human fibula."

I swallowed down the bile that rose up to sting my throat. "Why do you suspect a mountain lion?"

"Well, I told you we'd found lion tracks and scat around here, but we don't know for sure it was a lion. Lions hunt alone, usually at night. They like to jump on their prey from behind and kill with a bite that breaks the neck. They'll open up the body cavity and eat the large or-gans, like the heart, and then eat the thigh meat. Sometimes, a lion will hide his kill under dirt or leaves and come back to feed on it over a few days. All we've found so far are two bones."

"So the bones wouldn't be spread all over?" Jessup asked.

"They could be. After a lion is done, the coyotes and wild boar take over. They'll move things around. The bite marks on the bone look like coyote to me."

I crouched down and looked at the bone. Not much flesh remained, just a few tattered ligaments. Was this what was left of Paul?

Rowena moved away a few steps and threw up.

I looked back at her. She raised her head and produced a wan smile. When I started to move toward her, she shook me away. I then turned my gaze to Jessup. He had been watching me. So that was the game. I had been brought here so that my reaction could be examined. Maybe seeing the bones would make me break down and confess. Did they still suspect me? Jessup snickered as he swiveled his head toward Rowena. I turned to Alvarez.

"So we've found Paul's wallet and ring and a leg bone. What else?" I asked.

"One more bone," Alvarez said.

"We'll get more people out here and find more," Jessup said.

"Where is the bone?" I asked Alvarez.

"Fifty yards from here."

"Let's go," I said.

This time Rowena and I couldn't hold hands; the path was too narrow. Again with Alvarez leading the way, the four of us pushed through ferns and thorns. There, beside another flag, crouched a man.

"Hey." He stood up, camera around his neck.

"This is Dr. Doherty from the coroner's office," Alvarez said.

"What bone is that?" I asked Doherty, pointing to the longish bone beside the flag. This bone rested in plain sight, haloed by a circle of sunlight.

"Looks like a human right tibia to me. That's one of the two bones in the lower leg."

"But you're not sure?"

"I know it's a bone from the right side of some animal. Pretty sure it's human, too," the assistant coroner said. "Need lab confirmation to be absolutely certain, though."

I crouched down and put my head inches away from the bone. I observed bite marks, but no ligaments this time.

"Could this have happened to Paul last Saturday?" I asked.

"Why Saturday?" Jessup asked in response.

"I last saw Paul early Saturday morning. Doctor?"

"Seems like the bones are pretty well stripped for only five days out here, but it's possible," Doherty said. "Only sure way to know who these belong to is DNA testing. We can get DNA from the bones and then compare it to the DNA of the deceased or even a blood relative." He looked down again at the reputed shin bone. So did I.

For the first time that day, I felt a pang of hope.

TWENTY-NINE

WE DROVE WITHOUT SPEAKING. Hearing only the occasional squeal from my Michelins, I kept my foot on the gas as we descended from the park and twisted through the crosshatch of Palo Alto's residential streets. My mind chewed over the facts. Bones were found with Paul's wallet nearby. No one had seen Paul since Saturday. The police still had me pegged as suspect number one. But I knew those bones were not—could not be—Paul's. I pulled into the driveway on Lincoln, turned the ignition key counterclockwise, heard the engine grunt goodbye, and looked at Rowena.

"There's an evil force at work here," she said.

A melodramatic line to be sure, yet one that fit. "Yeah."

We walked in the house. I cupped her chin and tilted her face up. She looked right back at me. She had been sick, had to know she didn't look her best. Most women I knew would have told me not to look until they cleaned up. There was something fearless about her.

"How do you feel?" I asked.

She shrugged.

"My mom would say you look peaked," I told her.

"Yeah. 'Pea-ked.' That's about right, I'll bet." She began untying the laces of her Nikes. She shook them off. "You know what I need? A good run. Something to get the blood flowing into my brain. I need to think."

"You're up for it?"

"Right after I brush my teeth." She started putting her shoes back on.

"Can I come along?"

"Sure. You have any regular running routes?"

Thirty minutes later, we were loping through the Stanford campus on our way to the circuit around the Dish. I usually ran for ninety minutes in the hills four or five times a week. Even though I had slacked off a little since the murder, I was still in shape. I didn't want to run too fast for Rowena, so I ran behind and let her set the pace. She sailed along, ponytail bobbing out the back of the baseball cap I'd loaned her. I wondered if she was running faster than normal to impress me.

I called out directions through the campus, but otherwise we didn't speak. We twisted through the turnstile gate that the university had placed on the pathway up the hill leading to the Dish. There had been too many dirt bikers skidding down the hill, so now asphalt covered the path. I looked at my watch; we'd made it the three miles to the turnstile in under twenty minutes. As we began climbing, I pulled up the bottom of my shirt to wipe my forehead. The weather wasn't too warm, but Rowena was *moving*. The muscles under the skin of her legs quivered and darted like trout in a stream. She didn't look back, but I sensed she knew where I was. We passed day hikers carrying cardboard coffee cups with their Starbucks wrappers and undergraduate couples strolling hand in hand. There were others running—no, they were jogging; *we* were running. Rowena carried me along in her slipstream. We raced along the aqueduct carrying the gurgling waters of the Sierra to the parched throats of Silicon Valley. When we reached the old radio antenna known as the Dish, she looked back at me. *You okay?* her look inquired. I nodded yes, and we turned around for the run back. The city of Palo Alto, partly hidden beneath a canopy of trees, stretched across the horizon. From here, the distance from my house to the Berks' appeared a matter of inches.

Back we went, downhill now, then out the turnstile and through the campus. I stopped thinking. Those endorphins—natural heroin—had kicked in for me. I felt no pain; I just followed the bouncing black ponytail. The sun had set. Rowena only slowed when we neared the house. We walked the last two blocks through the gloaming. I shuddered as an evening breeze cut through my sweat-soaked shirt. A streetlight flicked on as we walked underneath. I could see Rowena's shirt plastered to her torso by perspiration, but unlike me, she wasn't breathing that hard.

Once back in my foyer, I asked, "You're a runner?"

"How do you mean?"

"Okay. I'll ask it this way. What was the last race you ran?"

"The Orange County Marathon."

"How'd you do?"

"About a dozen runners finished ahead of me."

"A dozen women beat you?"

"No. Just one woman. The rest were men."

"*I* would have needed three golden apples to catch you."

"I love the myth of Atalanta," she said, laughing as she tilted her head back. And my lips were on her neck. My face was hot. Her neck was cool. She purred. Our lips ground together, tongues thrusting. She moaned. We slid onto the floor in the living room. She grabbed. No dreamy lovemaking like last night or unhurried intimacy like this morning. This was primal. Her fingers were slipping under my shirt, then digging into my back as our lips remained cemented. I was yanking down her running shorts and didn't care as I heard the cotton panties underneath rip. *Now* she was breathing hard.

A loud thump on the front door froze us. Another thump and Rowena sat up. Her T-shirt fell like a curtain from her shoulders, down her chest, and then over her stomach.

"C'mon, Ian. Open up. I need to talk to you."

Fletcher.

Rowena shrugged. "Just a sec," I called out. We stood up and re-assembled ourselves, smoothing and tucking.

I opened the door. Fletcher, clad in another nondescript pantsuit, raised an eyebrow.

"Yeah, come on in."

"Just finished a run?" she asked.

"Yup."

Rowena came around the corner into the foyer. "You here, too, Ms. Goldberg?" Fletcher asked.

"Yes, Officer."

"Call me Susan."

"Please call me Rowena," came her response.

"All right. Enough polite chitchat," I interrupted. "Listen, Susan, you're not exactly winning friends and influencing people hereabouts. Hauling us up to the park to see how I dealt with those bones. No wonder you let Rowena come along—two reactions to judge for the price of one. I thought we were on the same side."

"It was Jessup's idea. And I figured you'd want to look around. Seemed like a fair trade." Fletcher raised her hand before I could say more. "It was you who insisted on bringing along Ms. Goldberg."

Right, the retching was my fault. "And so?"

"We had the bones tested."

Rowena's fingers flew up to her mouth.

"And?" I asked.

223

"They're human."

"And?" I asked again.

"Well, Paul's blood was type O."

"And?" Even though I knew that the bones weren't Paul's, I suspected what was coming.

"The bones came from a person, a man, with type O blood."

I inspected Rowena. The pinkish flushing brought to her face by running and our curtailed lovemaking had vanished. Her lips formed two white lines. But she looked steady on her feet.

I looked back at Fletcher. She was no sadist. This wasn't fun for her either. "What about DNA testing?" I asked.

"That's why I'm here."

"Let's hear it."

"We need to get a sample of Paul's DNA."

"Where did you find out his blood type?"

"His doctor."

"Ask him for a sample." I wondered how they'd found old Dr. Dubitzky.

"Doesn't know where to get one."

"You want me to come up with a sample of Paul's DNA?" I asked.

"You want *me* to go wake up Kathy Berk?" Fletcher replied. "She's got a concussion and is over at Stanford. 'Hi, Mrs. Berk. We've found some bones that might be your husband's. Can you help us?' Sound good? Maybe you can come up with a better plan."

"What do you need? Some hair, some blood, a fingernail clipping?"

"Any of the above," Fletcher replied.

"So you want to go poking around the bathrooms at the Berks' place? Couldn't you get a warrant?"

"No need. You told me you have regular access with permission? If so, you can let me in."

"She's right, you know," said Rowena's voice from behind me. "And besides," she added, "who's going to protest? Kathy's not living there, and Paul . . ." Her voice trailed off.

"And if Officer Susan here had to get a warrant," I said, "she'd need to bring Mikulski and Jessup and the whole gang into the party. This way she can find a critical clue all by herself."

Fletcher laughed.

When I walked down the brick path toward her city-issued Crown Victoria, I turned and looked back into the house through the big picture window. The drapes were open, and I could see the spot on the living room floor where Rowena and I had been a few minutes before. Maybe Fletcher was a little sadistic after all.

———————

The crime-fighting trio of Fletcher, Goldberg, and Michaels entered the Berks' master bedroom suite. We stopped for a huddle. Before we could touch anything, Fletcher handed us latex gloves, the kind doctors use during exams.

We snaked our way into the bathroom, a room of marble, mirrors, and porcelain bigger than my bedroom. Next to the mirror on the left, surrounded by light bulbs, was a switch with settings that read Sunlight, Indoor, and Night. A better bet for Paul's space was by the other mirror, which had an oval area on its lower half that magnified as it reflected. In the medicine cabinet behind this mirror was a congeries of bottles and tubes. In the top drawer under Paul's sink, we found two brushes and three combs. Fletcher wouldn't let us touch them, even with our gloves. We all scrutinized each bristle and tooth for an errant curl.

"We'll send these down to the lab boys in San Jose," Fletcher said. But we could tell they weren't going to find anything. I knew from the times I had stayed with the Berks that Florrie, a damnably efficient maid, cleaned the bathrooms every day. We could see that the towels on the chromed racks were freshly laundered. The four slots in the toothbrush holder held nothing. The shower stall gleamed. Intel's clean rooms should be so pristine. The bedroom appeared much the same. Not a single imperfection, let alone a hair, marred the line of suits, handcrafted in Italy and England, arrayed in Paul's closet.

Thirty minutes more of inspecting increased both my admiration of Florrie's housekeeping skills and the flow of invective that ran through my mind. I sat down on the floor and crossed my legs.

"Giving up?" Fletcher asked.

"Not yet. Let me think a minute."

The two women looked at me, shrugged, and restarted their search.

A few minutes later, I got up and went back to the shower. I took out my Swiss army knife and unscrewed the drain cover. I reached down expecting to find the same kind of slippery agglomeration of soap, dirt, and hair that I found when my shower refused to drain. Nothing. Nothing in the trap under the sink either.

I had one more idea. "Let's try the basement."

"Dirty laundry?" Rowena guessed.

I nodded.

In the basement, the laundry baskets stood empty. The cavernous innards of the commercial-style stainless steel washer and dryer held only air. When Fletcher had suggested that I let her into the Berks', I felt confident I was doing the right thing. In fact, I figured I was doing several right things: helping to resolve Gwendolyn's death, figuring out what had happened to Paul, sheltering Kathy until I could explain how the bones of a type O human ended up in Foothills Park. Now I wondered whether going through Paul's bathroom, bedroom drawers, and laundry represented another betrayal of our friendship. I felt like the seedy impresario of a peep show. Still, I would make the same decision again.

"That's enough," Fletcher said after a quick tour of the rest of the house. "I'll get the lab guys over here, but they won't find anything." She shook her head. She had been expecting a big break, maybe a career-making break, and wasn't going to get it.

"I'm not letting *them* in," I said. There was no longer any reason to cut corners.

"Not ready to join the force yet, are you?" Fletcher said, continuing to shake her head. "Doesn't matter. I'll have someone posted in front of the house tonight and get a warrant tomorrow morning." She brightened. "Of course, we don't need to do a DNA check on Paul. We could get what we needed from a parent or sibling."

"Nope. Paul's parents passed away years ago, and he's an only child."

"Damn."

"And don't go thinking of digging his parents up. I'm pretty sure they were cremated."

"Damn. Damn."

THIRTY

WE FILED BACK DOWN the stairs, Fletcher, Rowena, then me. I stepped in front of the two women to reset the alarm at the back door. From the time I entered the code, we had thirty seconds to leave.

I punched in the numbers and had just touched the knob when I heard a key scratch at the lock from the outside. Then the knob twisted through my fingers. Rowena grabbed my arm, but otherwise we didn't move. I held my breath. Could it be Paul? He could explain where he'd been, describe his relationship with Gwendolyn, and outline a plan for catching her murderer. He would be here in an instant. At last.

The door swung open. I looked down to see a woman's graying head. The mouth on the head formed an O and let loose a ululating scream that would have won her the role of the bereaved mother in any Greek tragedy.

"Florrie! Stop!" I shouted.

She did stop when she saw it was me. "Oh, Mr. Michaels. You made my heart stop." She held her hand over her ample bosom. Seeing Florrie—late fifties, hair in a bun, long black skirt, vague Eastern European accent—made me recognize the basis for my original picture of Gwendolyn the housekeeper.

"You frightened us, too. Look, this is Rowena Goldberg, a friend of mine. And this is Officer Fletcher from the Palo Alto police."

Florrie's eyes narrowed. "Something the matter?"

"Don't know," I replied. "When was the last time you saw Mr. Berk?"

"I've been visiting my sister Marina in Los Angeles for the last week."

"You haven't been here in a week?" Fletcher interrupted.

Then a deafening hee-haw began. We'd been talking with the alarm set and the door open. All four of us threw our hands up to cover our ears. I had to take one hand down to punch in the code. The alarm ceased immediately, but the ringing in my ears subsided only gradually.

"Sorry, that was dumb," I said.

Fletcher turned back to Florrie and asked, "When did you last see Paul Berk?"

"A week ago."

"When you last cleaned up, did you clean out the drain in the master bedroom's shower?" Fletcher asked next.

Florrie's eyes narrowed again and then turned to me. "Go ahead," I said.

"No," she answered.

As we walked around the block to where Fletcher had parked her car, Rowena asked the obvious question. "Who cleaned the shower drain if it wasn't Florrie?"

———

"That's Jason's car," said Rowena, pointing to the red Boxster parked on Lincoln across the street from my place.

I didn't need to ask how she knew. Plates reading "BLITZ" told the tale.

As Fletcher's car pulled to a stop, Rowena opened the door, ran to the front porch, where he waited, and cried, "Jason, what are you doing here?" I was far from delighted to see the two of them hug.

I stuck out my hand as I climbed onto the porch. Jason released Rowena from his clutches and shook my hand.

"How ya doing?" he asked. He looked over my shoulder. "Good evening, Officer Fletcher." I remembered that Fletcher had questioned Jason in LA.

Fletcher nodded. "Listen, you two," she said, addressing Rowena and me. "If you think of someplace else to look or if something comes up, you let me know. Anytime. The dispatcher will find me." She looked straight at me. "Thanks anyway." And she turned back to her car.

"Come on in, Jason."

We sat at three corners of a triangle, Jason in my favorite chair with his feet on the ottoman, Rowena cross-legged on the couch, and I on a straight-backed chair dragged in from the kitchen. Ever the host, I had brought Jason the bottle of Sierra Nevada beer he was now sucking and Rowena the glass of Diet Coke she sipped.

"So, Jason." That was me—such a witty conversationalist.

"Well, I got sick of sitting around waiting to hear what was up. I spoke to Mrs. Goldberg."

"Mom doesn't even know I'm here. I should've called," Rowena said.

"She told me you were probably up here."

"Really?" Rowena said in surprise.

"Yup. So I hopped in the car and drove on up."

"Have Porsche, will travel," I said. What was it about these Southern Californians that impelled them to show up unannounced at my doorstep? For them, a quick five hours up I-5 meant no more than a drive across town for me. I stopped myself. Throwing Rowena and Jason into the same bucket demonstrated my irritation. Rowena coming had been wonderful. Having the Goldberg sisters' wannabe beau in my house uninvited and unwelcome was the real-life equivalent to spam e-mail.

"I called you last night," Jason said. "You weren't there. Tried your cell phone all morning, too. No answer."

"Oh. Must still be in the car," Rowena said.

"I called your house. Like I said, your mom guessed you were here, and I thought I'd drive up. Even if Row wasn't here, it would give us a chance to talk." Jason nodded at me.

"What about?" I asked.

"Kind of to apologize."

"You already did that at your office," I said.

"Maybe. But that was only words. I still thought you had something to do with Gwennie's death."

I thought so, too. She was killed in my house, and she had been telling people we had a relationship. Some responsibility ended up with me. Just how much I still aimed to find out. To Jason, I just nodded.

"Gwennie and I had been drifting apart, slowly but surely for years. But it still hurt." Jason's head swung down, and he looked at the brown bottle in his hands before picking up his narrative again. "She'd said there was someone else. I asked if she'd met him at school. She laughed and said no, she'd met him through work. She was teasing me a little, I think. I didn't know she was working as a maid and didn't even ask what kind of work she was talking about. But she was wearing this baseball cap that said Accelenet on it. And I asked if her new boyfriend had given it to her. She said yes. Then we talked about other stuff."

"And when you saw in the papers that Gwennie was killed while working for Ian . . . ," Rowena put in.

"Yeah. I figured Ian here was the person from Accelenet. Met through work, she'd said. So that's why I was mad. But after I met you, I started thinking. Maybe you *were* lying. But then again, maybe I'd jumped to the wrong conclusion. Maybe she took care of other houses for Accelenet employees. Maybe she'd started cleaning here because someone had recommended her to you."

"That's not it," I said. "But an interesting thought."

"So I called the investor relations guy at Accelenet, what's-his-name, and told him that I wanted to do an interview with Paul Berk for a piece I was working on."

My pulse picked up. "Tony Chow heads public relations," I told him. Tony would swallow that lure in a New York minute.

"Yeah, that's it. Anyway, he set up an interview with Paul. It was just the two of us, Paul and me." That arrangement was part of Paul's shtick. He would meet with reporters and analysts without any PR watchdog there. He didn't need handlers, he'd say. He wanted the people interviewing him to feel like his best buddy, to think they were getting insights that Paul would entrust only to them. Nobody could match Paul's personal magnetism, and he knew someone else's presence would break the spell.

"So you met with Paul just last week?" I asked, trying to keep my voice steady.

"Let's see. Over the weekend. On Saturday. For an interview with Paul Berk, I'd give up a weekend, no problem."

"You met in his office?"

"We started there, but he wanted to take a walk."

"Along Shoreline?" That sounded like Paul, too. Take a walk with the person you're trying to win over. So it's informal, so you're a friend, not an analyst or reporter.

"How did you know?" Jason asked.

"A guess. Did you just talk about business?"

"For a while. But then I told him I'd known Gwennie."

"And?" asked Rowena.

"And he said the newspaper accounts made her sound like someone special and that he was very sorry." Jason looked at Rowena, and when he received no cluck of sympathy from that quarter, turned to me. No luck there either. He picked up the story. "I told him all about our relationship. How it hadn't worked out."

He had spilled his guts to Paul. Berk magic.

"Just like I'm telling you," Jason continued, "I told him about Gwennie saying she'd had a relationship with someone at Accelenet and how I figured it was you. He told me he'd known you"—Jason squinted at me—"for nine years and that he would bet his life against you having anything to do with her death."

In other circumstances, I might have savored this avowal of loyalty more. "When did you finish up?" I asked.

"Just before noon," Jason responded.

"And where?"

"What do you mean?"

"Did you go back to his office?"

"No. We said goodbye in the parking lot."

I sighed. "Listen, Jason, you need to call the police. You were the last person to see Paul. He's gone. Vanished. Your story will help the police set the time for his disappearance."

"You think he should talk to Fletcher?" asked Rowena.

Why not throw this one to her? She had missed the one she really wanted at the Berks' late that afternoon. "I do," I said.

"Sure. Okay," said Jason. He picked up his beer and finished off the last two inches of liquid.

I called the police. Fletcher picked Jason up ten minutes later.

––––––––––

"Poor Jason," she was saying.

"Yeah." I did feel sorry for him, but it was hard when I remembered finding Rowena at his place in LA.

Rowena and I were sitting at the kitchen table, dirty dishes in front of us. There hadn't been much to choose from, but she'd put together an omelet with refrigerator leftovers. Whatever she hadn't used, I had thrown in a salad. The omelet had been delicious, the salad passable.

"After Gwennie died, he went a little nuts. I stayed with him a bit."

"I know."

A flush started climbing from just over her T-shirt up to her face. "Yes. You found me there."

"Yes, I did."

"Well, I—"

I held my hand up with the sense that I didn't want to hear what came next. "I don't require any explanations," I told her.

"Just listen. At the time, I didn't think I needed to explain. It wasn't your business. *I* wasn't your business. But now? Anyway, the poor boy was going nuts." Poor boy. Probably pulling in well over a hundred thou at age twenty-three. Disconsolate, maybe. Poor, no. "I spent a lot of time with him, holding his hand, listening to his stories. I even stayed over at his place a couple of nights. He needed the company."

Rowena looked at me, and I looked back.

"Okay," she continued. "He did try something one night, but he was pretty easily discouraged. I was just a substitute for Gwennie." Tears ran down her cheeks. I pulled my chair over and put my arms around her.

That's where we were when the phone rang—with her head on my shoulder and my arms around her. I scowled, but Rowena picked up the receiver and handed it to me. It was Jason. "What's going on? You need a place to stay?"

"No. Won't need one. The police are holding me as a material witness. They think it's funny that I was just before Gwennie died and on the day Paul disappeared."

"You need a lawyer. You being held downtown?" Rowena came over and pressed her head against mine to hear what Jason was saying.

"Yes," he said. I knew that little holding cell all too well.

"Okay. I'll get a lawyer there tonight."

"Yeah. Listen, thanks, Ian. And about me and Rowena, I wanted to, but there was nothing . . ."

"Don't worry about that now. Let's get you some help." I hung up.

"The police think Jason killed Gwennie?" Rowena asked, wide-eyed. "That makes no sense. He wouldn't, he couldn't. He loved her." She glanced out the window, frowned, and looked back at me. "You don't think he did it, do you, Ian?"

"No, I don't."

"You are going to help him?"

"Yeah. I'll do what I can." I dialed Ms. Ishiyama's cell phone.

"Hello. Ian Michaels. Sorry to call so late." I looked down at my watch. A few minutes before ten.

"It's okay. Tell me what's happened," Ms. Ishiyama said into my ear.

"Jason Blitzer, Gwendolyn's old boyfriend, is being held by the police. He admits seeing her the day she died. And he was with Paul just before he disappeared."

"He sounds very unlucky or very guilty."

"You'll have to trust me. It's the former," I said.

"What do you want me to do?"

"Go get him out of jail. Help him."

"I cannot represent you *and* him."

"I know. Please go help him."

"Are you sure? The moment I go to work for Jason, I'll be looking after his interests, not yours. The police weren't convinced you were innocent this morning. If they start sniffing around again, I won't be able to help. This is no time for a foolhardy gesture."

"I'm sure. He needs your help now."

"Okay." She hung up.

Rowena threw her arms around me. "Thank you."

Had I done the right thing? Was I trying to impress Rowena? Would I have done the same thing if she had told me something had happened between her and Jason? I didn't know. But I did know he hadn't killed either Gwendolyn or Paul, and I guess that was enough.

"Let's go," I said to Rowena.

"Where? It's after ten."

"To the hospital."

THIRTY-ONE

"Do you know where Kathy's room is?" Rowena asked, pulling me toward the hospital's information desk.

"We're not going to see Kathy," I said.

She let go of my arm. "I thought that was the whole point. I thought you were worried about her."

"I am. But that's not why we're here. We're looking for the pathology department."

"Do you want to explain?" She stood before me, hands on hips.

I saw the menace in her eyes and said, "It's a long shot. I'm hoping to find out whether I'm right or wrong in a few minutes, or we might have to come back in the morning. Anyway, you'll find out the same time I do."

Rowena shook her head, stood aside, and, as I passed, hooked my arm with hers.

"Where is the pathology department?" she asked me.

"Don't know."

"We can ask them." She jerked her head toward the two women at the information station.

"Wouldn't it seem a mite peculiar to be asking where the pathology department is after ten at night? Let's check the map."

After a thirty-second scan, we realized the pathology department didn't appear on the map. That made sense. Why would members of the public need to find the labs where doctors peered through microscopes at human flesh?

"So where we headed?" Rowena asked.

"Second floor."

"Pathology is there?"

"Surgery is there, and I'd guess pathology is nearby."

We walked toward the elevators. It must have been well past any sort of regular visiting hours, but the hospital, of course, ran on a twenty-four-hour basis. A woman in a hospital gown pushed a Rube Goldberg contraption that held high a red bag of blood and a clear bag marked "Glucose," each connected to her arm by a curlicuing hose. A man and a woman, both about thirty, both in navy blue uniforms, rolled a gurney holding an ashen-faced patient. As we passed them, I turned and saw the large yellow letters EMT on their backs. But they weren't rushing. They talked over the man on the gurney; the lack of urgency on their faces, their calm tone of voice, and their sense of familiarity with each other said they weren't talking about the third member of their party. They were just coworkers chatting at the office water cooler.

A minute later, the elevator spit us out on the second floor. With a left turn, we would head to the family waiting area. I knew that even at this time of night we'd find lingering spouses and children speaking in hushed tones, anxious for word on how their husband or wife, father or mother, was faring. That left turn would pry open the lid on my box of memories stored since my father's death. Room C227 is where he'd been till just before the end. So I steered Rowena to the right.

"Why this way?" she asked.

I shrugged, and we walked down the deserted main hall. First one door and then another with signs reading, "Restricted Area. Authorized Personnel Only. Scrub Attire Required." No one had asked us for an ID, but I knew we didn't belong here. I felt an echo of that sense of trespassing I'd had in Paul's place. We swung into the first open corridor. The second door down read, "Room H2335, Surgical Pathology."

"Couldn't have got here much faster with a map," Rowena said in surprise. "How did you do that?"

"Let's see if our luck holds," I said, reaching out for the knob. I exhaled as the knob twisted, and we walked into a short hall. After a dozen steps, we came to a T. To our right, I saw an open area with cubes, desks, phones, and computers. A closed gray door materialized to our left. At the back of the open area, I saw some movement.

"Hello," I called out. "Sir?"

"Me?" A man in blue scrubs stopped and looked back at us.

"Yes, please. I'm Ian Michaels, and this is my friend Rowena Goldberg."

"Jeremy Trudeau," he replied as he approached. As we shook hands, I could see from the ID badge dangling around his neck that he was a pathology resident. Doctor or not, he was still young enough to have a couple of pimples on his forehead. Black smudges under his eyes, too.

"You're a resident here in pathology?" I asked.

"Yeah. I'll tell you. They say, 'Come to work in pathology. No long hours. Nine to five.' But here I am. What time is it?" He looked down at his watch. "They sure get their money's worth out of me."

"Listen, Jeremy. This is going to sound a little crazy, but I want to know how easy it would be to take an amputated leg from the hospital."

So here I stood, ten thirty at night in the pathology department, asking a resident how to purloin severed limbs. A modern-day William Burke, the notorious nineteenth-century grave robber. I put the odds at even that I would be explaining myself to Mikulski or Jessup before midnight.

Trudeau brightened. "Easy as pie," he said. "Let me show you."

He had not asked why we were querying him about amputated legs. I had a story fabricated and ready but really didn't want to use it, not in front of Rowena. I didn't want her to see me lie. Maybe she'd think I was too good at it.

The two of us trailed after Trudeau as he pushed open the gray door. He stopped in front of what looked like a built-in Sub-Zero refrigerator for storing wines—the Berks had one in their kitchen. Same brushed-stainless-steel edges, same glass door. But instead of cabernets and merlots inside, there were half a dozen packages wrapped in what looked like butcher paper and Zip-Loc bags. The bundles ranged in size from test tube to paperback.

Trudeau waved a hand toward the refrigerator. "Here's where we put specimens for the lab."

I sniffed, expecting an odor of decay or at least formaldehyde. Nothing. "We just walked in," I said. "Nobody stopped us."

"Yup." He grinned. "You probably could walk right out with any of this stuff. Hmm." He thought for a moment. "There are a fair number of people around here until about six. And then around eleven, maybe midnight, security locks the doors. So it would be best to make your move between six and eleven."

"That's now."

"Yup."

"What's brought here? Amputated limbs?" I asked.

"Everything. Earlier today, I did a histopathology on three limbs taken off by trauma."

"By trauma?" I repeated.

"Guy fell in front of the Cal Train. Sliced off his legs and left arm."

"But that's kind of unusual," I said.

"Absolutely." He looked at the ceiling for a moment. "An amputated leg? Most often, that would stem from diabetes. A diabetic starts feeling pins and needles in his foot. Poof. A few months later, the leg has to come off."

"But why examine the legs of that poor guy this morning, or of a diabetic? You know why they came off. What's there to see?"

"We do an exam on everything. What if I spotted some tumors? I'd let oncology know. What if there'd been some flesh-eating staph infection? The guy'd have to get some antibiotics."

"Uh, wouldn't someone notice if one of these packages disappeared?" Rowena spoke for the first time.

"Nope. If the surgeon isn't waiting for a biopsy or something, nine out of ten wouldn't notice or wouldn't care that they got no report."

"Really?" Rowena asked.

He grinned again. "But wait, I've got a better idea. Just walk into the operating room wearing scrubs and a badge. You could take the limb, and we here in pathology would never know."

"And if you don't have a badge?" Rowena asked.

"Then you could still get the leg right here." He pointed at the refrigerator, folded his arms, and gave us a lopsided smile of triumph.

"Are those specimens marked with a name or blood type?"

"They have the name, but no blood type."

"Thanks a lot. How long you been here?"

"I'm ready to retire, but I've only been here a year and a half. Let me tell you something. Never go to work at a place where they have beds and showers."

"Good advice."

Back on the first floor, I had the sense we had returned to civilization, such as it was. I examined each person we passed. You knew which ones were patients—most were wearing dressing gowns. But even without that, the tentative shuffling, downward-cast eyes, bald patches, or thick bandages gave an external manifestation to the burden of disease they bore. The doctors, nurses, and other hospital employees were just as easy to spot. The light blue scrubs or white coats announced their status as caregivers. The occasional person in civilian clothes went into the visitor category. Their grave faces supported my hypothesis.

Then it was back into the night's cool air. We sat on one of the ornate wooden benches outside the entrance. I looked at Rowena, and she looked right back at me. My stomach still felt a little queasy from our interview with Dr. Trudeau. I myself kept pushing away thoughts of what those refrigerated packages held, and our field trip to Foothills Park showed that Rowena's stomach was hardly cast iron. But she had pluck and showed no signs of nausea in her unwavering gaze.

"Okay," she said, "you've shown that someone could get their hands on a leg bone and leave it in the park. Guess we know now that it wouldn't be hard to do. In fact, if you've got nerve, it would be incredibly easy to do." She shuddered. "But just because that could've happened doesn't mean it did. I know you don't want to believe the bones we saw were Paul's. I admire you for your faith. But did it look like any legs were in the fridge upstairs just now?"

"No, but there were two there this morning," I pointed out.

"Exactly. How would you know when a leg would show up? One that belonged to a person with type O blood?"

Rowena had reached the heart of the matter in just a few logical steps. "Bingo," I said. "Those are the questions we need to answer."

"You got any ideas?"

242

"Yeah. Maybe. Remember, Conan Doyle wrote something like, 'When you have eliminated the impossible, whatever remains, no matter how improbable, must be the truth'?"

"Yes?" Elongating the final sound with a sibilant hiss, Rowena sounded wary.

"Well, I have an improbable idea that I'd like to check out."

Rowena stood up. "Okay, Sherlock. Let's go."

THIRTY-TWO

"Hi, Sylvia. It's Ian Michaels. I'm sorry to call this late. Is Dr. Dubitzky still awake?"

Frank Dubitzky had been my doctor since Paul recommended him nine years before. He had been Paul's for another decade before that and had passed to the experienced side of seventy. He told me to call him Frank, but he was older than my father would have been, and I didn't always remember to do so. I saw him at his office every other year for a physical and, along with his wife, Sylvia, every few months at the odd dinner party or fundraising affair. I saw more of her than of him. Gray pageboy swaying, arms thrusting, Nikes pumping, Sylvia power-walked past my place on Lincoln almost every morning. This was the first time that I had called them at home.

"Ian, well, you wouldn't call if it weren't important. And you're not waking me up. I'm waiting for Frank. That man is still at the office. Can you believe it? Call 327-2220. That's the phone on his desk. Otherwise you'll get the service. You're okay, aren't you, dear?"

"Health-wise, just fine, Sylvia. Thanks so much."

Rowena and I were sitting in my Acura's front seat, still in the dark hospital garage. My cell phone glowed amber as I dialed Frank.

"Hello?"

"Yeah, Doc—Frank. Ian Michaels. Sylvia said you were there."

"You okay?"

"I'm fine, but—"

"Police came and saw me about Paul," he interrupted. "Wanted to know his blood type." Like so many people, Dr. Dubitzky saw me through my relationship to Paul.

"I heard. Listen, Frank, I know it's late, but I'd like to stop by and talk to you about him."

"Is Paul dead?" I heard the anxiety in his voice.

"No."

I heard a sigh of relief and then, "Come on over then."

I knocked on the doctor's door ten minutes later.

"Ian," said the good doctor, extending his hand. Dubitzky, a sartorial atavism, wore gray slacks, striped tie, and herringbone jacket. His work habits were a throwback as well. Not too many Palo Alto internists remained in their offices half an hour before midnight.

I introduced Rowena, and we found ourselves in two leather chairs in front of Frank's walnut desk. This was where I sat after my biennial physical as Frank wagged his finger, warning me about the increased risk for heart disease and colon cancer my genes had bequeathed to me. On the wall just behind him, I scanned diplomas from Dartmouth College and Stanford Medical School.

"So what's going on, Ian? The police said Paul was missing."

"He is, Dr. Dubitzky," Rowena interjected. "We're trying to figure out just where he's gone missing to."

"So what can I do? Can't reveal any privileged stuff, you understand."

"When did you last see Paul?" I asked.

"Okay. I'm figuring Paul's in trouble, and you're his friend." The doctor whirled in his chair and started stabbing at his keyboard with his index fingers. "Says here," he said, pointing to his PC monitor, "that he was here a week ago Thursday."

"Now, Frank, this is a shot in the dark. You have any patients who have lost a leg recently? Maybe a diabetic who had to have an amputation?"

Dubitzky's eyes narrowed. "I don't have to look that up. I did. How did you know?"

"Lucky guess?" I hazarded with a shrug of the shoulders.

"And why does it matter?"

"Play along with us just a few more minutes," I asked, looking straight at the doctor. "When was that patient last in here?" My imaginary bow was sending another arrow of inquiry into the gloom.

The doctor's liver-spotted hands tapped at the computer again. "A week ago Thursday, too."

"Who was it?"

"Jim Pavlik."

Blinking in surprise, I said, "I know him. Poor guy. He used to work at Berk Technology. He had one of those insulin pumps he wore inside his shirt. Didn't know his diabetes had gotten that bad. Did he know he was going to lose the leg?" Paul would have known him, too.

Frank thought for a minute. "I guess I can answer that. I told him he probably would."

"What time was his appointment?"

"Ten thirty."

"And Paul's?"

"Eleven."

"So chances are good they ran into each other in the waiting room."

"They could have. Do you know where you're going with this?"

"We'll see," I replied and pushed on. "Which leg did he lose?"

"The right leg."

"Was it amputated above the knee?"

"Yes, just above. But in a few weeks, he'll be fitted with a prosthetic. They're pretty good nowadays. He should be up and around in no time."

"Let's hope so," I said. "Do you know what blood type Jim is?"

Frank shook his head. "I don't think I can tell you that."

As one of the doctor's patients, I appreciated the line he had drawn. "Now, Frank, I'm off in a different direction. You remember when Paul and I went to China."

"Sure. He came back with a broken leg, fibula and tibia both snapped right in half. I had that orthopedic guy Prescott take a look at it. Told me that those Chinese doctors knew what they were doing. But you know all that."

"Right," I said. "Now, here's my question. Would an x-ray show you where Paul's leg had snapped?"

"I'm no orthopedic guy, but sure, for years."

"Let's assume someone with a break like Paul's had died and donated his body to science. When the med students were looking just at the bones in the leg, would they be able to see where the bones had broken?"

"Same answer as the x-ray question. There'd be a very visible line on both bones if the break happened in the ten years before death." Frank pulled himself back to reality from the abstract realm of science and leaned across his desk. "But I thought you said Paul wasn't dead."

That afternoon at Foothills Park, I had inspected the bones for signs of a break. There had been none. "He's not," I said.

As I swung the car into my driveway, the headlights illuminated the figure of Officer Susan Fletcher sitting on my front steps. I didn't pull into the garage. Rowena and I got out.

"Where've you been?" Fletcher asked.

"Come on, Susan, did you forget? I'm not a suspect anymore. The brains on your side have decided it's Jason's feet that fit the murderer's shoes." I knew I sounded sarcastic and didn't much care.

She shook her head. "I don't figure him for it. Jessup is grasping at straws. But that attorney you gave him is sharp. Jason's being released."

Another pair of headlights approached. The car jerked along as the driver peered at addresses before stopping in front of my place. Jason Blitzer emerged through the passenger door to see a welcoming committee consisting of his deceased ex-girlfriend's sister, a Palo Alto police officer who had just finished interrogating him, and a former target of his right hook. "Left my car here," he said, pointing at the murky outline of his Boxster across the street.

I turned my gaze inside the car Jason was exiting to identify his erstwhile chauffeur. Made opalescent by the car's interior light, a ring of pearls highlighted the countenance of Ellen Ishiyama.

"Just dropping my new client off," she said, her soft voice just audible over the idling engine.

"I know it's late," I said to Ms. Ishiyama. A quick look at my watch showed the two hands to be straight up. "Or maybe I should say early. In any case, why don't you come in for a cup of coffee?"

"I do have a conference call at eight tomorrow—no, this morning," she said with an apologetic tilt of her head.

"I'm not just being polite. I think you should come in."

"Thank you. I could use a cup," she said, and stepped out of her car.

"And how about you, Jason?" I asked.

Some ten minutes later, I was perched on an ottoman in my living room. Rowena, hair still in her runner's ponytail, sat to my right, embraced by the arms of one of the club chairs. Jason, legs crossed, foot wagging, sat on the other. Fletcher and Ms. Ishiyama looked like mismatched bookends across from me on the sofa—the one stocky, hair cut short, in a light blue pantsuit almost certainly with a label inside proclaiming it one hundred percent polyester, and the other slight, with straight hair halfway down her back, in a beautiful ivory suit almost certainly with some designer's name just inside the collar. One thing was the same: both held pencils poised over open notebooks on their laps.

"So?" said Ms. Ishiyama.

"So." I blew out a lungful of air. "I don't know how they met, but I can guess. One day last November, Paul dropped off some papers on the way to the airport when I was out of town."

"What kind of papers?" Fletcher asked.

"We were setting up a European sub, and my signature was needed as a board member. I figured he'd slipped them through the mail slot, like he's done a few other times."

"And it was a Wednesday," Rowena said, looking down at her running shoes.

"Right. I checked Paul's and my calendars. I think I remember—not well enough to testify under oath—but I still think I remember that I found the papers on the table in the foyer with the mail. Logical enough for me to assume that Gwendolyn picked up the folder and put it there. But maybe when he dropped it through the slot, she opened the door. Or he might have seen her inside and rung the doorbell. Or even used the spare key and surprised her."

"So one way or another they met," said Rowena.

"Must have. Don't know what Paul thought when he faced your sister and not a senior citizen with a mop, but we can be pretty sure what happened. Easy enough to strike up a conversation. Anyway, he and Gwendolyn began seeing each other."

"Her calls started dropping off in December," Jason said with some bitterness, his foot swinging to an even faster beat.

"Okay," I nodded. "Paul was married and not eager to be found out. But he and Gwendolyn had the ideal hideaway for their rendezvous. My place. I wasn't there during the day. But after four or five months, the affair between Gwendolyn and Paul began to cool down."

"She started falling in love with you," Rowena whispered.

"She didn't really know me, but it does look as though she started fantasizing about the person who lived here." Uncomfortable, I looked at Rowena. Tears rimmed her lower eyelids. "She did use my name as the password to her computer, and she wrote a novel about a maid who fell in love with her employer."

"How do you know that?" Fletcher asked.

"I found a copy of it at Paul's."

"And that means Paul had seen it," Ms. Ishiyama said.

"But I haven't," said Fletcher.

"I'll get it to you." I told her that I'd mailed it to my office and that it must be sitting on my desk at Accelent by now.

She opened her mouth, but closed it before a single word emerged. I could see her mental machinery at work. No reason to ask me right now why I had mailed it to myself. She had broken my momentum by asking about where I'd found the manuscript; she didn't want to do that again.

"Okay, now. As Ms. Ishiyama pointed out, Paul must have gotten wind of Gwendolyn's obsession."

Jason shot up. "So he killed her!" he shouted, his right hand smacking into his left palm.

"Sit down, Jason," Rowena said. "That won't help." Jason looked puzzled, as if he didn't know why he was standing. Then his eyes focused on Rowena, and he followed her admonition.

"Let me go ahead a bit. Chances are very good that Paul left the house shortly after Gwendolyn was killed. Mrs. O'Flaherty thought she saw me, but now thinks it might have been Paul. Susan, you find out where he was parking?"

"The trouble with this neighborhood is that cars like Paul's BMW are a dime a dozen," Fletcher said. "But Mrs. O'Flaherty told me originally that you came home during the day, once or twice a week. If she mistook Paul for you all those times . . ."

"Then that would confirm they met here at this house," I finished. Fletcher nodded.

"It was Paul who hit you over the head, then?" asked Rowena.

"I think it was Kathy. She was there looking for Paul at the regular time. She thought I was Paul and let me have it."

"That's a guess," suggested the velvet voice of Ms. Ishiyama.

"Certainly. I'd also guess it was Paul who used my computer to write a letter from me to Gwendolyn. He did that to make the police think I did in fact know her."

"He made love to my sister and then murdered her. He practically adopted Ian and then tried to set him up for a capital crime." Rowena spit out these words with contempt and even hatred. "He's so low, so evil. And then when it looked as though he might become a suspect, he arranged to disappear."

"You mean he died, or maybe he was killed," Fletcher said. "We found his leg bones at the park."

"The bones aren't his," I said. "He had a clean break in his right leg less than two years ago. That would have been obvious on the bones if they were Paul's."

"Then whose bones were they?" Fletcher asked.

"Jim Pavlik's," I answered. "Paul knew him. Jim and Paul had the same doctor. Maybe Paul recommended Dr. Dubitzky to Jim just as he had to me. Paul must have seen Jim in the doctor's waiting room.

No one can think quicker than Paul. I'll bet he had the whole plan worked out a few seconds after hearing that Jim was losing his leg. He found out they were the same blood type—maybe he asked Jim if he could donate blood for him—and he found out when the operation was."

"And he stole the leg," said Ms. Ishiyama in a tone approaching admiration.

"Oh, come on," Fletcher snorted. "From the hospital? With all that security?"

"I went over to surgical pathology with Ian, Officer," Rowena said. "A ten-year-old could walk out of there with any body parts he wanted. Arms, ears, noses, legs, whatever. No problem."

Fletcher's pencil flew down the steno pad. "You take shorthand, Susan?" I asked.

"I worked as a secretary for a couple of years." She wasn't just taking notes; she was transcribing what everyone said. Bully for her.

"I apologize for this gruesome question," Fletcher said, looking up from her pad first at Ms. Ishiyama and then Rowena. "But if Paul walked out of the hospital with an amputated leg, it would have been cut with a surgical saw. There would be no mistaking a leg like that for one eaten by animals."

"That's why it was important that the amputation happened above the knee," I responded. "Paul pulled off the thigh bone at the knee. I think he himself stripped most of the flesh off the tibia and fibula bones. Then he left them up at the park to be gnawed on by animals and put his wallet and ring close by. When the bones were found, he figured the police would count him dead."

"And the poetic justice of a killer being killed that way himself would appeal to Assistant DA Jessup. Nobody would come looking for him," said Ms. Ishiyama.

Fletcher's writing hand came to a stop. The five of us were all thinking over the consequences of what we'd discussed. Fletcher stood up. "They'll think I'm crazy," she said. "But I'm going to get everyone from the FBI to the school crossing guards to start searching for Paul Berk."

"Just a minute," I said. But Fletcher, head down, was making for my door. "Susan, hold on," I called louder.

She turned around with her hand on the doorknob. "Why?" she asked.

Rowena looked at me and then at Fletcher. "Because Ian doesn't think Paul killed anyone," she said.

How did she know what I was thinking? I shook my head. "No, I don't." Fletcher came back and sat down on the sofa.

THIRTY-THREE

"WHY DON'T YOU THINK Paul Berk killed Gwendolyn?" asked Ms. Ishiyama. We had all returned to our seats. Jason's foot started wagging again, and I perched on the forward edge of the ottoman.

I shook my head. "I've known Paul for more than ten years. It doesn't fit. He's going to kill a woman more than twenty years younger than he is in a crime of passion? Don't think so." I hit my clenched right hand into my left palm. "If anything, his marriage withered because what he was passionate about was work, his company. Paul doesn't do things impetuously. He has an analytical mind that can see the implications and results of a given situation in seconds. Fast decisions, yes. Impetuous ones, no. Look how quickly he took advantage of meeting Jim Pavlik in the doctor's waiting room. I guess a case could be made that he had motive, means, and opportunity, but the MO doesn't fit the man I know."

Jason put both feet on the ground and leaned forward, which stopped the metronomic shaking of his foot. "But if he didn't do it, why did he try to cover it up?" Jason asked.

Rowena looked at me. Returning her gaze, I saw she got it. "He'd ignored his wife, slept with Gwennie, and blamed himself for what happened even if he didn't commit the murder himself," she said.

Looking around, I could see both Ms. Ishiyama and Fletcher nodding their heads in unison from either end of the sofa. Jason still looked perplexed. "So?" he asked.

"Imagine this," Rowena continued. "Your husband's interest in you has dwindled, and then you find out he's been sleeping with someone twenty-five years younger than you. You start turning your attention to another man, but then you find out that that same younger woman now has her sights set on him."

"Berk's wife killed Gwendolyn?" Jason asked in a voice fraught with doubt.

"I'd bet on it," Rowena said.

I picked up the story. "Kathy showed up here late morning on that Thursday. She had a key. Paul did, too, but he would have made a copy so that Kathy didn't notice it was missing when he used it. Anyway, Kathy picked up the key she kept in her kitchen desk and came over. I don't know if Paul was still here and Kathy saw them both or if Kathy confronted Gwendolyn after he left. My guess is that Paul had already left. Gwendolyn called me that morning and left a voicemail message. Maybe Kathy heard her leaving it. I think Kathy came over here to have things out with Gwendolyn."

"It wasn't premeditated?" Rowena asked.

"My guess is no."

"You think Kathy hit you over the head?" was Rowena's next question.

"I do. When I saw her earlier today, she acted like she was guessing Paul met Gwendolyn at my house on Wednesdays. But I think she knew and didn't much like it. I had my assailant figured as a man, because the blow landed on the top of my head. So it would have to be someone at least as tall as I am. I'm six foot one. Paul is an inch shorter. Doesn't matter much. But Kathy is only an inch shorter than Paul, so she's five-eleven, and with heels on . . . well, the arithmetic works."

"And she probably thought it was Paul coming in," Rowena said. "She read the note on the refrigerator postponing Gwennie's weekly cleanup and came back the next day. Maybe Paul was there and she surprised them, maybe not. But Paul knew that Kathy had killed Gwendolyn."

"If he had left already, she called Paul after stabbing Gwendolyn," Fletcher said.

"Probably," I said. "If it was a call on her cell phone, you could check with the carrier. She might have just called from my regular phone, though. Anyway, Paul was either there or came over. What did he do? He wiped off the kitchen knife. He put something in my computer to make me look like a suspect—"

"Why would he want the evidence pointing at you?" Ms. Ishiyama asked.

"I don't think he really meant to get me convicted. I was a red herring. He would have known that the accusation wouldn't stick."

I was giving voice to my hope. Paul must have decided in a few seconds to make me the suspect to divert attention from Kathy. Now I wanted to believe he never would have let me take the blame in the end. He must have figured I would be found innocent, leaving an unknown intruder or burglar as the suspect in Gwendolyn's murder. But he had a backup plan. When I shed the mantle of suspicion, he decided to put it on himself.

"Paul put me in touch with Bryce Smithwick, the top lawyer in the Valley," I said. "When I needed support, I turned to Paul. He's my best friend."

"A somewhat presumptuous best friend," Ms. Ishiyama commented, and then turned her head toward her new client. "You know, Mr. Blitzer, it appears that Mr. Michaels has saved you a considerable sum in legal fees."

Fletcher interrupted. "Okay, okay. Mr. Blitzer didn't look good for the crime before and looks even less good now." The way Fletcher said "Mr. Blitzer" seemed a jab at the lawyer's formality.

"Paul knew what Kathy had done," Rowena said. "That must be why they stopped living together. Paul decided to help her, but not live with her."

"I appreciate this theorizing," Fletcher said. "But not a word of it's proven. I'll have the lab see if the bones found in the park really do belong to this Jim Pavlik. They can do a DNA match with him. And I'm going over to Stanford Hospital to see Kathy Berk. When she talks, we'll know just what happened."

"You'll have to Mirandize her," Ms. Ishiyama said.

"I will once I get over there," Fletcher said.

"We're going too," I said. "Aboard at the takeoff, aboard at the landing."

Fletcher looked at me, started to say something, and then sighed. "Can't stop you."

———————

It was after one in the morning, and Rowena and I sat in my Acura, hospital-bound again. And this time we really were going to see Kathy. Fletcher couldn't stop us, but she didn't give us a ride either. She had taken off in her cruiser with her lights flashing. I couldn't guess whom she expected to get out of her way at this time of the morning.

"I can understand how you knew the bone wasn't Paul's," Rowena was saying, "but how did you know he stole it from the pathology lab?"

"I didn't know. I just started speculating on where one would get a fresh human leg bone. The hospital seemed the best guess. And then when we saw how easy it was . . ."

"Okay, then. Why did we go to Dr. Dubitzky's office?"

"Paul needed to know when a leg would show up in pathology and what blood type it was. It didn't seem likely that he had decided to find a leg and then started searching for one. I figured Paul had kind of stumbled across a leg scheduled for amputation. Where is that most likely to happen? First choice had to be a doctor's office. Which doctor's office? Why not Paul's own?"

"And Paul knew the police would come looking for hair samples or such for a DNA test."

"Yup."

"He cleaned up his house so that blood type would be the only way to match? He was pretty lucky that his blood matched Jim's."

"He checked in advance. That was part of what made the opportunity compelling. But the match wasn't such a long shot. Almost forty percent of all people are O positive." I had looked up blood types once when I found out I was AB negative, the rarest blood type of all.

"You did some pretty good guesswork," Rowena said, reaching across the gearshift and patting my thigh.

"Well, we don't know that my guesses are right. But Kathy does know what happened, and this time we *are* going to see her. We'll find out."

A few moments later, car parked in the same space as three hours before, we were passing the wall of concrete blocks on our way into the hospital again. This time, we walked straight up to the information desk.

"Hello." Rowena smiled at a sullen-eyed woman. "I'm Frances Berk, Kathy Berk's daughter. What room is she in, please?"

"It's past regular visiting hours," said the woman.

"Oh yes, but my mother just awoke. She called and asked me to come right over."

The woman pressed a few buttons on her keyboard and said, "Room C232A. It's up one floor, off the main corridor. Just go that way," she made a vague pointing motion, "and you'll see the elevators. Check at the nurses' station before you go in."

"Thank you so much, ma'am," Rowena said with another genuine smile.

My compunction about telling an untruth in front of Rowena ran only one way.

We held hands as we walked through the corridor and ended up taking the stairs to the second floor. As we approached the C wing, Rowena slowed.

"Nervous?" she asked.

"Yeah. You, too?"

She nodded.

Here we were. She was going to confront her sister's murderer. She had told me at the airport to find her sister's killer. I was delivering on that directive right now. We swung open the double doors. Up on a white board, we saw a list of patients and their room numbers. Kathy was indeed listed in Room 232A; no one was in 232B.

We followed the curving corridor past patient rooms. Lights were out in almost all of them. Several had curtains pulled around the beds. The only door that was fully closed displayed a yellow warning sign: "Patient Sensitive to Latex. Wear Non-Latex Gloves." In another room, I could see what I supposed was a wife slumped sleeping in an armchair next to her snoring spouse on the hospital bed.

We came to the nursing station, where a man and a woman, both RNs according to their badges, were filling out forms. No sign of Fletcher. I couldn't understand how, ignoring speed limits, she hadn't beaten us here.

"Excuse me," I said. "This is Mrs. Berk's daughter, who just got in town. Can she peek in and see her mom?"

The male nurse, bespectacled and graying, looked up. "June," he said, turning to his late-night coworker. "Is Mrs. Berk awake?"

"Bad blow to the head, but she was awake a couple of hours ago when her brother came by," said the Filipina nurse.

Her words struck me in my solar plexus. I took a clumsy step backward. "Her brother?" Like Paul, Kathy was an only child.

"Yes, nice man." She peered at me for a moment. "You related, too?"

I didn't answer. I grabbed Rowena's hand and pulled her with a jerk that elicited a gasp. We started running farther down the corridor.

"Be quiet going in," the nurse whispered loudly after us.

"Damn," I said under my breath, dragging Rowena along.

The lights were out in Room 232. I flicked them on. The bed closest to the door, marked 232B, was freshly made and empty. With a rushing whoosh of metal sliding against metal, I threw back the curtain surrounding the other bed. Though unmade, it, too, stood empty.

"Check the bathroom," said Rowena.

I turned the stainless steel handle and opened that door. Drops still hung on the shower curtain. A wet towel covered the floor. A bluish hospital gown was wedged against the small tiles in the far corner. No Kathy. Damn again. Paul remained a step ahead of me.

I heard steps and whirled toward the door. Fletcher and Mikulski stepped into Room 232.

"Stopped to pick him up," Fletcher explained, nodding toward her partner. "Where is she?"

"Gone," Rowena said.

"Gone," I echoed.

EPILOGUE

I GROUND THE GLASS under the heel of my gleaming black shoes. Applause erupted. Relieved, I lifted my hand in a small, triumphant wave. I had feared nothing more at my wedding than a failure to crush that glass on the first try.

Jewish tradition holds that even in a time of great joy, we should remember that all is not right in the world—a contrarian view holding that behind every silver lining a cloud looms. So at a Jewish wedding, the groom breaks a glass as a reminder of the tragedies that abound in Jewish history and life in general.

The doubts that I had expected to gnaw at me over getting married had never come. As I looked at Rowena standing beside me, I felt sublimely content. At the same time, I knew this portrait of happiness was drawn on used canvas, where the old painting's figures of jealousy, rage, and murder continued to peek through. And here was the irony: if not for Gwendolyn's death eight months before, I would not have met Rowena, and I would not be standing beside her under the *chuppah*, the Jewish wedding canopy, in the same sanctuary of wood and windows where Gwendolyn's memorial service had been held. Thus, shattering the glass after our vows—mixing a drop of lamentation into our cup of joy—validated ancient wisdom. I saw tears flowing down Rowena's cheeks and realized that my face, too, was wet. I squeezed her hand.

Rabbi Kahn said, "Mazel tov," and gave me an encouraging nod. I reached out to Rowena, put my palms on her moistened cheeks, and kissed her. When we pulled apart, applause and congratulatory shouts greeted us again. My sister, Allison, wrapped her arms around me and whispered, "That kiss must have lasted a minute." She looked up at me with mock disapproval. And then, allowing the skin around her eyes to relax, she said, "Now we've *both* found what we were really looking for." At one time, Paul would have been my best man—who else?—but he and Kathy had been missing without a trace for over six months. So I hadn't thought long before asking my sister to stand up for me. Why not? The idea had appealed to my mother's twin values of family and unconventionality. Rowena thought it made perfect sense. Allison was moved. I was delighted.

Twenty minutes later, Rowena and I were bouncing up and down on chairs borne aloft by triumphant guests. She teetered, then I teetered, in time with the klezmer band's trumpets and fiddles and the guests' loud choruses of "Mazel tov!" Jason Blitzer was tossing me up with more energy than my bearers at the other three corners, beads of sweat hanging from the furrows that crossed his forehead. My right buttock rose from the chair at the apogee of each of his heaves. I could see Fletcher, who had opted for the lighter load, among those jolting Rowena with the same fervor. In the far corner of the room, Roger, the Berks' former chef, waggled his hand in salute even as he growled orders to a regiment of servers. A few months before, we'd found Roger playing hermit in his condo and talked him into starting a catering business. I caught Rowena's eye at the zenith of her chair's trajectory and jerked my head toward the burly figure in his toque. She, too, could see that Roger had come back to life. Making people happy by feeding them was how he himself found contentment.

Three hours later—filled with the salmon Roger had smoked, the chocolate cake he had baked, and the champagne he had selected—I sat with Rowena in the back of a Lincoln Town Car limousine. We were heading to her parents' house at four o'clock on a bright, sunny, and warm Sunday afternoon. Once Rowena and I had decided to get married, neither of us wanted to dilly-dally. And this morning had been the first opening Rabbi Kahn had. Didn't matter to us. Neither of us wanted a large, swanky nighttime affair at a hotel—not in the same year as Gwendolyn's death. We invited only people who really wanted to be there. I remembered being a teenager and hearing my father complain about this wedding or that bar mitzvah he had to go to. "I don't even know them," he'd moan to my mother. We'd invited a hundred guests. With Allison's family, my mother, a few cousins, about a dozen of my friends, and Susan Fletcher, now a sergeant, I had accounted for about a quarter of them.

I contemplated Rowena, resplendent in her mother's wedding gown—once white, I suspected, but now a mellow ivory. Her face was flushed, her chin sat on her chest, her eyes looked downward.

"Your mother wore a dress that low-cut to her wedding?" I asked. The dress was cut into a deep V in front that showed the crevice between Rowena's breasts. The tight bodice, decorated with intricate beadwork, further emphasized her figure.

Rowena reached over and punched my upper arm. "How do you do that?"

"Do what?" I asked, my hands extended upward in innocence.

"Know exactly what I'm thinking. It was the sixties when she got married anyway—not a modest time." Rowena kissed me on the cheek. "Did I ever tell you that my mother said she knew you and I would get married the first time she met you? For her, it proves that good can come out of even the worst tragedy."

Mrs. Goldberg had asked me to help Rowena pack up her sister's stuff, making sure we'd see each other again. Even in the midst of mourning for one daughter, she was worrying about the other's future.

After a few minutes of silence, Rowena brightened. "Maybe Mom should go to work for one of those dating services, maybe set up her own website—e-yenta.com."

"That would be perfect for her. Shall I mention it when we get to the house?"

"I dare you," she laughed. "Let's talk about the honeymoon."

"Yeah, let's," I said, and then exhaled. For our wedding present, Rowena's parents were sending us to Bora Bora for two weeks. I hadn't been anxious to spend my first married night in an airplane; it took twenty hours to get there and required changing planes in Los Angeles and Tahiti. But the pictures of isolated thatched *farés*—Tahitian for "home," the brochure said—extending into a lagoon had sold me on the idea. Plus, Rowena had promised that our cell phones wouldn't work there. "We'll be like Paul Gauguin running away from civilization to Polynesia," she'd said.

She knew I wanted—or even needed—to get away from the furor caused by Paul's disappearance. DNA testing had verified that the bones at Foothills Park were not his, but Jim Pavlik's. Kathy's cell phone carrier had confirmed that she called Paul around the time of the murder. Back at Accelenet, Paul's office stood just as he'd left it. I felt like a parent keeping a child's room unchanged while he went off to college. I had wanted to become president of the company, and the board had appointed me. But when the moment came, it meant little. With the gimlet-eyed clarity that passing time provides, I saw that I had worked so hard for the job because I wanted to win—no, earn—Paul's approval. And that wasn't important anymore. I'd given some thought to turning down the CEO position, but I knew I was needed for continuity, to reassure our two hundred employees and the investors who had put over seventy million of their unearned money in the company. In the end, though, climbing up the greasy pole meant more than being perched on the top.

"It will be good for you to get away," Rowena was saying. She could tell what was going on in my head, too.

"Sure will." I did have one more good reason to take the position. The enlarged Bonds project team was, in Silicon Valley vernacular, "pushing pedal to the metal." If I proved wrong on that bet, the company would have another CEO soon enough.

"You know what I'm thinking about doing?" Rowena asked after a few minutes.

"No." I hadn't a clue.

"I met with the Santa Clara County DA last week."

"Really." She had my full attention now. "About Gwendolyn?"

"That's how the conversation started."

"And how did it end?"

"He offered me a job."

Rowena had resigned from Tatum and Schulman and was scheduled to start in the litigation department at Bryce Smithwick's firm after we returned from Bora Bora. "And what are you going to do?"

"I thought working for a hotshot Silicon Valley firm would be exciting."

"And Bryce's is the hottest," I said.

"But with Gwennie gone . . ." Her voice trailed off for a moment. "Here's what I want." Her voice was husky. "I want to pursue justice."

"I'm not sure assistant DAs find justice in every case," I said.

"You don't have to tell me that."

"But you're going to tell Bryce that you're giving up an astronomical salary for a pittance from the taxpayer anyway?"

"You think he's going to be upset?"

"Bryce hates to lose at anything, anytime. He'll think you're nuts. So what? He'll get over it."

"And what do you think? Are you mad that I didn't discuss it with you before now?"

I closed my eyes and pictured life as the spouse of a crusading DA. I liked what I saw. "Good for you. I think you should pursue justice." And I reached over and kissed her soft lips. After I came up for air, I looked around. No mock disapproval from Allison this time. And the limo driver still had his eyes on the road.

We sat in companionable silence for a few minutes, and then Rowena asked, "Ian, what do you think of what's happened?"

I knew what she meant. Gwendolyn dead, Kathy a murderer, Paul missing, she and I married. How could we make sense of all that? "Maybe we're just dots in a pointillist painting."

"Like something of Seurat's?"

"Yeah, but huge, infinite in scope. We are living out our lives and looking at the painting from about an inch away. We don't get the chance to see it from a distance so that all the twists and turns of our lives, which make no sense to us, can be seen as part of the whole. Why is that red dot next to the green one? Why did Gwendolyn die? How does everything that happens fit into the overall picture? We don't know. I don't know. My mind's eye is too close to the painting."

"If we could get far enough away from what's happened, it would make more sense?" Rowena's tone mixed hope and skepticism.

"Maybe. I want to believe so."

We were at the Goldbergs', unwrapping the last of the presents that the guests had left for us at the synagogue. We could open a boutique featuring Haviland china, Gorham silver, and Waterford crystal with our takings. Anytime we wanted to have a couple of dozen people over for a formal sit-down dinner, we would be ready.

"What is this?" I asked, holding up a large round disk with silver handles.

"A cake plate," Rowena answered.

"Does everyone in the world know that but me?"

"Pretty much," she nodded. "Give me the card." I handed her the card, and she wrote down the names of the donors of the fanciest platform any cake could hope to stand on.

"Your turn," I said.

Rowena ripped the paper off a box about eighteen inches tall and six inches wide.

"I don't see a card," she said.

"Probably inside."

She used a scissors to open the box, pulled out four or five balls of crumpled tissue paper, and extracted a Toby jug of Sherlock Holmes in his familiar deerstalker. A magnifying glass and meerschaum pipe were linked together to form a handle.

I leaned forward and asked, "Any card?"

Rowena peered into the jug and uncrumpled the paper balls. "No, can't find one."

I took the outside wrapping paper and flattened it. It was possible that the giver had written a name on the paper, but I knew he hadn't.

"What's the matter?" Rowena asked.

"It's from Paul."

"How can you tell? How would he have known about the wedding? How would he have had it delivered?"

"He'd know. Don't know how he arranged to have it delivered, but I know the man. This is his sense of humor. You called me Sherlock once. Now he's doing the same thing."

"He's saying you've been playing detective? Or maybe that you tracked Kathy down using Holmes-like reasoning?"

"Something like that."

"Are they going to find them?"

"Don't think so. Paul's not only the smartest man I've ever known, the police figure he cashed in millions in stocks and bonds just before he disappeared." I shook my head. "No, I don't think so," I repeated. "If justice means standing trial, there's not going to be any justice done here. But if the punishment is seeing the life you built melt away, if it's living with someone you no longer love but are still bound to, maybe."

"We're too close to know," Rowena said.

"Or to ever know."

Rowena smiled and took my hand. "Come on. We need to get to the airport. We'll be in Bora Bora tomorrow."

ACKNOWLEDGMENTS

The seeds for *Dot Dead* were inadvertently planted by Silicon Valley luminary Ken Oshman when he took a flier and hired a person with no high-tech experience to work for him. How many regrets he has for that decision I do not know; I have had none. The book itself began to germinate in classes on mystery fiction taught by the inspiring Margaret Lucke and on novel writing led by the supportive Donna Levin. My muse for the past several years has been the virtuoso novelist and teacher Ellen Sussman. Her writing classes and critiques moved the book along while improving it at each step. In those classes I found my first two fans, Terri Bullock and Karen Nelson, who, along with Ann Eisenberg, provided the kind of encouragement any first-time novelist craves. My college friend Rick Wolff showed true generosity in his willingness to extend a helping hand. Literary agent *par excellence* Randi Murray saw the potential in my manuscript and has been steadfast in her belief in it and in me. Barbara Moore, acquisitions editor at Midnight Ink, has been gracious, helpful, and patient with this newcomer to the world of publishing, as have Alison Aten, Brett Fechheimer, Gavin Duffy, and the entire Midnight Ink team. Wade Ostrowski, Pat Holt, and Peggy Vincent all proved to be perceptive and understanding editors—other authors should be so lucky. With a fine sense of humor and an unmatched eye, Doug Peck did his best to make the author look presentable. When expertise was required, my polymathic brothers Corey and Wes offered it. Stuart Kaminsky is not only a grand master; he is a prince.

Each chapter, each word of the manuscript was read to and critiqued by my wondrous wife. She claims to have enjoyed the story. Worth almost an Edgar Award would be *Dot Dead* meeting the selection standards of her book group.

If you enjoyed *Dot Dead,* read on for an excerpt from the
first book in Chuck Zito's Nicky D'Amico Mystery series

A Habit for Death

AVAILABLE FROM MIDNIGHT INK

ONE

AT FIRST, IT HAD seemed like a good idea: June, July, and August outside Manhattan in the clean air of the beautiful, tree-filled, sun-drenched western Pennsylvania countryside. There would only be three shows, the first and last musicals. I wanted a chance not to swelter in the August humidity of New York City, an escape from the grinding pace of making a living to pay for my tiny studio in the West Fifties. The trip was made more appealing by the idea of subletting my apartment at a small profit and paying off some back rent. And, yes, there was the ques-tion of getting away from a failed romance—the kind of affair where you know it's over but you still walk by his favorite restaurant or "unex-pectedly" find yourself in front of his building. We'd met just before Thanksgiving. From November to April we passed quickly through in-fatuation (mutual) to infidelity (his) and on to inanity (mine). When I'd started thinking about trailing him at night as he went out for a drink, I knew I needed to get out of town. What can I say? I was still trying to master the dating thing. In the end, western Pennsylvania seemed barely far enough away.

St. Gilbert's College sat in the middle of Appalachian coal country, part of the town of Huber's Landing. Huber, whoever he was, was long gone, and so were the coal mines. The countryside was left to tiny farms and small towns that once thrived near industrial activity but now sat with indifference in the middle of a mountain range covered in pines, small creeks, and mid-sized lakes. St. Gilbert's itself was a private school with a student body of two thousand from which no one famous had ever graduated and no one infamous had ever dropped out. Its buildings, all red brick and vines, were a little gone to seed. It had no claim to fame, unless you counted the magnificent scenery.

That scenery was the only part of my ideal summer that didn't disappoint me. I learned one of those lessons they can't teach you at a theater conservatory: when someone promises you fulfillment, cash, and free time, run away fast.

Benny Singleton, the artistic director, turned out to be an autocratic six-year-old disguised as a middle-aged man. It was a discouraging sight watching him hack his way through a play day after day.

That the play should be *Convent of Fear*, a musical thriller about a serial nun killer, only added to my disappointment.

The convent in question runs a school for orphan boys. Enemies plague the convent with trouble. A local developer wants the land. The church diocese, tired of losing money, wants to shut them down. It goes on from there, but the real fun starts with the murder of a young nun. There are singing police, frightened children, and dancing suspects. More nuns are murdered and more music slaughtered. In the end the murderer turns out to be the groundskeeper, whose only child drowned while on an outing from the school orphanage forty-five years earlier. How does a child with a father end up in an orphanage? Think amnesia. Think how you'd rather be watching a good movie.

The scene that orphan number six had just interrupted on the Monday of the final week of rehearsals was the killing of young Sister Klarissa, love interest of the policeman. She had just finished singing about leaving the convent for her "true love." In the previous scene her true love had sung the show-stopping tune "Gonna Make a Habit of You." Does it matter that the Mother Superior is on the take?

After I'd announced that everyone should take ten, the musical director, a principal actor, and the prop master approached me simultaneously. I've never lost my childhood faith in first-come first-served, so I started with the musical director.

While actors at least have to give lip service to sharing the stage with someone else, musical directors often mistake themselves for God. Edward Rossoff was so confused he conducted everything around him. The best way to hold a conversation with Edward was at a distance safely out of reach of his extended hand gestures.

"I need more time in this schedule," he said. He waved one hand and poked with the other. "You have to get me more time. They all sound like shit. Like shit." Edward had a way with language completely at odds with his appearance: a man neatly attired in a dark suit and thick glasses, mostly bald and pushing sixty. He punctuated each "shit" with an ominous downbeat of his left hand. "I need time now. Today."

"Edward, I don't make the schedule," I said. "That's Benny's job. I just execute it."

"Well, you can just execute this music, because this schedule is shit. And that fat twit wouldn't know the difference." Edward was waving both hands in four-four time.

"Maybe you should ask him—"

A sudden cut. "You are not serious, are you, young man? Of course you are, you have never been in this pit of hell before. This shitting waste of space. Benny Singleton"—and here Edward raised his voice and both arms to crescendo—"wouldn't know how to schedule a six a.m. wake-up call. Well, I am not letting him embarrass me again. Bad enough I have to suffer with this shit of a score. I will not—do you hear me, Singleton?—I will not be embarrassed again. I will expect a new schedule by tomorrow. *Shit.*"

Edward turned on his heel and strode across the front of the house to the piano on the far side. This put him far away from me and far away from Benny Singleton, who was deeply involved in counting the number of pieces of fuzz on the seat in front of him. I guess he wasn't interested in sharing any rehearsal time today.

There was an audible sigh behind me. It came from Sister Mary Corinne, a nun who spent a lot of her free time watching rehearsals. Sister Mary Corinne was Edward's age. She had the harsh look that sometimes develops from too many years of self-effacement in the service of too many good causes. Her hair was gray and pulled back, framing a pair of wire-rimmed glasses that accentuated her sharp blue eyes. Like all the nuns of her order, she no longer wore a habit, but that didn't mean she looked relaxed in jeans and a white blouse.

"He really is a nice man." I assume she said it for my benefit. Despite her severe angular appearance, she was obviously not without some charitable views toward humanity. Edward Rossoff was an excellent musical director, but I was definitely immune to his personal charms.

"I'm sure he is, Sister," I said.

"Nicholas, it's bad luck to lie to a nun," she said without any trace of humor in her voice.

I turned to the next person in line. Joe Sobieski Jr. played the young cop who falls in love with Klarissa. He was a few years younger than me and looked even younger. He had the dark-hair, pale-eyes combination that dominated that part of the country. I might have considered him cute—I do like dark hair and pale eyes—but even when he was trying to be pleasant, Joe couldn't keep his entire face from frowning, eyebrows and mouth drooping downward into a scowl. As usual he was wearing nothing but dark clothing. For Joe the year was always 1984 and the location was always the Lower East Side. A year he no more than vaguely remembered, a location he'd never been.

"Will we get to my scene tonight?" he asked. "If we start over with these kids, I'm never going to get onstage." Joe put an emphasis on "kids" that turned it into a true four-letter word. He switched to a tone that hinted at his busy life outside the theater. "I just don't want to hang out here all night for no reason."

Now, I may, at times, be cranky and difficult, but when it comes to children, I figure seven-year-olds at least have an excuse to behave like seven-year-olds. With adults I am often not so patient. Nonetheless, I assured him that we weren't wasting his time and that we would be in serious need of him at any moment. Confidently assuring actors that time was not being wasted is one of the first tasks any good stage manager learns.

My internal clock was ticking urgently now, telling me that I needed to end this break. I took the prop master, Marty Friedman, by the arm and started toward my table.

"Walk and talk, Marty," I said, gently guiding him along the aisle. "What can I do for you?"

"I need petty cash."

That was another peculiarity of St. Gilbert's. Normally, as stage manager, I would be getting my petty cash supply for those handy incidentals—pens, paper, coffee, the occasional new novel for personal entertainment (yes, that could technically be considered stealing, but you take your perks where you can)—from the company manager just like everyone else. Or maybe the business manager. But at St. Gilbert's there was no business manager or company manager. So I dispensed cash and collected receipts and tried to keep an accurate count, though math was never my specialty.

"Receipts?" I asked.

"I don't have them on me, but I have to go shopping first thing tomorrow morning. I'm running out of time."

Marty Friedman was nervous. The type of guy whose first thought when the alarm goes off in the morning is "Oh my God, what's wrong now?" Marty was a former St. Gilbert's student who still returned summers to play at theater. In the off-season he taught high school English to children who are learning disabled. I have no idea how he ever managed to get through a day of such potentially anxiety-producing work. The oddest part of the entire package was his size. Marty Friedman was six feet three inches tall and nearly two hundred pounds. I literally looked up to him, always asking myself, "What could make this man so nervous?"

"Marty, you know I need receipts. Receipts in, cash out."

"I know, I know, Nicky. But I left all my paperwork at home. I've got to shop. We tech in three days and I'm not finished buying. And then I have to paint stuff. And then it has to dry, and the weather is way too humid, and you know how that is on paint. It will all dry tacky and have to be redone. I don't have time."

I had a choice. Lay out cash or listen to him for another five minutes.

"How much?" I asked.

"Another hundred."

That was twenty dollars a minute for the whining.

"OK, tell you what. Take a seat, and once this break is over we'll go to my office and do the cash."

"Oh, great. That's great. Thanks, Nicky. Really. Thanks."

The thank-yous alone could take yet another five minutes. I waved him away toward a back row.

It was time to start again. I chased two orphans from under my work table, where they were busy playing cavemen. The rest of the cast was scattered around the auditorium and stage. For a few seconds everything was peaceful. Then I noticed a bundle of black cloth heaped on stage left. I looked at it for several seconds to see if it would move. It didn't. I asked it to.

"Ah, Sister Sally. Sister? I think you can get up now."

For a moment there was no response. I was just beginning to think something was wrong when the bundle of cloth slowly unrolled itself into the shape of the young nun so recently bludgeoned to death in the orphans' dormitory.

"Oh, I knew we were done. I knew we were on break," she said. "I was just trying to get into character as a dead person. After all, I'm going to have to lie there for a long time." Sister Sally stood up and brushed dirt off her habit. Like all the nuns at the college, she'd abandoned the traditional black habit as everyday wear. The robes she was dressed in were actually produced by the St. Gilbert's costume shop.

"I am sorry that I got this nice new costume dirty, but the costume people wanted me to start working with it tonight. You know, we don't wear these things anymore. Anyway," she said, "I have to confess, I'm not feeling all that well. But I think resting there for a while helped."

In one of the few theatrically interesting twists of the summer, Benny convinced several nuns from the St. Gilbert's convent to perform as nuns in *Convent of Fear*. Not all the nuns of St. Gilbert's approved of the production, but the college administration thought the production would help liberalize the institution's image and increase its success rate at recruiting new students.

Sister Sally was one of the nuns who approved. She played young Sister Klarissa. Every theater group attached to a Catholic school has one nun like Sister Sally: young, energetic, perky-perky-perky. Sally genuinely loved the theater. She had a laugh like the sound of a helium balloon losing gas.

"I'm sorry you're not well, Sister," I said. "Do you need anything?"

"No. No. I'll be just fine. I believe in a positive attitude. Don't you?" All the while she was fingering the wooden cross at the end of the rosary that hung from her waist.

"Absolutely," I said. "Now remember, all you need to do is lie there. You don't really have to do any acting to play dead." Anything to cut down on the melodrama.

"Oh, I knew that too." Sister Sally laughed.

I winced.

"I just wanted to make my time in the theater as interesting as possible," she said. "I don't believe in wasting any of life's moments. Do you?" She laughed again. Very loudly.

I knew just where to start rehearsal.

"OK, everyone. Back onstage. Let's kill the nun one more time."

Once rehearsal was under way, the prop master and I headed for my office at the back of the house. I left Patsy, my assistant, to "sit book." This involved using the prompt book to cue the actors onstage if they should forget what to say or do next.

We were halfway up the aisle when *he* entered the auditorium. I know it's just begging for trouble for a stage manager to get involved with a cast member, but he was beautiful: about three inches taller than me, dark brown hair, light blue eyes, and muscles with just enough body fat to cushion them to the touch. He had a long torso but was wearing denim shorts slung low on his hips and ending just below the knees, which balanced him perfectly. A tight T-shirt clung to a V-shaped upper body that swept up from his waist with a natural, non-gymed, toned definition. His face and arms were smooth, suggesting only the lightest scattering of body hair. I am a big fan of the diversity of human genetics that can produce so beautiful a man. David Scott, member of the chorus and genetic delight, was the textbook answer to my broken heart. OK, maybe just a bandage on my wounded pride. All right, so it was lust. At least it seemed mutual.

Our eyes locked onto each other's with a decidedly reciprocal interest, anticipating smiles, nods, brushing lips, and late-night rendezvous. My imagination leapt several hours ahead to see the two of us sitting on a picnic table under a sliver of a moon and a field of stars. The sound of the lake lapping against outgrown tree roots mingled with violin music. We'd kiss, and then, as the score rumbled an incessant bass, we'd slowly lean back along the length of the table, the sweet, fresh, clean country air mingling with the now-raging scent of our bodies. And we'd scream and scream . . .

Scream?

Someone was screaming onstage.